Rational Innocence

J.A. Commodore

ISBN: 978-1-957203-65-2 (sc)
ISBN: 978-1-957203-66-9 (hc)
ISBN: 978-1-957203-67-6 (e)

One Galleria Blvd., Suite 1900, Metairie, LA 70001
1-888-421-2397

To
Madelyn Gabriel DeMarco
Chloe Lia DeMarco
Jameson Grant Lindner
Graham Michael Lindner

To my Dear and Long time Friend who has passed away,
Donald Morzenti

RATIONAL INNOCENCE

Whenever you gaze upon a newborn in complete innocence, realize that every villain and every hero and all of us in between were once just as innocent, and the difference between them is a result of how rationality affected their maturity.

CHARACTERS AND EVENTS

1982: story flashback to law school

John Castano: family lawyer and main character

1983: John graduates from University of Minnesota law school

Elizabeth "Liz" Danfurth: John's friend in law school, maiden name was Ruffalo

James Boilen: longtime friend from college

Deatra "Malone" Boilen: James's wife

1985: James and Deatra are married

Dan Danfurth: Liz's husband dies September 1989

Pauli, Pauli & Steinman: law firm for whom John works

Carolyn Danfurth: Liz and John's daughter

1986: Carolyn is born

December 1989: the story begins

Alexi Antonoff: Dan's friend, GBI-S4 agent

Sandi: Liz's boss

Dorothy: Liz's mother

Paul: John's father

Isabel: John's mother

Nancy Williamson: John's older sister (two years), husband Josh, sons Chad and Grant

Betty Stefano: John's younger sister (one and one-half years), husband Terry

Gilson Road: road Dan and Liz's cabin is on

Mildred Hansen: neighbor at Dan and Liz's cabin, husband is George

Willie Durante: private investigator

Robel & Associates: Willie's employer offices on south side on the third floor

Murray's: Minneapolis restaurant

Lynn Markeson: John's ex-fiancé
Brett Malone: Deidra's younger brother
Paul Greco: John's good friend
UFAC: United Front against Animal Cruelty
Rudy: John's law clerk
Paul Runyon: Dan's coworker
Ollas Sorenson: Dan and Liz's neighbor in Minneapolis
Al Reitbrock: UFAC national chairman
Albert Wertz: UFAC local chairman and lives in Uptown
Phillip Longhouse: mysterious author of the memo
Project WASP: mysterious research project Dan was involved in
SIAIBM: mysterious organization for which John was doing research
Celia: John's law secretary
Phil Roland: Dan's friend from the Athletic Club, real name is Garson Petroff
Bill: Liz's brother who lives in Duluth, his wife is Toni, and Lana his daughter
Ron Tomlinson: John's landlord
Norbert: Liz's neighbor
Harold Kapinsky: Detective Hennepin County Detectives
Maggie: manager of Wanda's Diner
Sean O'Riley and Tom Stanford: Minneapolis police officers
Robert Jerome and Joe Foley: GBI Agents
Capitan Robertson: Hennepin County Detective
Greg Steinman: senior partner in John's law firm
Hillary Holden: Brett's significant other
Ronald Ziegler: Hillary's public defender
Bill Fabiano: used-car salesman
Susan Greenfield and Gloria Cook: friends from Mexican vacation
Capitan Nick and Ishmael: crew of fishing boat
Scott and Sandy, Rick Phelps and Gustav: acquaints on Mexican vacation
Dr. Cumson: research analyst who works for Willie

Life seems so simple when you are young, then life's experiences make everything very complicated.

The drive up Highway 47 was lonesome. Traffic was light, not true of the urban chaos I left behind, and I needed some stimulation to stay awake after a long day at the office. The radio was loud, the jazz stimulating, and I had the driver's side window open somewhat, and the cool December air chilled my car. I'm John Castano, and this is my story.

I spotted the road I needed to turn on, slowed, and made a left turn. I passed a row of mailboxes, and the only light was that from my headlights. It was a dark, cold night; snow was in the air. A sharp wind clattered the leafless branches of the trees that lined the narrow asphalt road. It was as if I drove in a tunnel as my headlights illuminated the tree trunks just ahead. There were no driveways or signs since I left the main highway. Just for a second, I felt as if I was the only person left on earth.

As I rounded a sharp curve, my headlights lit a reddish gravel driveway a hundred feet ahead. I slowed to a crawl and turned right into the drive, just wide enough for a single car. The darkness seemed to close in even more, the stones crunching under my tires as I slowly drove up a slight hill. Cresting the hill, the drive opened into a large clearing, in the middle of which I saw the glow from two windows.

As I approached, my headlights reflected off a log cabin. Nearing the cabin and approaching the end of the drive brought my silver-gray BMW Coupe to a halt. I turned off the ignition and exited the car. The door of the cabin opened, and the silhouette of a woman appeared in the doorway. She was tall with a shapely, slender build.

A soft tender voice said, "I was getting worried, John. You're so late."

It was Liz, Elizabeth Danfurth.

I ascended the three steps to the porch and was greeted with a warm hug. All the cold dampness seemed to vanish as Liz's hug grew longer. I gave her a kiss on the cheek, and we entered the cabin, locking out all the dark loneness.

"Have you eaten yet?" Liz questioned.

"I'm starved," I replied.

"I have dinner for you. I hope you like homemade beef stew?" Liz responded.

"Sounds fantastic."

I woke to bright sunlight slipping around the window shade in my bedroom. I got out of bed and fumbled for my trousers. Finally getting them into the right position, I slipped them on. Next was my polo shirt. I walked to the door, opened it, and stepped onto a small balcony overlooking the great room from my loft bedroom. The smell of fresh brewed coffee and cinnamon rolls tickled my nostrils. As I descended the stairs, a new fire crackled in the large, natural fireplace.

I walked from the living area to the small kitchen, passing the master bedroom. The door was open, the bed was made, and Liz was nowhere in the cabin. Two cups sat in front of the coffee maker; I filled one with fresh brewed coffee. Next to the coffee maker were half-dozen fresh baked cinnamon rolls. Liz was up early. I glanced at the stove clock, and it was 8:38 a.m.

I walked to the front door, opening it to the startling glare of the winter sun. It snowed lightly during the night, just enough to cover the ground. Footprints descended the porch steps and tracked down the drive and out of sight. I closed the door and walked to the living area, sitting in an overstuffed leather chair off to the side of the fireplace and took a sip of coffee. It was just as I liked my coffee, strong and hot.

My thoughts drifted to Liz; Elizabeth Ruffalo was her maiden name. We met when she was in the final year of MBA studies at the University of Minnesota, and I was in my final year of law school. It was fall; the year was 1982. We met one evening at the Big Ten, a university student hangout on the edge of campus. Liz was there with some friends. My buddy, James Boilen, and I were playing darts. I lost, and Liz remarked that she had the bet on me. I apologized and said I was off my best game. We started to talk and talk for some time until she was prompted to leave, as her friends were heading back to campus.

James was a big man, not tall, just big. He had jet-black hair, deep-set brown eyes, and a slightly ruddy complexion. Yet his voice was soft and clear. He was my roommate in law school, where we first met. Our interests were similar, and we both enjoyed fishing, as he came from Northern Minnesota and grew up with a fishing rod in one hand.

The next time we met Liz was again at the Big Ten on a Saturday some days later. We came to watch U of M take on Wisconsin for Paul Bunyan's Ax, a rivalry that has a long UM/UW tradition. She was at a table for four with one of her friends. James and I walked over and asked if we could join them. Liz replied "yes" without hesitation.

After traditional pleasantries, James struck up a conversation with Liz's friend, Deatra. Deatra was in nursing school, while Liz was in business. Both were tall, thin, shapely ladies with a definite glowing complexion. Deatra and Liz met at a party held by a common friend and became close immediately.

The friendship between James and Deatra flourished, and they were married three years later. They still enjoy each other's companionship to this day. Liz and I became dear friends, just dear friends. Many doubted if a young man and woman could have just a friendship, but that was all it was. Liz met her husband-to-be, Dan Danfurth, just after graduation and were married a year later. They had one child, Carolyn, two years after they married.

All of us watched the game together; Wisconsin won the game. After the game, I commented about college football, "College football is all about money, and the sport is secondary."

"Why do you feel that way?" asked Liz, who was sitting next to James.

"Major-league baseball has farm clubs where they develop potential players, but the rest of professional sports uses the colleges and universities as their farm clubs. With the blessings of the NCAA, colleges and universities found that they can make huge amounts of money on their sports programs. As a result, they recruit just as professional sports teams do."

"So what's wrong with that?" piped James.

"Colleges and universities can only admit a limited number of new students. Many of these guys on sports scholarships are not there to be educated. They just want to play their sport in the hopes a major-league team will draft them. They get special exemptions so they can be admitted to the institution that otherwise they would never get into. The rub comes in that these people take the spot of someone who wanted to be there to get an education but was denied because this football player took their place, all because the institution wanted to make money."

"I sort of understand," Liz offered. "The sports programs are done to make money first, and education is secondary."

"Right," I concluded.

We changed the conversation to a more positive note, discussing our plans for the future and various academic ideas. We finished the evening with a round of darts, ladies against men (isn't it always that way?), and the ladies won by a point. We left agreeing to see each other again soon.

We met many times during the coming academic year. It became obvious that James and Deatra were in a serious relationship. Liz and I remained friends, although I felt that it could have become more serious. At that time, I was into law and getting established and really didn't consider a more serious relationship.

After graduation, Liz joined a large investment firm as a personal consultant and was rapidly promoted to management where she works today. She met Dan while working as a consultant. He was an associate professor of applied physics at the U. I joined the law firm of Pauli, Pauli, & Steinman as an associate. It was a general law firm, and I worked in the family law area. Both Liz and Dan became my close friends, and I consulted them on most of their legal matters.

I heard footsteps on the front porch, and the door opened. Liz stood there, and I realized again her great beauty: long black hair streamed from beneath the white-and-green stocking cap; her large round brown eyes were hallowed by her long black eyelashes; and her checks, nose, and tip of her chin were pink from the winter chill.

"Good morning. Did you sleep well?" she asked as she dropped the newspaper on the mail table.

"Sure did," I replied as she began to remove her mittens and cap.

She stuffed them into both coat pockets, removed her coat, and hung it on the coat tree on the opposite side of the door, as the mail table then slid off the fur-topped boots.

"A bit chilly out there this morning," she quipped. "I took my morning walk to the main road for the newspaper.

It is exactly four miles down and back. It really gets me ready for the new day."

"See you found the coffee. The cinnamon rolls were for your wake-up snack," directed Liz. "I'll start breakfast now."

Liz walked to the kitchen, and I followed, taking a stool at the breakfast counter. I placed my cup on the counter, as Liz swung around with the coffeepot in one hand and the cinnamon rolls in the other.

"Refill?" she quizzed. "Have a roll. I'll have breakfast in a few minutes. How do you like your eggs?"

"Over easy, plenty of butter on the toast."

After breakfast, we cleared the table. It was time to do the unpleasant task that brought me here. I began taking the various documents from my briefcase.

"As tough as this is, it is best we begin. It will only take a few minutes, and we'll have the rest of the day to do some walking and explore the area," I advised.

The documents were to finalize the estate of Liz's late husband, Dan. He died on Friday, September 22, 1989, in a tragic accident right here at the cabin.

Dan took a long weekend to do some ruffed grouse hunting at the cabin with his friend, Alexi Antonoff. Dan arrived on Thursday evening. Early Friday morning, as he planned, he left to cut down a good-sized, dead maple tree behind the cabin at the edge of the clearing as his woodpile was shrinking. The tree had been dead for several years, so the wood should be plenty dry to use immediately.

Alexi, Dan's friend and hunting buddy, arrived midafternoon, and when Dan did not respond to his knocks, he entered the cabin; no one locked doors during the day up here. Dan was not in the cabin, and Alexi went to the garage to see if Dan was there with no luck, though his car was in the garage. Outside he looked around and spotted the fallen tree some one hundred yards behind the cabin. He decided to check it out, and as he approached the fallen tree, he spotted some blaze-orange under the branches. His pace quickened, and as he approached, he realized the branches buried Dan.

Alexi pulled away as many branches as possible but realized Dan was dead. He rushed back to the cabin, dialed the operator, and had her connect him to the local sheriff's office. Ten minutes later a squad sped up the drive, red lights flashing. Two officers exited the car, and Alex escorted them to where Dan lied.

About ten minutes later a second squad arrived, and a single officer walked back. The coroner was called after the arrival of the third officer, and he was on scene in less than an hour. One of the officers contacted the Minneapolis police after getting Liz's work address and phone number and asked that an officer notify Liz of her husband's death and whom she should contact locally.

Dan's body was extracted from beneath the tree, bagged, and taken to the morgue at the local hospital. The coroner would examine the body there and make a final judgment as to cause of death. Since this had all the indications of an accidental death, no investigation was conducted other than describing the scene.

Liz's coworker in the office next to hers related this to me at the wake for Dan. Liz was at her desk in her office when the receptionist called to inform her that a police officer wished to talk with her. Instantly she knew it was bad news about Dan. She asked the receptionist to escort the officer to her office. Her large brown eyes constricted as the officer approached, and her face became uncharacteristically pale.

"Are you Elizabeth Danforth?"

"Yes."

"Is Daniel Danforth your husband?"

"What's wrong, what's happened?"

"Well, mam, this is the part of my job I really don't like doing. It seems your husband was cutting a tree down and somehow was struck by it. He is deceased."

Liz slumped over in her chair, burying her face from view. There was a long silence before the officer spoke and asked if there was someone he could get for her.

Liz nodded "no" without raising herself from the slumped position.

The officer offered his condolences and said he would leave the contact information with the secretary. He left.

As the rest of the story goes, on the way out, the officer stopped at the receptionist's desk and informed the receptionist of his business with Liz and left the necessary contact information so she could get it to Liz. The receptionist apprised Liz's manager, Sandi, of the situation and gave all the contact information to her.

Dan was a tall, slim man, clean-shaven, hard but handsome features. He had black hair, as did Liz, which was shoulder length and well kept. His demeanor was all business and a serious health nut who worked out daily, but when he was in social situations, he was lighthearted and charming. He was also a devoted husband and dad. I could see why Liz loved him so.

Sandi had two coworkers drive Liz home. Liz and Dan lived in a modest house in Plymouth. Her mother, Dorothy, was at the house; she lived in separate living quarters, which were attached to the house, and she tended to Liz's daughter, Carolyn, during the day. Her mother was also shocked but managed to keep her composure and helped Liz explain the situation to Carolyn, who, even at her young age, seem to understand what just happened.

She did not cry but asked, "Will I never see Daddy again?"

After Liz gained some composure, she called me at the office and said to the receptionist, "This is Elizabeth Danfurth. May I speak with John Castano?"

The call was transferred direct to my desk.

"John Castano."

"Oh John, this is Liz; Dan died."

"What, how?"

Liz gave me a brief explanation. I told her I would be right over.

I immediately left the office, telling my secretary I would be gone the rest of the day due to an emergency. I was going to Liz's not as her attorney, but as a close friend to console, support, and help her in any way I was able. This is what good friends do.

When I arrived, Dorothy answered the door, "Please come in. Liz is in the family room."

"You have my deepest sympathy," I offered.

I went directly to the family room, and Liz met me. I wrapped my arms around her and held her for several minutes in silence with her head on my shoulder. She was not crying, but I could feel her anxiety and fear.

Liz asked me to contact the coroner and make the arrangements to bring Dan's body back. Since he had identification on his person, and Alexi made positive identification, the coroner released his remains. There was no autopsy as the obvious cause of death was due to being crushed by a falling tree, an accident.

A local funeral home would pick up the remains and handle all funeral arrangements. The funeral was set for Wednesday, September 27. The visitation and funeral were attended by several hundred friends and associates of Liz and Dan. Dan was buried in a cemetery just a short distance from their home. As the grave side services concluded, Liz, Carolyn, and I walked to the suspended coffin.

Liz slipped a single rose from the flower cluster on the top of the coffin, and in a sweet soft voice, Carolyn said,

"Bye-bye, Daddy. I love you."

Sitting at the dining room table in the cabin, I began explaining the various legal forms that were required to transfer Dan's assets to Liz. There was also the matter of the insurance claims, one for the life insurance through his work at the U of M, and the other a whole life policy he had since graduating from college. Both life insurances required a certified copy of Dan's death certificate. Some of the asset-transfer documents also required death certificates.

During this process, Liz read the death certificate for the first time. This must have confirmed the reality that Dan was really dead, as her morning cheeriness vanished into a gray, solemn gloom. Tears welled up in both her big, brown eyes then tumbled one after the other down her once rosy cheeks. I placed my hand over hers and gave her a gentle squeeze. She looked directly into my eyes, smiled weakly, and wiped the tears away with her other hand.

After we finished, it was late morning. Liz tossed more wood on the fire, and we sat in the family room, I in the overstuffed leather chair, and Liz on the love seat. We just chatted about various things not related to Dan. After about an hour, Liz went to the kitchen to make lunch.

"I have some chicken soup I made at home and brought up with me. Would you like some and a sandwich?"

"Sure," I replied, still sitting in the overstuffed chair.

"I have some egg salad or chicken salad. Which would you like?" she asked.

"Egg salad is fine."

"Whole wheat or white?" she asked.

"White for me," I answered. "You sound like my local lunch waitress."

After lunch, we agreed on taking a walk. The weather warmed up a little, and much of the night snow was gone.

This time of year, early December, weather systems and fronts moved swiftly in Minnesota and can change every few hours. We walked down the drive, down the narrow asphalt road that I drove on the way to the cabin—it seemed nearly as lonely and hostile as it did last night—and out to the main road. At the side of the road was a line of four mailboxes, one Liz's and the other three for houses up the narrow asphalt road past Liz's. Liz checked her mailbox.

"I don't have mail delivered here, but sometimes people put filers and ads in the mailboxes."

There was a slot for newspapers. I inquired, "You obviously have newspapers delivered?"

"Just weekends, and when we are not here—I'm sorry—when I'm not here, I have our neighbor pick them up."

"I see four mailboxes, but I didn't pass any houses on the way to yours."

"They are up the road a half mile or so. I have Mildred pick up the papers. She lives at the end of the road."

We reversed our walk and headed back to the cabin. As we approached the cabin, I indicated I would like to see the tree and area where Dan had his accident. Liz took me around to the back of the cabin and pointed out the fallen tree but did not accompany me to the site. The walk took a couple of minutes, but it was a very long couple of minutes.

As I stood over the spot where the tree felled Dan, an eerie thought began rolling around in my head. Dan was well experienced in cutting trees as he did much of the clearing of the meadow the cabin sets in the middle of. It only takes a couple of seconds for a tree to fall. How would Dan get so far from the tree trunk, where he was cutting about twenty-five feet, and why would he go in the direction the tree was falling? Something didn't add up.

Back at the cabin, I said nothing of my thoughts to Liz as she had enough to think about. I told her I would be heading back to the Cities. She said I was welcome to stay the night. I thanked her and said the offer was very tempting, but I had to be back, as I had to lecture at the 8:00 a.m. mass at church.

On the drive back to the Cities, I kept mulling over the idea that Dan was far too experienced a tree cutter to be killed in the way he was. The why, and more importantly, the how continued to concern me. I have no police training, but I could not understand why the police did not ask the same kinds of questions. It must be that our thought process must encourage us to make quick decisions, a process necessary during our prehistoric times, but not necessarily good in modern-day society. Once we come to a conclusion, we tend not to look critically and without bias at the situation.

The officers arrived on the scene of the accident and saw a tree on top of Dan. An accident is the obvious conclusion. From that point on, little thought is given to any other possibility unless we are smacked across the face with a glaring inconsistency. Small inconsistencies get overlooked. So the officers never asked the why-and-how question.

I decided to contact the police officers involved and asked them if they would allow me to review their accident report. This should not be a problem, as I am, in fact, the attorney for Liz. On Monday morning, I would call the department and make arrangements to review their report.

I arrived at my duplex, just a short distance from the law offices in downtown Minneapolis. It is a comfortable two-bedroom, two-bath, 1,400-square-foot duplex with a single car garage. It suites my needs, and I don't have to fight Minneapolis traffic traveling to and from the suburbs. I rented the property two years ago. Prior to the duplex, I lived in my law school apartment.

I pulled into the garage, went out the garage door, and grabbed the mail. I closed the door and went into the house. It was six thirty in the evening, and I was thirsty and hungry. I ordered a pizza from my favorite pizzeria; I consider myself a pizza connoisseur and Gardetto's was the best in the Cities. I went to the refrigerator, grabbed a Heineken and a glass from the freezer, and retired to the front room to glance over the mail while waiting for my pizza.

As I waited, I began to think back to my childhood. How simple everything was then. I was born and grew up in a medium-sized town, La Crosse, Wisconsin. My father, Paul, was a strict disciplinarian, but my mother, Isabel, was a bit of a pushover unless we really got her pissed off, which I managed to do every once in a while. I had two sisters, Nancy, who was two years older than me, and Betty, who was eighteen months younger. Dad wanted to get the children over early and broke with an old Catholic tradition of six to twelve children. It wasn't that he did not love children, but he felt his energies would be better focused on the three of us.

My childhood was tame. I liked school but was not big into sports. My father and I shared many hours hunting or fishing on the Mississippi river. I had several friends of similar background with whom I hung out. We were a mischievous bunch but never got into any serious trouble. We were just sort of the local neighborhood irritants, and an occasional neighbor would complain to Mom that we were too loud or that we tossed some scrap on the sidewalk.

This would be one of the things that got Mom pissed. After one of those incidents, I would be grounded for a day or two; the length depended on which neighbor made the complaint.

After graduating high school, I decided to attend the U of M, as Minnesota and Wisconsin had a reciprocity agreement where I could attend U of M at University of Wisconsin–resident tuition cost, and a Minnesota resident could attend UW under the same arrangement. I studied under a prelaw program and applied and was admitted to the U of M law school upon graduation.

Just then the doorbell rang. It was my pizza.

We should not make assumptions, as they impose a conclusion before the truth is known, but to suspect is acceptable.

Monday morning, I called the sheriff's office for the county in which Liz's cabin was located. The receptionist connected me to the sheriff, who happened to be the third officer to arrive at the accident scene. After introducing myself, I asked if I could see the complete accident report, and the sheriff was most agreeable. I could come in any time, and the secretary would get the report and provide a place where to review it. If I wanted to speak with the two officers who were first on the scene, then some arrangements must be made in advance. I indicated I had no need to talk with the officers, but if after review of the accident report I did, I would let the secretary know. I told the sheriff I would be up Wednesday midmorning.

After concluding of that call, I called Liz at her office. I felt I needed to keep her in the loop on the accident report review, as I was doing it under the cover of being her attorney.

"Elizabeth Danfurth," I asked the operator.

"Who may I say is calling?"

"John Castano."

The phone rang four times.

"Elizabeth Danfurth," came back.

"Hi, Liz, it's John."

"Oh, John, how are you? How was the drive back?"

"I'm fine, and the drive was uneventful."

"What's up?" Liz queried.

"I called the sheriff's office this morning and asked to review Dan's accident report. I'm going up on Wednesday. I just wanted to keep you in the loop," I informed her.

"Why do you want to review that report?"

"Well, on the way home, I was thinking about the accident and had a few questions. They probably are nothing, but I wanted to see if the report would give me some answers. It is nothing you need to concern yourself over."

"What sort of questions?"

"Really nothing important, just some technical information. If anything important turns up, I'll let you know."

"Okay, John," she said reluctantly without pressing me any further.

We chatted a few minutes, and I suggested paying her and Carolyn a visit on Sunday afternoon. She agreed without much enthusiasm, which I considered a result of lingering depression from our Saturday estate session. Now I wished I stayed Saturday night to give her some support. Stupid me. Stupidity is a dangerous thing that we need to guard against constantly. It's an easy trap to fall into, and habitually doing stupid things is dangerous. Most of the time, our ego prevents us from recognizing our own stupidity.

Wednesday morning, I left my duplex at six thirty to go to the sheriff's office. After leaving the office Tuesday evening, I told my secretary I would not be in on Wednesday until after lunch. The day was dry and cold. It was dark, as sunrise is not until almost eight o'clock. I got to the sheriff's office at 8:22 a.m., and the sun was just peeking over the trees onto the street in front of the station. I parked my Beamer in an angle slot just down from the main entrance.

It was a small, red-brick, single-story building. I went in and was cheerfully greeted by the secretary, who sat at a desk in the center of the room. She was a little older, maybe midfifties, with salt-and-pepper hair. I could see some young attractiveness in her, but she did not age well. I introduced myself, and she remembered that I wanted to view the officer's report of the Danfurth accident. She got up and went to the bank of file cabinets behind her desk. She extracted Dan's file, turned to me, and asked me to follow her. We went through a door into a short hallway and into a small interrogation room with a table and two chairs opposing each other. I took the seat facing the door, and she placed the file in the table.

"When you're done, just bring the file back to me," and the secretary left.

I got a pencil and notepad out of my briefcase and opened the file. The right flap had several pictures taped to it in clear plastic sleeves. I did not want to look at those first, as I was afraid the images would cloud my objective review of the report. The first report was from the corner and more complete than the "Cause of Death" section on the death certificate. It read in part, "Death was caused by a blunt-force trauma to the back of the skull, causing a massive skull fracture and fatal trauma to the lower brain and brain stem. There were numerous contusions and scratches to the right side of the face; none of which were capable of causing death. There was no bruising on the right side of the face."

I copied this part down then turned to the officers' report. This indicated that Daniel Danfurth was found "twenty-four feet, six inches from the nearest part of the stump to the closest part of his body, his right foot. Mr. Danfurth's body was lying on the ground, on his stomach, feet toward the tree. It was clear Mr. Danfurth was deceased. His body was covered by numerous tree branches from one-half inch to three inches in diameter."

It continued on with the disposition of the body, but all I copied down was his location with regard to the tree.

I then looked at the pictures. Dan was shown from several angles with the branches covering him and when all the branches were removed. There were several views of the accident scene. What I found most interesting was the stump.

The only way Dan could have been hit by the tree where he was found is to have notched the tree in the direction of fall, began cutting from the opposite side, but before making a complete cut, stopped, put down the chainsaw, and walked away from the tree in direction of the fall. Then a breeze could have unexpectedly pushed the tree over. He had to be looking straight down when a tree limb hit him. If that was how it happened, there would be a thick section of the trunk that was not sawed but broken, leaving gagged splinters of wood poking up from the stump. The picture showed a cut almost completely through the trunk. The tree then fell in a couple of seconds—not enough time for Dan to walk or run that far from the stump.

I checked the section of the police report on weather conditions. It stated, "The weather was mild with a broken overcast and a light wind from the south." Not strong enough wind to push a partially cut tree of that size over, and from the wrong direction as the tree fell to the east or south east. That brought up another thought—the cabin was due south of the tree, so why was Dan walking southeast? One final observation from the picture of the spot, Dan's body lay after it was moved. There was no blood on the grass under where his head lay. With the trauma he suffered, there should have been some blood.

I was done here, so I returned the file to the secretary and left. I decided to go the cabin on my way back to the Cities. I wondered if someone from one of the other three houses on the road noticed anything unusual the day of the accident. I passed the four mailboxes at the turnoff into Gilson Road, the narrow asphalt road Liz's cabin was on, and had a thought.

I passed Liz's drive and drove about a half mile when I came upon the second house's drive, which turned off to the left. The drive continued about a quarter mile and ended at a small cabin set into the woods. Obviously, it was a vacation cabin, and no one was here. I turned my Beamer around and drove back to Gilson Road, made a left, and drove a couple of hundred yards where the third house's drive turned off to the left. I went down the drive again to a small, unoccupied vacation cabin.

Back on Gilson Road, I drove another half mile, where the road ended at a house which was obviously year around. There was a car in the drive, and smoke billowed from the chimney. I parked, went to the front door, and knocked. After a few seconds, the inner door opened, and an older woman looked out at me. I introduced myself and explained that I was investigating Mr. Danfurth's accident.

She introduced herself as Mildred Hansen and that she knew the Danfurths. Mildred was an elderly lady, maybe in her seventies, with a distinct dowager's hump. She had a plain dress on, dark support hose on the legs, with some beat-up slippers.

I asked, "Did you see anything or anyone unusual the day of the accident?"

"Well," she hesitated. "Well, it seems there was a van, dark in color, which I drove by while I was on the way to the mailbox in the morning. I glanced at the driver as I squeezed past the van. I had never seen him before. It was parked just before the Danfurths. The van was nowhere in sight when I returned."

"Do you remember about what time it was?"

"Ah, I usually go to get the mail around nine thirty."

I thanked her, gave her my card, and suggested she should call me if she thinks of anything else. I worked my way back to Highway 47 and headed to the Cities. I was thinking that Dan's death was not an accident. Going to the sheriff with this information could get me laughed out of the office, so I needed more corroborating evidence. At this point, I was about to the end of my investigational abilities. I needed to go to the next level.

Our firm uses a detective firm for client investigational purposes, Robell and Associates, and I have used one of their detectives, Willie Durante. I used Willie for a few of the cases where a client needed information on their spouse or someone else. Tomorrow I would call and set up a meeting with Willie and determine if he would be interested in continuing my investigation.

Suddenly I glanced in my rearview mirror and noticed a beige Ford 150 pickup speeding up on me. I glanced at my speed; I was going sixty-three in a fifty-five zone. The truck slowed what looked like inches from my rear bumper. We were in a long no-passing section of road. As I usually do when being tailgated, I dropped my speed to fifty-five. He continued, and I dropped to fifty. This made the driver of the pickup truck very agitated. He was offering me the one-finger salute. I continued at fifty until we reached a passing zone, and he roared around me, cut in short, missed the front of my car by inches, and again offered the one-finger salute probably because he wanted to be sure I understood his displeasure with my driving. An asshole, I thought, as he roared off down the road. Life without humor is like living in perpetual darkness.

There are two kinds of assholes. There is one that's all puckered up between two cheeks with maybe a hemorrhoid peeking out to get some air. The other is an individual who feels the world was made for only their pleasure and anything less upsets them.

An asshole is probably the most used noun in the English language a person uses to describe someone they do not like. There are hundreds of definitions for its use. My definition is simple—it is someone who has very little respect for custom, law, and other people, and it is demonstrated in their behavior.

10

I arrived back at the office at one forty-four in the afternoon and checked my messages. Nothing urgent. I checked my Rolodex for Willie's number and called his office. Willie was out, so I left a message asking him to call me at the office ASAP. If after six, call my home, and I left my number. I then called Liz's office. The receptionist passed my call through.

"Hi, John," Liz sounded much more cheerful today.

"How are things going, Liz?"

"Much better today," she offered. "Are we still on for Sunday? What do you think about going to the zoo with Carolyn? It's great in winter. We can spend some time in there then have an early dinner."

"That sounds really good. I was at the sheriff's office today."

"Did you find anything interesting?" Liz asked.

"I did, but I don't want to talk about it on the phone. Could we meet somewhere for a few minutes and discuss it?"

"It sounds like something bad," Liz responded with concern in her voice.

"I won't lie to you, it could change everything."

"So what is it?"

"It is complicated and theoretical, and I feel it best to talk face to face," I explained.

"I just can't imagine what it might be, but let's meet at the bar at Murray's at five thirty if that's okay with you," Liz instructed.

"Sure, five thirty at Murray's."

The rest of the afternoon I returned phone calls and caught up on some paper work. About four thirty, my phone rang, and my secretary told me, "Mr. Durante is on line one."

"Hello, Willie, thanks for getting back to me so quickly."

"Hey, no problem, John. What are you calling about?"

"I have a personal matter not related to the firm that I would like you to look at."

"What, you're finally thinking of getting married, and you want me to check out the chick?"

"No, no, no, nothing like that. It's about an accident."

"So you ran a little old lady over in the crosswalk, hey."

"*Nah,* nothing like that either. Can I meet you in your office?"

"Sure, say, first thing in the morning."

"What's first thing?"

"I'm working late tonight, so I won't be in until 10:30 a.m. or so."

"How about eleven o'clock in your office?"

"Sure, see you then."

Willie probably had to follow some cavorting husband around from bar to bar and will probably get a snootful before the evening is over. He'll have to sleep late in the morning. While night is thought of as a culprit for all bad happenings, in reality, most bad things happen during bright daylight.

I got to Murray's at 5:15 p.m. and went to the bar. Liz was not there yet. It was crowded as always. I spotted an open table in the back and grabbed it. The waitress came over and asked what I wanted. I ordered a Heineken. It came with a frosted mug, and she poured the entire bottle perfectly into the mug with just the proper-sized head; she was a pro.

"I'm expecting a lady friend, brown eyes with long black hair. Her name is Elizabeth. If you see her, direct her to my table."

It wasn't five minutes, and I spotted Liz at the entrance. My waitress went over to her, said something, and directed her back to my table. As Liz approached, her appearance dazzled me as usual. I got up, and we gave each other a big hug; I so enjoyed these embraces. Liz and I sat down.

"How was your day?" I inquired.

"Exceptionally well," Liz responded. "And yours?"

"Very, very busy."

The waitress came over, and Liz ordered a Whiskey Old Fashion with sweet and two olives.

"The olives are the best part. Well, what's this all about?" Liz asked.

"On the way back Saturday night, I began thinking that Dan was a better woodsman than to walk under a falling tree he was cutting down. So I decided to check the accident report. If it was an accident, Dan would have cut through the tree, put down the chain saw, walked some twenty feet in the direction of the fall, and get struck down by the tree. The blow was to the lower back of his head, which means when the tree hit him, he had to be looking straight down at his feet. Finally, there was no blood on the grass beneath where his head lay," I explained.

"Oh my god! So you don't think it was an accident! Dan didn't have any enemies. Why would someone kill him? I cannot believe anyone would murder him! You're sure it wasn't just a freak accident?"

"If it was, it would be one of the most unusual accidents I ever heard of. I don't know if it would even be possible."

"What do we do now?" asked Liz.

"I don't think I have enough to go to the police, so I am meeting with a private detective. His name is Willie Durante. I am going to ask him to check into this for us, and he'll probably want to talk with you first."

"About what!" Liz said with an air of indignation.

"Just background about Dan, that's all."

"I guess that's okay, but not at the office. I don't want inquiring minds trying to come up with why some detective is questioning me. Have him come to the house some evening."

Liz's drink came, and I was still nursing my beer. We chatted about memories of Dan. Liz indicated she was very thankful I was there for support and help.

"I don't think I could have made it through this far without you."

"Liz, you're one of my best friends, and that's what good friends do for each other. I just wish I could have done more. Anytime you need some advice, help, or just a shoulder to lean on, I'm here for you."

"Oh, thank you, John. I've always known that, and you are such a good friend."

We continued to chat until our drinks were just about finished.

I asked Liz, "Do you have time for dinner? It's a bit crowded but maybe they would have a table.

Her instant reply was, "Sure. I need to call home and let Mom know I'll be late and not to hold dinner."

I motioned our waitress over and asked her if she could check to see if we could get a table for two in the dining room. She returned a few minutes later with a positive answer. I paid our tab and gave the waitress a handsome tip. Liz made her call and joined me at the table.

Murray's was a popular restaurant which was known for steak. They've been around since 1946. I've been known to pound down a steak or two in my day, and this was perfect for me. Liz picked the place, so she must like the food.

Liz ordered rack of lamb, and I had a New York strip, medium rare, more to the rare side. I knew these chefs would get it right. I really cannot stand overdone beef. I ordered a bottle of red wine. Dinner was pleasant, and dessert was a big hug on the sidewalk in front of the restaurant. It was 8:30 p.m., and I walked Liz to her car after deflecting several slight protests. I needed one more of those warm hugs Liz always gives me.

The key to rational life is to educate innocence.

I got into the office at 7:30 a.m. Taking off had me a bit behind, and I wanted to get caught up before meeting with Willie. At ten thirty, I left for Willie's, about a fifteen-minute drive from the office. I parked in the parking lot outside a seven-floor office building on the south side of town. I entered and went to the directory. I had never been to Willie's office; he always had come to mine. Robell and Associates were located on the third floor.

I entered through double glass doors, into a small waiting area with six soft chairs and two end tables each with a lamp. There were no magazines. The reception desk was to the left behind a wall with a large, glassless window.

I went to the window, and a young lady, blond hair and bright-red lipstick, asked, "Can I help you?"

I felt like saying, "I hope so since you're the only one here," but then being a smart-ass would not gain anything, just make me feel good.

"Yes, I have an appointment with Mr. Durante."

"Mr. Durante is not in yet. Take a seat," she popped back.

I placed my briefcase in front of the table and sat in a chair next to it facing the door. I took out some case reviews to update me on a case I was handling. It was about twenty minutes later, 11:10 a.m., and Willie swept into the office.

With a huff, he said, "Mornin', John, sorry I'm late. Come in."

"Good morning, Willie. Late night, hey?"

"You got it, pal."

Willie was middle-aged with a robust build, about six feet one inch, with rounded shoulders. He had a full saltand- pepper mustache that covered his nostrils and very little dirty-gray hair on his almost bald head. His blue-gray eyes were barely visible from beneath his puffed eyelids. Willie had large, weather-beaten hands, which complemented his size-fourteen feet on which he had two well-worn brown shoes, which had not been touched with a polish rag since the day he bought them or found them in a dumpster. Also, he seemed to have missed his shave this morning. He was the sort of person who would not stick out in a crowd, an essential characteristic for someone in his business.

I followed Willie to his office, the second in a bank of four against the back wall of a large room with four desks and several file cabinets. It wasn't much, ten by twelve, a desk and chair, two chairs in front of the desk, and a credenza. A window behind the desk overlooked the parking lot. The top of the credenza was covered with a scuffle of file folders, magazines, newspapers, and other documents. Willie opened an old, ragged leather briefcase, which opened from the top and began to add to the pile on the top of the credenza. I put down my briefcase and sat.

As he emptied the briefcase, he quizzed, "So, John, what the hell is this all about?"

Willie sat down in his chair, and I explained the circumstances surrounding Dan's death. I pulled out the file with the information I gathered and handed it to Willie.

"Here's what I have. Let me know your thoughts."

Willie took some time to read and reread some parts of the information I provided him.

He looked up at me with his puffy blue-gray eyes and said, "This doesn't appear to be an accident. It appears someone did the poor bastard in. It had to be someone who knew him well enough to know where he was going and what he was going to be doing. So what do you want me to do?"

"Well, I think I've gone as far as I can. Now I need to get you to dig around and see if you can get more incriminating information. When you feel it's time to involve law enforcement, we can go that route."

"I can do that. It might take a couple of weeks."

"That's fine. Bill your time to me, not the firm, as this has nothing to do with them. This is my personal investigation."

"So why have you taken such an interest in this fellow?"

"His wife, Elizabeth, and I have been good friends since law school. Plus, I am her attorney. I feel it is my duty to resolve this, so she can put it behind her."

"Aha! Is there a little 'step in and take Dan's place' in all this?"

"Willie, why do you always go back to an ulterior motive?"

"Don't know. You being single, I guess. I just like to stick a friendly thorn in you. Plus, most of what I do involves romance."

I guess a lot of my friends and associates wonder why, at thirty-four, I never married. I was engaged to a Lynn Markeson, a fine lady, just after joining Pauli, Pauli & Steinman. We dated for a few months then decided to marry.

She was an English teacher for a suburban school district. We loved the theater, art museum, and the nightlife in the Cities. It seemed a certain union.

It came time to plan the wedding. She insisted on a Baptist wedding, I was a lifelong Catholic, and it should at least involve a priest. Her family would have nothing of that, and it came down to dropping my religion in order to get married. The impasse could not be resolved, and our engagement was dissolved. We remained friends and do see each other every now and then. She eventually married a fellow Baptist, which made her family happy, but she seemed less than fulfilled.

I thought to myself, *Why do so many people refuse to compromise?* and it is not just religion, but politics and cultural beliefs. It troubles me because this rigid, uncompromising attitude is the same that drove people to injure those of different beliefs. Just think, throughout history how many people were exterminated in the Crusades, the Inquisition, and in Germany during the dominance of Hitler, and in many other situations just because they did not have the same belief?

Religion has been the foundation on which humanity has built its societies, and it is required to maintain societal continuance. But it seems there is some sort of flaw in the human psyche, which forces normally good, honest people to do evil deeds to those who do not believe exactly the way they do. That flaw, which goes against religious teachings, could be the undoing of all human society.

Since then I've dated various other ladies, but none developed into anything serious. I've been most happy living alone and having a strong circle of friends. It certainly makes life less complicated, or so I thought. Marriage is demanding, intolerant, and time-consuming. I do value all my friends, but they, too, can be demanding, intolerant, and time-consuming.

"Okay," Willie broke my thoughts. "What I need is this Elizabeth's phone number. I want to talk to her first."

"I anticipated that. Liz and I met last night, and I briefed her on what I found and that I was going to ask you to investigate. I said you would want to talk with her."

"Well, what's the phone number?"

"It's best to contact her in the evening at home." I handed him a slip of paper. "This has her home phone and address."

"Fine, I'll try to call her tonight unless you have some plans together."

"You're a skunk, Willie."

He just smiled.

I drove back to my office. It was one fifteen in the afternoon when I got to my desk. There was a stack of messages, which I thumbed through quickly until I reached the one from my friend, James. I pulled it from the stack. He wanted me to call ASAP.

James and Deatra live in Rochester. Deatra is some sort of medical administrator and works for a local clinic. James joined a Rochester law firm. They have a very nice house—neat as a pin, as they have no children yet.

Children have a need to turn everything they come into contact with into total disaster. It must have something to do with their lack of responsibility.

I picked up the phone and dialed his office number.

"Hello, how may I direct your call?" a pleasant feminine voice came back.

"Hi, this is John Castano. I am returning James Boilen's call."

"One moment, please."

The phone rang, and James picked it up on the first ring.

"Boilen."

"Hello, James."

"It's you, John. How the hell are you?"

"I'm getting along. How is Deatra?"

"She's fine, expecting in May."

"Congratulations, you old dog. How does it feel to be a daddy soon?"

"Shit, I haven't had time to even think about that."

"I'm going to guess your call was more than just to tell me about your looming fatherhood. What's up?"

"Well, Deatra has this younger brother, who I guess just sort of goes to the U of M. Well, he's into some kind of animal rights group. It's not PETA, but some local movement. He was at this protest at the zoology building and got busted for disorderly conduct. He could just pay the fine and walk away, but he wants to take the whole thing to court. I guess he wants to make some sort of statement. All this has Deatra's mother upset, and when she is upset, Deatra is upset; and when Deatra is upset, it's hell for me. Now, I don't care what the dumb-ass does. As far as I'm concerned, he can just rot, but Deatra is on my ass to help this stupid shit."

"So where do I come in? You know I don't handle criminal defense. Don't you think this kid needs a shrink, not a lawyer?"

"He would never see a shrink. He's so dumb he's been working on this BS degree for five years, and he's still a freshman. I think it's in basket weaving."

"So how can I help?"

"Just talk to him. I'll have Deatra set up a meeting with him at a coffee shop or something. Talk to him and let him know what the potential consequences are if he pursues this thing. Scare the hell out of him if you can."

"James, if you were not a very good friend, I would be giving you the names of some excellent defense lawyers, but I'll do it. Weekends are best, just not this Sunday, as I have plans with Liz."

"Oh. How is Liz getting along these days?"

"She's getting there."

"Give her my regards," James finished.

We said our goodbyes, and we hung up.

My next call was to Liz. Not only did I want to inform her of Deatra's pregnancy, but I wanted to let her know that Willie would probably be calling her this evening. Liz was in her office.

"Hi, John."

"Liz, I got some good news for a change."

"Oh, good. I sure could use some good news."

"I talked with James today. He sends his best, and Deatra is pregnant. She is due in May."

"Oh, that's great. I'll have to call her. Where did you see him?"

"He called me while I was out seeing Willie. I returned his call."

"So you talked with this Willie guy?"

"Yes. He is going to call you tonight at home. I don't know if he will want to meet with you, or he can get the information over the phone. Let me know how it goes."

"What kind of information will he want?"

"Probably stuff like who were Dan's friends, what kind of work Dan was doing, things like that."

"Okay, John."

We chatted for about fifteen minutes before Liz had another call. I confirmed Sunday, and I would meet her and Carolyn at their home at one o'clock. The rest of the afternoon was just the usual. I had two consults on estate maters. I left the office about 5:30 p.m. and was thinking of a nice, cold Heineken when I got home. I just wanted to kick off my shoes, plop into my La-Z-Boy, sip my beer, and "veg" out for an hour.

It was Friday. I was in the office at 8:30 a.m. after the usual unmemorable evening at home. The secretaries stayed late last night to decorate the office for Christmas. I thought that was very nice of them to take their personal time each holiday to decorate our office. It made it feel a bit more like home, not like mine, as I have yet to decorate. I decided to do something about that tomorrow and get a tree.

About ten thirty, James called.

"John, Deatra has set up a meeting with her brother, Brett Malone. He will meet you at the Big Ten tomorrow at eleven o'clock. He'll be wearing a San Francisco 49ers sweatshirt. he's into California. I don't know why he just doesn't move there, except he wouldn't have his family there to wipe his ass."

"James, I get the distinct feeling you don't like your brother-in-law."

"Oh really, John? I don't know where you could have gotten such an idea? He's a stupid ass."

"Well, for you and Deatra's well-being, I'll meet, him but I won't promise it'll do any good."

"Thanks a whole lot, John. Next time we get to the Cities, we'll take you and Liz to dinner."

"Sounds good, James. I'll call you at home after we meet."

"Thanks."

We hung up, and I started to wonder just what I was going to say to this fellow. Just then my phone rang, and my secretary informed me my next client was here. I had her escort them to my office.

When I got home that evening, the answering machine's message light was blinking. I pressed the Play button. It was Liz. She informed me that

Willie called, and he is meeting with her at her house tomorrow morning at nine o'clock. I didn't call her back, as I had to hurry and change, as I was meeting another friend, Paul Greco, as we had tickets to Timberwolves basketball. The Timberwolves were in their first year in the Cities.

The game was a struggle, but my friend was great company. Paul really was an avid fan, and all the excitement flowed from him with every play. I was upstream of Paul's excitement but enjoyed just watching his enthusiasm; to see someone so immersed into the event was worth the price of the ticket. I find my close friends are just a joy to be with, and Paul certainly was not an exception.

Paul was a thin but muscular man, with light-brown hair and a rough woodsman's look. I have never seen him in anything but blue jeans, sweatshirt, and sneakers, but I'm sure he must own a suit or two, since he sells medical equipment to hospitals and doctor's offices.

After the game, we poured over our plans and hopes and pounded down a few beers in a local pub. While I did not smoke, the cigarette smoke was so thick it really wasn't necessary as I got all the benefits while not having to light up. Despite that, the night went quickly.

"I'm really looking forward to our fishing jaunt to Mexico," Paul entered with a sense of anticipation and excitement.

"I sure am," I replied. "Let's hope we have good weather at both ends."

"Yes, let's hope. What do you think we'll catch?" Paul speculated.

Paul was the victim of marrying for love and only love, which he soon discovered was not nearly enough to sustain a marriage. A divorce ensued after he discovered his bride had additional consorts outside of the marriage.

The split was bitter, as Paul had come to me to handle the legalities. To this day, neither Paul nor his ex spoke with the other. It was from that encounter that our friendship grew.

The conversation then returned to tonight's game. We stayed in the pub until after midnight, finally finding our way to the parking lot and our cars.

Saturday morning I struggled out of bed after getting home late full of hotdogs, pizza, and beer. I managed to brew a cup of java, hot and strong, and flicked on the morning news. Nothing noteworthy happened overnight; the Timberwolves lost. The weather was going to be overcast with highs in the midthirties. I finished that cup and had a refill.

By the time I finished the second cup of coffee, the cobwebs cleared from my head, and I showered and got ready to meet Saturday head-on. At 9:45 a.m. the phone rang. It was Liz. She was crying.

"What's wrong?"

"That Willie fellow you hired thinks I had something to do with Dan's death."

"What!"

"Yes, he kept asking me questions like where I was on Friday morning. I was in a meeting from 8:00 a.m. to 12:00 noon. Then several of us went to lunch together. I didn't get back to the office until one o'clock."

"I'm so sorry I am causing you all this grief."

"That's okay, John. I know you are just trying to help. I just feel maybe it's best just to leave it as an accident. It would be so much easier."

"I think Willie is just trying to cover all the bases. I would not take this too seriously."

"Okay, John. See you tomorrow."

After Liz hung up, I had a few minutes to think before the phone rang again. Why is it we pursue the truth so vigorously? Maybe Liz was right, and it would really be better just to leave things as they are and not stir up the proverbial hornet's nest. Is it revenge in the guise of justice? Is it putting a final close on something that continues to gnaw at us? Is it just that we feel justice must be done? I'm a lawyer; I should know, but I don't.

Willie was on the phone.

"Hey, John, just finished with my meeting with Elizabeth. She is a fine lady. I got a lot of info from her."

"Yeah, I just got off the phone with her, and she was plenty upset."

"Upset? About what?"

"She thinks you suspect her in Dan's demise."

"No, no, I just needed to put together some timelines and need to know who was where when. Plus, if this does go to the police, they will talk to her first, and that is the first question they will ask, plus some harder ones like,

'Were you having marital or financial problems?' She has nothing to do with what happened to Dan. I did get a list of friends and acquaintances and plenty of background on Dan and what he has been doing at the U."

"Well, maybe we can get together the beginning of next week, and you can give me all the details."

"Sounds good. I'll call you first thing Monday morning and set something up."

"Okay, but I hope it's before eleven o'clock."

The key to become successful at anything is the ability to honestly and effectively self-evaluate. Anything less is a betrayal to yourself.

I was at the Big Ten at eleven o'clock, walked through the place looking for someone in a 49ers sweatshirt, saw no one, and decided to wait near the front entrance. There were only a few people there. At eleven fifteen, an earlytwenties fellow with red hair and a 49ers sweatshirt walked in.

"Are you Brett?"

"You got him. You're Deatra's friend?"

"Yes, John Castano."

"So what are you going to do for me?"

"Let's get a booth and talk."

"Well, fine," Brett said less than enthusiastically.

We took a booth and ordered a couple of Cokes. It was obvious that Brett really had no desire to be here.

"Your sister wanted me to talk to you about your disorderly conduct charge."

"What about it?"

"They said you want to take it to trial."

"That's right."

"Why?"

"The whole idea of the protest was to get arrested. That's the only way we can make people aware of our cause.

If I plead guilty and pay the fine, it will all go away. That's what the police and the U want. No way!"

"You think by taking this to trial will get you publicity and attention, forget it. You know how this will come down? This is not like a felony. It's only a misdemeanor. They will call you before the judge, and the charges will be read. He asks you how you plead. If you plead not guilty, the judge will read the officer's arrest report. He'll ask you for your side of the story, might ask a question or two, and pronounce sentence. You'll be fined and probably have to do some community service. That's it. No reporters, no camera, and no publicity. The best course is just pleading guilty and pay the fine."

Brett looked undeterred and really made no eye contact with me at all.

"That might be the simplest way to do this, but my people wouldn't like it much."

"Who are your people?"

"I belong to the UFAC. They're my people."

"What is UFAC?"

"United Front against Animal Cruelty."

"Have you considered your family? Your mother and sister are really upset."

"They'll get over it."

"Sure they will, but why cause them any grief?"

"That's life, man. It's my life!"

I knew that this encounter was going nowhere. If I was going to get through to this young man, we would need to find out some background on UFAC and their activities, then continue our discussions some other time, as this meeting was at an end. I needed some background information on UFAC and the incident in which Brett was involved.

"When is your court appearance?"

"Two weeks from Monday."

"Could we meet again before then?"

"Why?"

"Just to talk some more, and I'll look into the incident and its consequences."

"Okay, same time, same place next week."

"Great."

I gave him my card, and Brett got up and left. I sat a few minutes reminiscing about the great times I had here and meeting Liz and Deatra. Those were the good old days. To reminisce is a gift from God.

On the way home, I decided to pick up a small Christmas tree for my duplex. I didn't know who would be over and say, "Oh, what a beautiful little tree," but at least I would be prepared. I stopped at a lot not far from my duplex and took a look around. Everything I saw was eight to twenty feet tall. God forbid, I only wanted a tree three to four feet. Then someone asked me if he could help. I explained my interest, and he led me to the very back of the lot. There sat two spruce trees the size I was looking for. The lot attendant said they were the tops of bigger trees, which had been damaged. I pointed to one, and we concluded our deal.

At home I used the rest of the afternoon to put up and decorate my little tree. I put out a few other things, all stuff given to me by my mother. I could hear her instructions, "Christmas, it is not Christmas unless you have decorations." I didn't know what decorations had to do with celebrating the birth of Christ, but so be it. To me, Christmas was not about decorations and gifts, but about celebrating Christ with family.

Could it be that dreams are our subconscious minds' excursions into parallel worlds?

I woke to a familiar rumble, one I had not heard since last March, and looked at the clock on my end table; it was five after five Sunday morning. It obviously snowed during the night, and the rumble was that of the plow clearing one side of the street. It would be back in a few minutes to clear the other side. After it passed the second time, I dozed off again and lapsed into a dream sleep.

The dream was one of a type I had just about every night for the past couple of months. It's the last dream during my sleep. The situation is different with each dream, but the link is always the same. I am searching for something, someplace, or someone and encountering numerous obstacles, never finding or reaching what I am searching for. I don't know what it all means. I'm sure some dream gurus would have an answer and as many answers as gurus, but I am sure that in the jumble of nerve endings and synapses that make up my brain, there's some logic to it all.

I was awakened by the hum and pop of a snowblower. My landlord was out early, clearing the walks and drive. I struggled out of bed and, on my way to the kitchen, opened the front door to the sight of several inches of white, fluffy snow. The street lights created bright spots and shadows and made the new snow one of nature's wonders.

I brewed a pot of coffee made from fresh ground beans. It was strong and hot, just like I like it. I sat at the dinette table and flicked on the TV. Not much happened overnight, and the locals were focused on the first major snow of the season. The anchors were speculating on whether it would last until Christmas. I finally toasted an English muffin and smeared some Extra Crunchy Jif on both halves. After polishing off the muffin, it was time to get ready for mass.

After mass, I drove to a local diner to have a late breakfast. I grabbed a stool at the counter, and a waitress, who looked as if she had not been to bed in six days, asked me what I wanted to drink. I stop here often after mass, and their coffee is awful; they load it up with chicory.

I recognized several people from the church, a few who skipped out after taking communion, as this is a longstanding Catholic practice by many. Everyone seemed consumed by the conversation of the first snow. It was enthusiastic and favorable, but as the storms pile up week after week, the conversation changes from enthusiastic to just plain annoyance and disgust.

"No coffee?" the waitress quizzed.

"Sorry, not today, just a tomato juice and water and bring some Tabasco."

"Gotcha, bud." The waitress stomped off.

Despite her appearance, she was very efficient and returned quickly with glasses of water and the tomato juice and Tabasco.

"Ready to order?"

"Sure, a number one, eggs over easy, bacon, and white toast."

"Got it."

Breakfast over, I left the diner and went home to change. I departed for Liz's about twelve o'clock, as it was a good forty-five-minute drive, and I was to be there at one o'clock. Yes, I'll probably be there fifteen minutes early.

There are three types of people when it comes to making appointments: those who arrive early; those who arrive early and wait somewhere until it is the exact time of the appointment; and those who arrive late. I'm the first type. I arrive fifteen minutes early.

Liz and Carolyn were happy to see me. We exchanged some pleasantries and departed for the zoo. As one would expect, there were not many people there. The new fallen snow provided a great background for the bear, moose, elk, and wolf exhibits. On the other hand, the African and Australian exhibits were inside and very mundane.

As we walked toward the polar bears, Carolyn, who held my hand, looked up at me and said, "Are you going to be my new daddy?"

I was startled but composed. I stopped and knelt at Carolyn's side, still holding her hand.

"No, darling, I am your very special friend."

"Why can't you be my daddy?"

"Because being a daddy is something that your mommy must also be a part of."

"So I know Mommy likes you very much," she explained.

I was in a real spot. Carolyn needed a daddy figure in her life, so how do I redirect her thoughts without crushing her emotionally?

To my rescue, Liz interjected, "Let's go into the pavilion and get some hot chocolate."

After the warm drinks, we explored a few more outside exhibits and headed for an early dinner. Carolyn wanted pizza, and we went to a place that catered to children. Actually, pizza connoisseur as I consider myself, the pizza was not bad, and they served Heineken.

While Carolyn was occupied in the ball pen, Liz leaned over close to my ear and softly said, "I really don't know where Carolyn got the idea about you being her new daddy. I hope you were not offended?"

"Oh, heavens no. I was flattered."

"You're such a good friend," Liz whispered to me.

One of the choices in life is to become good at lots of things but master of none, or to be a master of one thing and mediocre at all the others. The first will let you be free, the other will enslave you the rest of your life.

Monday morning I was at the firm at nine. On the way back to my office, I asked one of the law clerks, Rudy, to come to the office. I wanted Rudy to do some research on the United Front against Animal Cruelty. I needed as much as he could find out about them by Thursday. That would give me Friday to go over it and come up with some sort of plan for my Saturday meeting with Brett. Rudy assured me he would have the info on my desk by noon Thursday.

Rudy no sooner left, and the receptionist rang and told me James was on the phone.

"Good morning, James, and how are you this fine day?"

"Okay," the answer came back. "So how did your meeting with Brett go on Saturday?"

"Nothing really came of it. He is a very headstrong young man and is not shy about his opinions. We talked for several minutes, and it seems this UFAC organization has him really sold on their cause. They want to make some sort of statement during their hearing."

"So that's it?"

"Well, as of today, I guess so, but we have another meeting set up for next Saturday. I am going to get some background on this organization and see if I can discredit them in some way in Bretts' mind."

"I didn't even know the name of the organization he belonged to," James offered. "What does UFAC' really mean?"

"United Front against Animal Cruelty."

"For God's sake, what else is this shithead into? Keep me in the loop."

Nothing more needed to be said.

The next couple of days slipped past in stealth fashion with the usual mundane meetings. The consultations were important, as I needed to feel I was helping my fellow man. It was six thirty Wednesday evening when the phone rang at home. It was Willie.

"John, I have plenty of information on Mr. Danfurth's accident. Could we meet somewhere at your convenience to go over this and determine what direction you would like me to take?"

"Sure, is tonight at my place good for you?"

"That sounds fine, John. In an hour?"

"Fine with me. See you in an hour," and I gave him my address.

Willie arrived exactly one hour later. I had him come in, and we sat at the dining room table. He hauled a few pages of notes from his briefcase.

"I talked with Mrs. Danfurth, and she gave me the names of several friends, associates, and acquaintances that Mr. Danfurth had frequent contact with prior to his death. I have eliminated most as possible suspects."

"Mrs. Danfurth is a fine lady. I think she felt I had her under the microscope, but all the personal questions I asked her were for background only. When you talk with her again, assure her I don't believe she had anything to do with her husband's death."

"There is this fellow who found the body, Alexi Antonoff, who was to bird hunt with Mr. Danfurth that weekend.

I could not find much about him. He's sort of a mystery. All I was able to find out is he works for some secret unit of the GBI called S-4. Their function is a complete secret. I couldn't find much personal history either. He was born to immigrant parents in 1960 in Arlington, Virginia. He graduated Annapolis in 1981 and served four years in Naval intelligence. Everything ends after his discharge, and that's all I have."

"Okay, sounds interesting."

"There's also a coworker of Mr. Danfurth who I found interesting. His name is Paul Runyon, and he's also a professor of physics at the U.

Mr. Danfurth and Mr. Runyon have had several confrontations over the past year. The nature of which I have not been able to determine. Most of the confrontations were verbal, but one did involve some shoving, but no blows. I have several people who witnessed these events mostly occurring just before or after departmental meetings. I thought some of the people at the U whom I talked to spoke in an almost foreign language."

"And how's that?" I questioned.

"The words they use. I don't know if they are even in the dictionary. Like this one TA said, 'I'm not sure what the incongruity was between the two.' Why didn't he say he didn't know what the hell the disagreement was about?"

"The English language is cluttered with synonyms for common words, which add nothing to the meaning except to confuse less literate people. I suppose that people use these words in order to impress others with their great knowledge," I offered.

"Well, I suppose so," Willie whimpered then continued.

"Finally, one of the Danfurth's neighbors, the one directly behind their house, Ollas Sorenson, has had an ongoing feud with Mr. Danfurth over a tree in their backyard, which has overgrown into his yard. He doesn't like the overhang and feels Mr. Danfurth should remove the overhang at his expense. Mr. Danfurth had a different view. Where do we go from here?" questioned Willie.

"Have you found out anything about Danfurth?"

"Not much. He's a full professor of physics. He's been doing some research as all these guys do in addition to their educational responsibilities."

"Well, with a lot of these professors, the research seems to be the most important duty, and the education of students is secondary," I injected.

"Naw, I understand your thinking. I don't think Mr. Danfurth was that way. He really took his educational responsibilities very strongly. Most of his students said he always had time for them and never demeaned them when they asked a question."

"Okay, Willie, see what more you can find on his students and research. We need to come up with possible motives for his murder. That's the only way we'll be able to interest the police. They will have to be involved at some point. We need to get as much as possible, or they may dismiss the whole thing."

"You got it, boss, but it's going to cost you."

"That's fine."

Thursday arrived as a bright new day, although it was cold as hell. Many told me hell is a hot place, but since it was created to punish sinners, I would guess it could be both, depending on what condition would be the greatest punishment for the individual interned.

I followed my usual weekday morning coffee, TV news and some grub, in that order. I began rolling over in my mind why am I going through all this with Liz and Dan; it could be traumatic for Liz and her family. It's costing me a bundle and could open a real Pandora's box. Maybe as a member of society, I am obligated to do this as society demands justice, and I'm just the instrument?

I figure these thoughts were just academic, as I was not about to drop the investigation. So my thoughts traveled to what to do next.

The phone rang. I answered, "Yo, John here."

"John, its Liz. You cannot believe what's happening now. The Internal Revenue Service is going to audit our tax returns for the last three years. God, I don't need this. What am I going to do?"

"Who did your taxes?"

"Dan."

"Do you have the copies and receipts?"

"I don't know. I'll have to go through Dan's files and the safe and see if I can find them."

"Are you at home?"

"Of course. I never go to work this early."

"When can you look for the records?"

"Tonight after work. Could you come over after work please, please. I'm so uptight."

"Of course. What time?"

"Five o'clock."

At the office, our legal clerk had a file on my desk. It was titled, *United Front against Animal Cruelty (UFAC).*

The group organized in Wisconsin in 1984 and applied for nonprofit status. Their mission statement was, "To make the public aware of the abuse of animals in research conducted at public institutions." There was a list of officers and "cells" at several universities all in the upper Midwest. Al Reitbrock was their chairman and was located at their "cell" in Madison.

They had offices. The cell chairmen were listed as the contact for that cell. Funding was obtained from public donations and the organization called United Workers for Public Justice. There was no information on them. The local cell chairman in the Cities cell is Albert Wertz. He lives in the Uptown area of Minneapolis, which is the cell's headquarters. He's not a student, but works as a bus driver for a private bus company.

The organization was involved in nonviolent protest at several universities including the U of M. Several of these protests resulted in arrests for trespassing and disorderly conduct. All were taken to a hearing, where the defendants made loud and raucous protests. Several of these outbreaks resulted in the defendants being convicted of contempt of court, in addition to the charges of which they were accused. The sentences ranged from thirty to sixty days in jail, fines up to one thousand dollars and community service.

The rest of my day was the usual. I left the office for Liz's at four fifteen, and at four forty-five, I was at Liz's. Carolyn and Grandma just finished up with dinner.

"I haven't eaten. Would you join me? It's just pizza and a salad," Liz invited. "It's from your favorite pizzeria."

"Sure, how can I refuse?"

I sat at the counter across Liz, and she passed the salad bowl. It was her special Italian parmesan dressing on a bed of fresh romaine. I loaded my plate, as I only had an egg salad sandwich for lunch. The pizza was, as usual, topnotch.

Liz explained, "I found the tax copies and receipts in the safe. I also found this."

She handed me a brown file envelope about an inch thick and tied down with two buttons by a red string.

"What's this?" I questioned.

"I don't know. I have never seen this before. It was Dan's and is full of technical data. It's not like Dan to store work stuff in our safe. He must have had some reason to put it there and not at work."

"Would you like me to represent you at the audit?"

"Yes, I was hoping you would."

"Can I take Dan's file along with your tax records? I need to spend some time with both."

"Yes," Liz agreed.

We finished dinner and retired to the family room, where we spent an hour or so chatting. Liz had to get Carolyn to bed; it was 7:30 p.m. We said our goodbyes, and I left.

At home, I opened Dan's brown file. The first portion consisted of ninety-two pages, numbered and clipped together by an expandable metal clip, of hand-printed calculations, graphs, charts, and data tables. It seemed to have something to do with how objects traveled at high speed through space. Dan was a professor of applied physics, so this would fit into his area of education and training. But why was all this handwritten and in his safe at home?

I looked at six pages that were not part of the bound file. They were letters with no letterhead or address and signed by a Phillip Longhouse. He was inquiring as to the progress of Project Wasp. They all ended simply with, "Please reply via the usual route." They were dated 7/16/87, 11/22/87, 3/5/88, 8/4/88, 1/15/89, and 10/10/89. The last one was dated only eight days before Dan's death. There was one other thing, a corporate credit card with an organization called SIAIBM, in Dan's file.

I had the feeling that this file should be kept in a very secure place, so in the morning, I would place it in my personal safe at the office. I used the rest of the night looking over the tax returns for the Danfurths. I didn't see anything that seemed like a red flag, but then I'm not a CPA. There was an income entry under miscellaneous income that listed the US Defense Department for 13,700 dollars. I decided to bounce them off our firm's CPA and see if they could come up with something. It was 12:30 a.m., and I retired for the evening.

August 1989
Washington, DC

The life of the cicada might seem unique. There are several species of cicadas, but the most common in North America has a seventeen-year life cycle. It begins when the eggs laid in a slit on a branch of a deciduous tree hatch, and the nymph falls to the ground, where it burrows down as much as eight feet using strong front feet to dig.

Attaching itself to the root of a tree, it sucks the juice from the root to sustain itself. It remains there until the seventeenth year, at which time it crawls to the surface and climbs up the trunk of a tree where it attaches itself.

Soon the mature cicada emerges and begins its mating ritual. The male makes the loud, shrill sound most of us know to attract the silent female. Mating complete, the male dies. The female then makes a slit in the bark of a branch and deposits her eggs in it. She then dies herself. The next life cycle begins.

The real story is how the organism grows, unseen, for years, sucking the life juices from its surroundings to emerge and dominate the scene for a brief period of time only to drop back into obscurity again. The plans of many follow a similar cycle. The key is to be able to discover and monitor those cycles and determine their impact on mankind, or to be prepared to take action when they emerge.

In a room in a somewhat seedy part of Washington, DC, three men sat on chairs around a small coffee table. It was evening, but some daylight hung on the western horizon. It was a warm and humid evening in late summer. The men had the only window open, but it did little to cool the room. Outside, the evening cicadas began their irritating cry for a mate. The noise was somewhat distracting, but not at the level of the heat and humidity in the room, so the window stayed open.

One of the men, a rather large, middle-aged man, well shaven wearing suit pants, white shirt and blue tie, which was loosened from his collar, asked with an Eastern European accent, "Do you understand what is required of you?"

"Yes," replied the second, a taller man one could tell even sitting. He was middle-aged with some graying hair and neat, business-casual clothes.

"Are you sure? Do you have a plan? We don't have much time before this project will be finished, and our opportunity will be lost."

"Alexi will give me the specific information, which I will use to determine my exact approach, but I have some of my soldiers already inside collecting what they are able to find," injected the third, who was slightly balding, midthirties, sort of a hippie-looking fellow.

"Good. What specific information are you expecting, Al?" replied the first.

"Time, place, and opportunity."

Alexi added, "I am very close to the situation, and that should not be a problem."

"Okay, then the operation is a go. I expect to have this resolved by the end of September, as the final meeting is set for October. Are you in agreement?" concluded the first.

"It'll be done!" affirmed Alexi.

"Good, gentlemen. Until October then. The meeting is over."

It was another sunny, cold day, and everyone at the office was in full holiday spirit. First thing I did was to place Dan's file in my personal wall safe. Next was to call Liz at her office, as I was hoping to meet her for lunch to discuss what I found in the tax records and Dan's file. She had lunch free, so we decided to meet at Murray's at twelve fifteen. My next call was to Willie's office, hoping he just might be in early, and I was in luck.

"Durante here."

"Willie, I didn't expect you in this early."

"Go ahead, be a smart-ass. I'm here early most mornings. What can I do for you?"

"I was wondering if we could meet at your convenience sometime this weekend. I have some interesting new information about Dan?"

"Sure. All I got going is tailing some bimbo on Sunday afternoon during the football game, whose husband thinks some other guy is banging her."

"Sounds like a good time to stray, during the football game, that is."

"Yeah, how about your place on Saturday at two?"

"Two is fine, but let's do it at my office."

"Sure, but why there?"

"The stuff is there. I'll be in the lobby at two to let you in."

"Okay, see you tomorrow at two, your office."

The morning flew by, and I suddenly realized it was noon. I rushed out of the office for my lunch meeting with Liz. Murray's was crowded as usual, but I had made a lunch reservation. Liz was there, and we were seated at a table off in the corner. After the usual pleasantries, we ordered. I suggested we wait to talk business until after we were done with lunch.

Liz ordered a Waldorf salad, and me a half-pound burger done medium with onion, bacon, and cheese. I felt I needed an unhealthy treat, but I did skip the fries. After lunch was done, I began the business.

"Liz, I reviewed your tax returns and couldn't see anything that would be a problem. I have one question. What was Dan doing for the Defense Department?"

"I have no idea," Liz responded. "I didn't know anything about work for the Defense Department."

"Okay. They paid him 13,700 dollars last year. Since I am not a CPA, I would like to have the firm's CPA take a look at the returns. Is that okay with you?"

"By all means, John. Is that all?"

"No. I went through Dan's file last night and have some questions. Most of what was there was very technical information, but I found six memos and a corporate credit card. Each memo was exactly the same. They inquired as to the progress of Project Wasp and instructed Dan to 'reply via the usual route.' These are the dates," I said as I slid my notes to Liz.

"Do these dates have any significance?"

I paused for several seconds while Liz read the dates.

"The corporate card was insured by an organization called SIAIBM. Do you know anything about SIAIMB?"

Liz grabbed her purse from the chair next to her, and after rustling in that bag of tricks for a while, she pulled out her day planner. It is absolutely amazing what a woman can get in such a small sack.

She searched the pages for a few seconds then answered, "Dan traveled to Washington, DC, on January 15 and was scheduled to travel there again on October 10. His accident, or murder, canceled that trip. He took two trips to Washington in 1987 and in 1988, but I am not sure of the dates."

"Interesting."

"As far as this company, SIAIBM, I never heard of it."

"Why did Dan travel to Washington?" I quizzed.

"He told me he was on some sort of scholastic board which reviewed advances in applied physics. They met twice a year or so."

"Did this board have a name?"

"If so, Dan never mentioned it to me."

"Where did he stay when he was there?"

"At a vacation inn."

"Do you know which one?"

"No, but I have a phone number. Dan always said if I needed to contact him, and he was out of his room, to ask for the day manager, and he would contact him."

"How long would Dan be gone?"

"Two days."

I copied the phone number down on my notes. We used the next twenty minutes or so just chatting.

"Carolyn really enjoyed last Sunday. Would you consider doing something again this Sunday?"

"Sure, what did you have in mind?"

"*The Nutcracker* is at a theater downtown, and I have four tickets I got before Dan died. Carolyn really wants to see it. Mom will come with, so that leaves a ticket for you."

"I don't want to break into a family thing."

"Come on, John, you're just like family."

"Okay, what time?"

"Be at the house at twelve thirty. The play is at two o'clock."

It was going to be a busy Saturday. I was to meet with Brett at eleven then meet with Willie at the office at two. I began thinking just what approach I was going to take with Brett. My thoughts were that the only chance I had was to expose the true intentions of UFAC and hope he realizes he is just a pawn. All they wanted from the hearing was to create publicity for their organization and to be disruptive to the legal process. I needed to emphasize the consequences of that action and that he would get little support from the group once the event was over. I had little hope this would work, but the small chance it would was worth the effort since it was a favor for a friend.

Before leaving for my meeting with Brett, I dialed the vacation-inn contact number Liz gave me.

"Vacation Inn West, can I help you?"

"Yes, please ring guest Dan Danfurth's room."

"One moment please."

There was a long silence, two to three minutes. I would have thought I was disconnected, except I could hear muffled, unintelligible voices. Then a different voice, "Sir, Mr. Danfurth is not registered and does not have a reservation. May I help you in some other way?"

"No, I must have the wrong inn."

I was at the Big Ten at eleven o'clock and got a booth. About eleven twenty, Brett strolled in, wearing the same 49ers sweatshirt. I wondered if it had been washed since last week; probably not.

"Brett, over here."

Brett walked over and sat across me in the booth.

"So why am I here?" he inquired.

"Because we need to talk about UFAC and your hearing."

"So what's to talk about?"

"Have you any idea that UFAC is using you?"

"Using me? Forget it."

"Yes, using you. They set you and a few of your comrades up to get busted. They then pumped you full of a lot of crap to get you angry. When you go before the judge at the hearing, you are instructed to be disruptive and defiant and create an incident all in the name of the cause. You and your pals are convicted of contempt of court and disorderly conduct and sentenced to thirty to sixty days in jail, fined around a thousand dollars, and have to do community service. That's the last time you will see a UFAC person. You will serve the time, pay the fine, and do community service by yourself."

"How do you know this?"

"Because I checked up on the organization and past events similar to yours."

"That's a bunch of bullshit. You're doing my sister's bidding. I'm out of here."

"Fine, but before you go, here are my notes. Take them and check them out. You might be surprised."

Brett grunted but took the notes and left. I grabbed a bite to eat then headed to the office.

I got to the office at 1:15 p.m. Willie was to be here at two. I cleaned up a few business things and brewed some fresh, hot, strong coffee. I usually don't drink coffee after breakfast, but Willie keeps his motor running on the stuff.

The coffee was still perking, and it was five until two. I took the elevator to the lobby and saw Willie driving into the parking lot. He pulled up and parked in the first handicapped space and headed for the door. I let him in.

"Don't see a handicap permit in your windshield."

"You the handicap police? I don't think any cripples are going to be looking for a spot here today."

"Ah, just giving you some shit."

We took the elevator to the office. I offered Willie a cup of coffee.

"It's fresh, strong, and hot."

"Sure, John," he said as he sat in a chair behind the coffee table. "What you got?"

I brought Dan's file over and sat next to Willie.

"Liz found this in the safe at home while she was searching for their tax records. She said it was unusual that Dan would have work at home."

Willie scanned the technical report then looked at the memos and credit card.

"What's this Project Wasp?"

"Liz doesn't know. It seems Dan was on some sort of technical board and traveled for meetings to Washington, DC, on the dates of the memos. She gave me the phone number of a vacation inn where Dan stayed. I called the number. It was the Vacation Inn West. She also knew nothing about the organization, SIAIBM, insuring the card. I checked the organization out but could find nothing on it."

"Where did you check out this SIAIBM?"

"Just stuff here at the office like list of US corporations, educational institutions, and charities."

"Interesting. Can I take this file with me? I need to go through the whole thing and make some notes. Then I'll get it back to you."

"I'm sure that'll be okay with Liz."

Before Willie left, a personal question popped into my mind; and since he always gave me some crap about being single, I wanted to get some background on him, so I asked him why he wasn't married.

He hesitated a while, and I kept expecting a response. Then he began, "I was. Her name was Clair Anne."

"You divorced?" I questioned.

After another long pause and with a tortured effort, Willie began, "We were married in 1977. She was a nurse at County, and I was a police officer. She worked the eleven to seven in the morning shift, so I worked the midnight to eight shift so we would have some time together during the day."

Willie paused again.

"We did everything together. We were so much in love, never had any kids, though, but were planning to do so.

On the night of July 14, 1984, Clair Anne was on the way to work when a drunk blew through a red light and slammed into the driver's side of her car."

I could see Willie's eyes begin to tear and realized how difficult this was for him.

"I can see this is bothering you. You don't need to continue, Willie."

"No, I want to. I haven't really told this to anyone since it happened. I was on my beat when the dispatcher informed me of the accident. I rushed to the hospital and into emergency. A doctor came out from a crash room and restrained me. He told me Clair Anne was dead on arrival. He also told me she was two months pregnant. The accident caused a miscarriage.

"I asked to see her, and the doctor suggested I not do that. He said, 'Remember her as she was,' but I insisted. I had worked many fatal accidents, and I didn't think it would be a problem. I was wrong.

"We went into the crash room, and in the center was a table with Clair Anne's body covered by a sheet. Blood had seeped through the sheet in several spots on her left side. The doctor took hold of the sheet and turned to me and said, 'Sure you want to do this?' I said yes, and he slowly pulled the sheet back to Clair Anne's waist.

"The left side of her head was a mass of mangled flesh and bone. Her left eye was gone. Her shoulder was crushed into her chest, and her arm was a mangled mess. From her right side, she looked as if she were sleeping. I don't remember what happened then, but the doctor told me I let out a loud cry, collapsed to my knees, and began to wail profusely. Two nurses came and, with the doctor, helped me into an empty exam room."

"God, I'm sorry to hear that, Willie."

"That's not the end of the tale. The drunk was not hurt. It was his third OWI. He was given a three-year license suspension, a thirty-day jail sentence, and two years' probation for OWI homicide with a motor vehicle. About a year later I was still working the late shift, when I saw him stumble from a bar and attempt to open his car door.

"I stopped, knowing he was still suspended and confronted him. He turned and spit on me. I proceeded to beat the shit out of him and almost killed him. He was in the hospital a month. I lost my job and landed where I am now.

That's the story."

"I'm so sorry about you losing your wife, and I can understand your reaction. Thank you for telling me."

After a few more minutes, Willie related this story, "There was this old farmer who had a horse whose name was Danny. He and Danny rode all over the farm and sometimes into town. They loved each other. But both got older. A time came when he couldn't ride Danny because Danny would just stand there if you mounted him, and if you hitched him to a wagon, he would back up until the wagon stopped against something.

"The farmer told his wife that he was thinking of taking old Danny to the glue factory, as he was not much good, and to take care of him was costing lots of money. That evening he sat with his wife at dinner. They were having pork chops. He took his first bite, chewed a bit with a quizzical look, then spit it out. He asked his wife what she put on the chops. She replied, 'Just a little glue. I thought you might want to see how old Danny is going to taste.'

"Danny lived a couple more years and died peacefully in his stall one night. The next day the farmer took his backhoe into the middle of the pasture that Donny loved so much and dug a big hole. He gently lifted Danny with the shovel and placed him in the hole and buried him.

"The moral of the story is sometimes we need a shock in our lives in order to get our priorities straight.

"Catch you later," said Willie as he left the office.

21

While at church—I usually get there earlier than most—a young lady, probably about twelve years old, with cerebral palsy and in a wheelchair was rolled in by her mother and father. They sat in the front where space is provided for wheelchairs. I was across the aisle and two pews behind. After the sermon, Father sat in his chair for the usual minute or so given for reflection. Suddenly an extremely bright pinpoint of light appeared over the altar table. The light grew rapidly into the size of a basketball, with light streams shooting from it.

The light ball slowly moved from over the altar to a position just above and slightly in front of the girl with CP. Suddenly the ball descended onto the child, and a flash of light, so bright it was as if tens of thousands of flashbulbs went off simultaneously, filled the church. I was temporarily blinded.

As my vision slowly came back, I saw that every candle in the church was lit: on the altar, in the prayer areas, and on the memorial tables. They glowed with a brightness I never witnessed before. It was then I saw the young lady with CP standing, looking at her hands. They were not shaking and twisting uncontrollably as they did a few seconds before.

She covered her face with her hands for a few moments then looked at them again. She turned to her parents then swung and faced the congregation, tears streaming from her eyes. She ran down the aisle as fast as any child her age could and threw open the doors outside. Standing on the church steps, sun streaming down on her tear-dampened face, she let out a loud cry of joy. Her imprisonment in a body over which she had no control was over. She was now like every other twelve-year-old girl. How little we make of our own normality!

I rolled over and looked at the clock next to my bed. It was 6:33 a.m. and time to get up. I rolled onto my back and looked up at the ceiling several minutes to gather my thoughts and reflect on my dream. Is it possible that the child represents all humanity which suffers from limitations that keep us from reaching our full potential, and we need to look for the ball of light?

Sunday morning was the usual. Mass was not as eventful as my dream. I had the usual at my Sunday breakfast.

The counter waitress was her grumpy, old self. The tomato juice was cold and sweet, the eggs hard, and the toast dry, but what would Sunday morning be without this? I went from the diner to Liz's and got there about twelve.

Grandma let me in, and Carolyn came running up.

"Hi, John. Are you going with us to the theater?"

"Yes, darling, are you excited about the play?"

"Oh yes, all the toys come to life. You know, my toys are alive too."

"They live in you, right?"

"Well, sort of, I guess."

Liz walked into the living room. She was dressed in a black silk pantsuit with a gold metal chain belt, and a black-fringe, red cape. Her dark-black hair framed her long, narrow face. Then there were those big brown eyes. She looked absolutely dazzling.

"Hello, John. Carolyn was so excited that you were coming with us."

"I wouldn't miss it," I assured her.

The Nutcracker was as I remembered it. My family attended the play when I was seven. My mother, Isabel, and father, Paul, took the three of us, my older sister, Nancy, my younger sister, Betty, and me. We were so excited, as we never attended a play before, and we traveled to Madison to see it. We were staying overnight in the Midway Motor Lodge. It was such an adventure.

I remember that during the play, Betty nodded off and began snoring. Mom was so embarrassed but couldn't reach Betty; she was on the other side of Dad, who was so captured by the play he never noticed, or didn't care. Nancy and I just giggled. Mom gave us *that look*, which, in our family, meant, "If you know what's good for, you'll stop what you're doing now." She nodded her head at Nancy. That meant, "Poke Betty now." Nancy followed orders, but it did little good, as Betty snored through the entire second half of *The Nutcracker.*

Carolyn never nodded nor blinked throughout the play. At intermission I got us all an ice cream from a vendor at the front of our isle.

Carolyn remarked, "I sure would like toys like that."

"You already do," I told her.

"*No,* I don't!"

"Yes, you do. You just don't know where to look."

"Then where do I look?"

I pointed to her forehead and said, "Right here."

"I don't understand," Carolyn questioned.

"Someday you will—then you will know how all your toys come alive."

After the play, we went to dinner at an upscale restaurant just a few blocks from Liz's house. Carolyn was a perfect lady during dinner.

We were finishing up with a cup of coffee when a tall, dark-haired man I had never met strolled over and greeted us, "Hi, Liz, out with the family?"

"Sort of, Phil. You know mom and Carolyn. This is my attorney, John Castano."

My thoughts started spinning. She knew this Phil well, and suddenly I'm her attorney—nothing about friend. I had a sinking feeling in my stomach, but why?

"Hello, John, I'm Phil Roland."

"Nice to meet you," but I really wasn't thinking that.

"Phil was Dan's good friend. They met playing handball, members of the same club and all that, you know," explained Liz. "Phil is sort of the club's bachelor."

After an exchange of a few meaningless pleasantries, Phil excused himself and returned to his table, where he sat with another couple. I began to wonder about the exchange. I think the thing that caused my troubled thoughts was being introduced as Liz's attorney. I always thought that I was something more than just her attorney. Maybe I was being too presumptive.

We returned to Liz's about 6:30 p.m. It was dark, and there were no lights on in Liz's house.

She remarked, "That's odd. My timer light is out."

"Maybe the bulb burned out," I suggested.

We went in, and after turning the foyer light on, Liz instantly said, "Something is wrong!"

"Stay here," she instructed Mom and Carolyn.

She began searching each room, starting with the living room. I followed. She entered the office and turned on the light. There was a large gasp, "Oh, god!"

The desk was littered with opened and scattered files from the file cabinet.

"Someone broke in!" she exclaimed.

"It certainly looks that way. I'll call the police," I offered.

"Please do."

Liz and I checked the house, and all the doors and windows were secure. The intruder was a professional. We must have interrupted the burglar in the act, as he was far too professional to leave files scattered around.

The police arrived in just a few minutes. They inspected the desk and files.

"Do you have any idea what the intruder was looking for?"

"No, these files contained various family communications. I don't know what someone would want with that. Nothing else seems to be disturbed."

"Have you found the point of entry?"

"No, none of the doors or windows looked as if they were opened."

"We'll have a look around if you don't mind."

"Sure," Liz agreed.

After a few minutes the police returned.

"Apparently, the culprit exited the side garage door, as it was unlocked, and fresh footprints in the snow led from the door behind the neighbor's house and ended at their drive. He must have had a car parked somewhere close. Did you see any unusual cars on the street?"

"No," I replied and turned to Liz. "Did you see any cars?"

"No, nothing on the street. How did this guy get in?"

"He must have come through the front door, probably picked the lock. I speculate when he saw you pull into the driveway, he ducked into the garage. Once you guys were in, he left via the garage door. He must have had his car somewhere close by."

The police filled out their incident report, had us sign off on it, and left. I offered to have Liz spend the night at my place, but she declined.

"I'll be okay, John."

"Well, if you need me, please don't hesitate to call."

I spent an hour or so helping Liz clean up and file the folders and spent some time talking about possible reasons for the break-in. Liz seemed calm and collected. She was not prone to hysteria or irrational behavior while under stress. I felt confident that she would be okay. This guy would not be back, but I suggested Liz secure all her doors and place a chair in front of each. If anyone would open the door, it would make some noise—a burglar's worst enemy.

The first thing I did Monday morning was to call Liz and check how the rest of her evening went. She didn't sleep well, but there was nothing unusual. I said I would stop by after work if she didn't mind. She didn't. I arrived at the office at nine. The office staff was in full holiday spirit. Christmas was a week from today. I grabbed a cup of coffee from the lounge and went to my office. My Monday schedule was on my desk, along with a return-call request from Brett. Then I noticed it. On my desk was a small notebook I used to keep tract of expenses. I always kept this in my locked drawer. I made an entry on Saturday, while waiting for Willie, but returned the notebook to the safe when I removed Dan's file.

The material in the locked drawer was not in the order I kept them; someone was in the drawer over the weekend. The only one other than me that has a key is my secretary.

I buzzed her and asked, "Were you in over this past weekend?"

"No, why do you ask?"

"Someone was in my locked drawer and rearranged the stuff in it and left my expense notebook on the desk.

Where do you keep your key?"

"Locked in my desk drawer. It certainly wasn't me."

"Hmm, could you check with the others and see if anyone was in the office Saturday late afternoon or Sunday? I was here Saturday from one thirty to three o'clock."

"Sure."

I called Brett at the number he left.

A young female voice answered, "Hello."

"Yes, Brett Malone, please."

"Sure, dude, just a moment."

About a minute passed before Brett answered, "It's Brett."

"John Castano, what can I help you with?"

"My hearing is in four hours. I checked out what you said, and you were right. After this is all over, these guys are going to hang me out to dry. What should I do?"

"You need to plead guilty, but your fellow rowdies will probably start a fuss right off the bat. I'll call the clerk for that court and explain the situation and see if we can get you split off from the others. If so, when the judge asks you how you plead, say 'guilty.' I'll call now and get back to you."

"Okay."

I called the court and talked with the clerk. He needed to speak with the judge and got back to me in a half hour. He said Brett would be called separately before the other defendants but cautioned me that there would be hell to pay if Brett did not plead out. I assured him he would, and I would be at the court only as his advisor.

I told Brett to be at the court at one o'clock, and I would be in the court to act as an advisor only. I cautioned him, because the judge is cutting him some slack, he needed to follow through with his plea, or it would be considerably worse than had he stood with the group.

As I was finishing up with Brett, Celia, my secretary, beeped me on the intercom.

"Yes, Celia."

"I talked with everyone but Randolph. He left with his family for the holiday and will not be back until the third. None of them were at the office on Saturday or Sunday. Is there anything else you would like me to do?"

"Thank you so much, Celia. No, nothing right now."

I needed to give Willie an update.

I called Willie and got his answering machine and left a message, "Willie, John here. Call me ASAP."

About eleven forty-five, Willie called, "Waz up, John?"

"We need to meet, say, my office. Could you make five?"

"Sounds important. Five is fine."

I left the office at twelve and grabbed a sandwich from the deli just down the street and headed for the courthouse. Arriving at the courthouse, I checked with the receptionist to see where municipal court was being held. Got to the courtroom and found Brett on the bench outside.

"Hello, Brett. Are you ready?"

"I guess."

"Do you have any questions?"

"I hope I'm doing the right thing. My friends are not going to be happy with me."

"They are not your friends. They are using you for their own purposes," I assured Brett.

At one o'clock the bailiff opened the courtroom door.

"Brett Malone."

I followed Brett and the bailiff in and had a seat on the aisle in the second row.

The judge read the charges, "Brett Malone, you are charged with disorderly conduct and trespassing. How do you plead?"

"Guilty, sir."

"I'll accept the plea for disorderly conduct and fine you seventy-five dollars. I am dropping the trespassing charge since you are a student, and this happened on university property. In the future, be more rational when expressing your frustrations. See the bailiff."

I got up and walked out to the courtroom. There were three fellows and a young lady sitting in the bench. I thought these must be Brett's cohorts. I waited at the elevators for Brett to finish with the bailiff.

As he came out, one of the older fellows questioned, "Why were you in the court?"

Brett replied, "I pleaded guilty."

"What! That's not the plan. You deserted us!"

"I'm sorry, but I felt this was best."

He glared at Brett but said nothing.

I went down in the elevator with Brett.

"Who was the guy talking to you?"

"Albert Wertz. He is the local chapter chairman."

"So that's Wertz."

We parted company in the lobby, and I returned to the office and called James. He seemed satisfied with the outcome.

Willie was at the office at 4:45 p.m. Celia escorted him to my office.

"Thank you, Celia. Have a seat, Willie."

"So tell me what is so important."

"Yesterday afternoon I went to The Nutcracker with Liz, Carolyn, and her mom. We went to dinner after the play. We got back to Liz's at seven thirty or so and interrupted an intruder. He was a professional, apparently picked the lock on her front door, and focused on going through the family files. He was looking for some sort of information. He snuck into the garage when he heard us coming and slipped out the side door once we were in. Then this morning I found someone had gone through my locked drawer sometime after we left on Saturday. I think he was looking for information I may have related to Dan and this SIAIBM."

"Sounds logical to me. Did he take anything from either you or Liz?"

"Liz didn't think he took anything. You have all I have of Dan's stuff. Nothing was taken from my drawer."

"How did he get into the drawer?"

"I haven't the foggiest idea! Must have picked the lock as he did at Liz's," I answered

"Call the building superintendent and see if I could get a look at the security cameras tapes from this weekend.

Maybe I can get a visual look at who may have gotten in here. I'm in the process of getting information on SIAIBM.

I'm taking Dan's file to someone I know who is educated in physics and math in order to get some idea of just what Dan was working on. I'm also trying to track down this Phillip Longhouse, but I don't have a shitload of information to go on. The Vacation Inn West in Washington is all I have."

"I'm sure the building superintendent is gone for the day, but I'll talk to him tomorrow and set something up. Keep that file secure since it looks like someone is after it," I emphasized.

It was 5:50 p.m. when I got to Liz's. Mom cooked a pot roast and had a place set for me.

"Liz said you were going to stop by, so I set a place for you. Do you like pot roast?"

“One of my favorites,” I responded.

“Liz brought some Heineken home. She said you liked it.”

“That’s very thoughtful of Liz.”

Liz and Carolyn greeted me in the kitchen.

“Hi, John, did they catch the burglar yet?” quizzed Carolyn.

“No, honey, but we’ll make sure he doesn’t get into your house again.”

“He wasn’t in my room, was he?”

“No, he was just in the office,” I consoled.

After dinner, which was the best pot roast I’ve had since leaving home because my mother was an expert potroast chef, Liz and I retired to the office.

“Have the police given you any kind of update?”

“No, not a word. I don’t think they will ever find out much more than they know now.”

“Someone got into my office at work over the weekend and went through my locked drawer. They didn’t find what they were looking for. I think it is the same chap that got into your house. I think they are looking for something of Dan’s. Willie has Dan’s file, and that may be what he’s after.”

“Really?”

“I have Willie checking into the whole thing. I’ll keep you posted.”

We chatted for a couple more hours about her work, mine, and the fast-approaching Christmas Day. I left for home at nine thirty.

The rest of the week was mundane, as Christmas cheer usually reduces people's need for legal services. It's good for my business that Christmas cheer only lasts a few days. I contacted James and told him I would like to have lunch with him and Deatra on Saturday in Rochester if they were free. I was going to be traveling home for Christmas and will be going through Rochester. We decided to meet at a downtown restaurant at eleven thirty.

Saturday morning, after my coffee, I headed for Rochester. I picked up a breakfast sandwich at McDonald's on the way out to the Cities. It was just a short distance from my duplex to Highway 52, and it was about an hour or so, depending on traffic, to Rochester. I usually like to take the River Road home on the Wisconsin side, as it is just a spectacular drive, but I wanted to see James and Deatra.

I got to the restaurant in Rochester at eleven twenty and spotted James and Deatra at a booth in front at the windows. They got up and waved me over. Deatra had a white-red-and-green turtleneck sweater with green cotton slacks. She looked lovely and in the Christmas spirit. Her pregnancy was not noticeable, at least to an untrained observer as me. James had dark-blue slacks, a light-blue cotton turtle neck pullover, and a gray smoking jacket. He looked very upscale and professional.

James moved over and sat next to Deatra; I sat across them. We exchanged all the pleasantries then spent some time getting up-to-date with each other's lives. It had been more than a year and a half since we saw each other. Both James and Deatra ordered chicken dumpling soup and a house salad with fresh baked rolls and water. I ordered the New York strip steak sandwich on a French roll with fries and coleslaw and an iced tea.

I knew it was not the healthiest choice, but, hell, how boring my life would be if all I ate were what some health guru says I "needed to eat." Just call me an independent kind of guy.

Eventually our conversation came to Brett. Both James and Deatra were very appreciative for convincing Brett to plead out.

I warned, "Keep in close touch with Brett, as he is an outcast from his support group. The head of that group, Albert Wertz, was very unhappy with him when he saw him at the courthouse."

"We will," agreed Deatra. "He's coming down tomorrow to be with Mom and us for Christmas."

"If you can, without putting him on the defensive, find out anything you can on this UFAC and his activity with them."

"Okay, we'll do what we can without ruining our Christmas," said Deatra, while James nodded his head in agreement.

I got to Mom and Dad's at three. When I walked into the house, the smell of baking sugar cookies filled my nostrils. Mom was where she spent most of her waking hours, the kitchen. We greeted, and she offered a cookie, still warm from the oven.

"Dad went to the hardware store to get replacement bulbs for the Christmas tree. Nancy will be here tomorrow with the family. Betty and Terry will come both days."

Nancy lives in Madison and works in the Department of Education for the state. Her husband, Josh Williamson, works as some sort of insurance executive. They have two boys, Chad and Grant. Nancy, Josh, and the kids celebrate Christmas on even years with Josh's family, who live in San Diego and odd years with us. That seems as good a system as possible; notice I didn't use the word fair—more about that later. Betty and Terry Stefano were just married last year, and they live in La Crosse. He is a contractor, and Betty is a clerk in a local store; as of yet, they have no children.

Mom had a simple meal for dinner, chicken casserole with a salad and fresh baked apple pie. It was just Mom, Dad, and me tonight. Sunday and Monday will be very hectic. With dinner finished, Mom directed me to the family room, while she and Dad cleaned up. As I gazed upon the Christmas tree, I could hear their loving squabbles, as dad would do something not just right, and both would dispute the issue.

I lapsed into a postmeal stupor and began to reminisce about Christmases past and how we looked so forward to the day. As kids, the anticipation and excitement within us was so great it often exploded into exaggerated behavior until Mom or Dad or both would finally have to "sit" on us to calm everything down. But as I think back to that extreme excitement, it did not arise from our desire to celebrate the birth of Christ, but to all the decorations, good food, family being all together, which is a noble thing, and, of course, the anticipation of all those gifts. This was not to say that we had no reverence for the meaning of the day—Mom and Dad made us fully aware of the significance of the day—but then, we were just kids.

Really, just what is Christmas? It should be the rejoicing of the birth of a savior, but that rejoicing has spilled over into the celebration of gifts, food, and parties. Is that irreverent? Muslims celebrate their holiday of Eid al-Adha and the Jewish celebrate Yom Kippur without the fanfare of Christmas. I would suggest it is not irreverent as long as the gifts, food, and parties do not overshadow the true meaning of the day. That's what we must guard against.

This heavy thought on top of a full stomach put me into an early stage of sleep, when Dad walked into the family room.

"Yo, John, wake up. It's too early to fall asleep."

"I wasn't sleeping."

"Oh, eyes closed, mouth open with deep, heavy breathing is not sleeping?"

"No, Dad, it's deep thought."

"So I guess it comes down to just what the definition of sleep is. What were you so deep in thought about? Not business, I hope?"

"No, I was thinking about all the good times we had on Christmases past."

"That we did, John, and I hope many more to come."

"So tell me, have you met any possible Mrs. John Castano candidates lately?"

"No, Dad. You'd be the first to know."

"So what's the problem. You still hung up on that Lynn?"

"Gosh, no. She's happily married and has a family. I just have not found the right woman yet."

"Maybe you're too picky."

"Dad, marriage is the single most important decision a person makes. I think it's critical to be, as you say it, 'picky.'"

"Point well taken, John," Dad conceded.

Mom, Dad, and I were up early Sunday morning. It was cold and cloudy with a hint of snow. We were going to the seven-thirty morning mass on Christmas Eve day, as it was Sunday. Nancy, Josh, and the boys would be here around three o'clock, and we would be going to the four-thirty children's mass with the boys, something we do every Christmas Eve. This fulfills the Christmas-Day obligation, but Mom and Dad always went to the nine thirty mass Christmas Day with Betty and Terry.

The Christmas Eve dinner was a family tradition of a variety of fish and pasta, even though the church no longer required a meatless meal. Mom and Dad spent the afternoon preparing for dinner. They cleaned the squid, soaked the dry, salted cod, and made the meatless tomato sauce, which will garnish the cheese ravioli and gnocchi. Mom made her special breads, and the entire house was filled with an aroma a king would die for. It all came together about an hour after returning from mass, although there were a variety of cheese, sausages, olives, and breads to tame the now raging appetite of us all immediately.

At three twenty, the Williamsons arrived in full Christmas attire.

"Hey, Nanc, how was the drive?" I said as I gave her a big hug.

"Slippery in spots. There is a little snow here and there."

"Merry Christmas, Josh," I said as I shook his hand.

"And a *ho, ho, ho* to you," Josh responded.

The boys came barging through the front door.

"What's the rush, guys? Give Uncle John a big hug."

They sort of stalled and shrugged, but I did get my hug from each.

"You guys been good?"

"Yeah, Uncle John."

The gifts poured in along with some additional goodies for dinner that Nancy brewed up. The boys vanished upstairs, and the adults invaded the kitchen, where food tasting was the order for the hour.

"Hey, guys, if you're taking communion at mass, no eating one hour before," Mom reminded.

"Just one of the hundreds of human-made rules to tells us how we must act so that we are in the good graces of God. I would like to invest in the telephone company all these holy men use to talk with God," I blasphemed.

And Mom warned, "Careful, John, lest God strike you down."

"Mom, I'll take my chances. I'm not going to be playing golf, and I'm almost always in the company of good pious people, so the proverbial lightning strike is out of the question."

Church was crowded and hot. The children's presentation was full of humorous flubs and doting parents squeezing their hands and shaking their heads. It made the mass. We got there a half hour early and had to split up in order to get a seat; not to mention we had to park two blocks from the church. The poor souls who came just as mass started had to stand and probably had to park six blocks away.

When we returned home, Betty and Terry were there. We did the usual family greetings. The Eve meal was as it could be and more. The fried squid with homemade cocktail sauce were a crispy delight, the cod in red sauce was excellent—Mom's sauce would take first place in any contest—and the ravioli and gnocchi were superb. Of course, most of us overindulged. After dinner, the ladies stayed in the kitchen to clean up, while Dad, Josh, Terry, and I retired to the family room. The boys disappeared when dinner was over.

"Terry, how's the work these days?" Dad inquired.

"Things are slow, but that happens every year just before the holidays. I have a number of new job prospects on some commercial construction, mostly finish work for new offices."

"That's great," Dad injected.

Josh asked, "What kind of offices?"

"Well, Gilson Clinic is building a new clinic, and it would be the doctors' offices, exam rooms and things like that."

"That's good. They have the dough, not like these guys building apartments who are trying to do it on a shoe string," I offered.

The conversation went back and forth for about forty-five minutes, when Mom, Nancy, and Betty appeared with a fabulous Christmas cake. I don't know how it happens, but the boys suddenly popped in with eager grins on their faces.

"Mom, how can you expect us to put another forkful of anything into our stomachs?" I asked.

"Well, speak for yourself," Terry injected.

"I want a huge piece!" shouted Chad.

Surprisingly, we finished most of that cake.

Now came personal-gift time; it is when we exchange the gifts we got for each other, you know, the ones we take back to the store the day after Christmas, or slip into a drawer or closet to be forgotten until we need room and clean the place out. What is important is not the gift, but the caring message that comes with the gift. The last thing Terry needed was another hammer, or I a book on tort law, but the true meaning of giving lies not in the gift, but in the loving thought that went into finding and giving that gift.

It was time for the boys to get to bed. Each followed Grandma to the kitchen, where she equipped them with the traditional cookies and milk for Santa. They placed them on a small table next to the tree.

"Doesn't Santa come in through the fireplace? Grandpa, you don't have a fireplace. How is he going to get in?" Chad quizzed.

Being well seasoned on the application of some sense of logic to the Santa story, Grandpa responded, "He is able to open the doors of the houses that do not have fireplaces."

"Does he have a key?" Chad retorted.

"Yes, if you are good, he takes the key to our house with him when he leaves the North Pole. Now it's time to go to bed," Grandpa injected before Chad could use a little more logic.

Christmas morning was keynoted by the big, wide, and wily eyes of Chad and Grant as they entered the family room with the tree fully lit, the cookies and milk gone, and a modest pile of gifts under the tree. The next forty-five minutes were spent by the boys shredding the gift wrapping to expose a box containing some long-desired toy. Mom and Dad left for mass at nine after a breakfast of French toast and sausage.

After returning home, Mom immediately began the Christmas banquet. There was ham, sweet potato casserole, mash potatoes, green beans, romaine salad, cranberry salad, and fruit compote. Desert was tiramisu for the adults and spumoni ice cream for the kids and anyone else.

Nancy, Josh, and the boys left for Madison at three. Betty and Terry left soon afterward. I stayed for about an hour, chatting with Mom and Dad. I left at four thirty for my duplex, about a two-hour drive. I thought to myself what a pleasant Christmas we had, no family fights, no angry words. That's what Christmas really is—a celebration of family.

Tuesday morning I was in the office at nine. The usual daily schedule was on my desk, along with a return call form Liz. I called her at home as she was off during Christmas week.

Liz answered, "Good morning."

"Hi, Liz, it's John. How was your Christmas?"

"That's what I wanted to ask you. We had a very good time. My brother, Bill, and his family came down from Duluth on Sunday and left last night. His daughter, Lana, and Carolyn had a lot of fun. His wife, Toni, is newly pregnant, and she and John were so excited. How about your Christmas?"

"The whole family was there. I overate, but I cannot help it when Mom cooks. Everyone is fine, and we got all caught up on our lives. You haven't had any problems with strangers hanging around, have you?" I asked.

"No, nothing. The police stopped by on Saturday to ask the same thing. They didn't think this guy would be back. They think he saw enough to convince him that what he was looking for was not there."

"I hope so, but don't let your guard down. Remember I'm here if you need something."

"Thanks, John."

"What plans do you have for New Year's Eve?" Liz inquired.

"Nothing. I usually stay home, have a few beers, and hit the sack early."

"Dan's club is having a party to which I and my guest have been invited. Would you consider breaking your routine and be my guest?"

"Sounds interesting, sure."

"The party starts at eight. Why don't you come for supper? If you're willing, you could stay over after the party as it will be very late and have New Year's dinner with Carolyn, Mom, and me."

"I don't want you to go through a lot just for me."

"I'm not doing anything more than I would if you were not going to be here."

"In that case, I'll come."

We chatted a bit more about Christmas then hung up.

The rest of the week was quieter than the previous, which was as expected. The only thing that was noteworthy was a divorce settlement which happened on Wednesday. The wife, whom I represented, sued for divorce based on infidelity, as her husband was involved in a late-night auto accident with a lady of the evening.

This was not the first time the husband was caught with or trying to buy sex on the street. I wondered why some guys have this undeniable need to stray. If they have an innate need to be with as many different women as possible, then why get married? Is marriage a cover for their weakness, or is it just a need to be like most of the other guys? Not just to point to men straying, I have had several divorces where the wife did the straying.

The settlement stripped the husband of much of the assets, as there were two children involved. At the end of the proceedings, the husband turned to his wife and me and said, "This is not fair!"

We did not reply, but after the proceedings ended, I had a chance to reflect on the husband's statement. The word "fair" is a term that describes a nonexistent situation. "Fair" is defined as "not exhibiting any bias; impartial; done by the rules." This divorce proceeding certainly did not meet that definition, as all involved brought biases, and the rules were up for personal interpretation. Nothing is fair; just forget the word—it's useless. Most of the time the word is used by politicians to either assign blame or excite a specific political constituency.

The weekend was achieved without incident. Saturday I played handball with Paul at the Y. After the latemorning game where Paul kicked my ass, we had lunch at a modest diner just down the block. I paid for lunch as part of the loser's obligation. We talked and planned our January fishing trip to Mexico. Paul was about the same age as me and an avid sports nut. If he doesn't play it, he watches it like a religion. I am pretty much a dunce when it comes to sports, but I do give it a half-ass try.

Saturday evening I had dinner with one of the partners in the law firm. We needed to get some social time on a one-to-one basis. I'm not sure if it was a preliminary interview toward being offered a partnership. While I have not pushed hard for partnership status, it is usually something that happens or one moves on. The dinner was pleasant, and the post-dinner cocktail hour turned to two or three with the arrival of another partner. All seemed to go well.

Sunday was routine until I arrived at Liz's at six. One would agree the smell of cooking was much more than routine. I arrived with a chilled bottle of Asti Spumante and gifts for Carolyn, Mom, and Liz. Liz had me place my overnight bag in the guest room, and I freshened up in the bathroom. I met mom and Liz in the family room.

"Where's Carolyn?"

"She's in her room playing with her dolls," Liz explained.

"What smells so good?" I inquired.

"I made Lobster Thermidor for dinner. I hope you like it?"

"It really smells and sounds good. I love lobster."

Carolyn came running in. "Hi, John. This is my doll I got from Santa. Isn't she pretty?"

"Yes, Carolyn, what is her name?"

"Betty."

"You know, I have a sister named Betty."

"Is she as pretty?"

"Yes, Carolyn, just as pretty. Maybe someday you will meet her."

"Where does she live?"

"A long way from here," I answered. "Carolyn, I have a gift for you." I handed her a brightly wrapped package
with a red bow.

"Oh, goody-goody!" she exclaimed as she ripped the paper off with great anticipation of what the package held.

It was a red-and-white sweater with matching hat and mittens.

"Thank you, Uncle John."

Then I handed Mom her gift. She blushed and said, "John, you didn't need to do that."

"I like doing things I don't have to."

She opened it to find a fine Sunday hat.

"Oh, it is so beautiful. Thank you, John."

It was Liz's turn, and I handed it to her very hesitantly. "I hope I got this right." The box contained a white-and black pantsuit with a peach blouse.

"God, John, it is gorgeous, and I see they are my size. How did you know? Thank you, thank you," and she gave me a big smooch on my cheek.

"That's my secret."

Next was my turn, and Liz and Carolyn presented a very large box to me.

"This is for you, Uncle John."

"Thank you, honey."

"I helped Mommy pick it out."

I opened it to find a new leather top-latch briefcase.

"I saw your briefcase was a bit beat up. Didn't you have that back in college?"

"Yes, and it was a bit on the shaggy side. Thank you, Carolyn and Liz," I said as I gave each a kiss on the cheek. Carolyn giggled, and Liz looked at me with a warm smile.

"I'll give the old one to Willie."

"Great, that'll fit well with his beat-up shoes and shaggy suit," Liz injected.

"Who's Willie?" Carolyn questioned.

"A friend of mine, darling."

Dinner was ready, and we all went to the dining room. Liz had me sit at one end of the table and her at the other. Mom and Carolyn were across each other.

Carolyn looked at me and said, "That is where Daddy used to sit."

I smiled and glanced at Liz, who immediately stood up and took the cover off the tureen.

"Lobster Thermidor. The rice is here. I like to pour the lobster over the rice. I have my Caesar salad here. John, would you do the honors and open the Asti Spumante?"

Dinner was excellent, and Mom and Carolyn did the dishes. Liz and I retired to the family room, where we exchanged Christmas and New Year stories.

Eight thirty we left for the club and got there just before nine. We took a seat at a table with two other couples Liz did not know. Liz introduced us, and the other two couples heard of Dan's accident and expressed their condolences. They had a four-piece band and a singer who were doing a mix of fifties, sixties, seventies, and eighties songs. Liz and I thought they were quite good, a feeling not shared by the other two couples, but then these are the same people who pay $150 for a bottle of Cabernet.

We danced several dances and were taking a break at the table when I spotted this Phil guy on the way over with a bimbo blonde on his arm.

"Hello, Liz," Phil slurred. Then he turned to me and said, "Phil Roland, we met a couple of weeks ago."

"Yes, I remember."

"You two are becoming quite an item," Phil injected.

"John is my close friend. We've known each other since college. He's also my advisor and attorney," explained Liz. "Oh, and just what does he advise you on?" smarted Phil.

"None of your goddamn business Phil!" Liz smashed back.

"Wow, a bit touchy, aren't we?" cracked Phil.

Liz turned to me and asked to dance, which we immediately did, leaving Phil and his still unintroduced bimbo standing at the table.

"Please excuse my crude comments, John, but that guy really annoys me," Liz commented.

"You don't need to apologize. He is an asshole."

As we danced to *Melody of Love* by the Four Aces, Liz crushed in very close, and I readily absorbed the crush. I now understood why she first introduced me as her attorney. It was because Phil was a medaling creep. What sort of friendship Dan found in this guy was beyond my comprehension. I hope he just goes away and doesn't make any kind of scene, as this was too nice a night to have it ruined by some asshole.

The next number was "The Day Before You Came" by ABBA. The dance seemed endless, and all consciousness of my surroundings faded from my mind; there was just Liz, in my arms, and me as we danced slowly at half the beat. When we returned to the table, we couldn't see Phil and the bimbo anywhere.

"Thank God they are gone," Liz appreciated.

Before we knew it, the countdown to the New Year began. The waitress came by, and we each grabbed a glass of the bubbly. It was the hour, and "Auld Lang Syne" (Old Angzine, as it is now said) began. Liz grabbed me said, "Happy 1990," and planted a good, ten-second smooch on my lips. It passed like the light of a flashbulb.

When we broke away, she and I looked into each other's eyes, a studied look in an effort to find the true meaning to what we just experienced. We said nothing but held each other close for another minute or so.

"Happy New Year," I said.

"Oh, I hope so, John."

We danced several more dances, and at one o'clock a.m. the band announced the last dance. It was "The First Time I Ever Saw Your Face." We danced it close and with a passion not usually seen between friends. But then I had a snootful, and Liz drove back home.

I woke New Year's Day to the smell of roasting beef. It took me a few seconds to realize I was in Liz's guest room. It was 9:12 a.m. I lifted my head, and it felt as if I just got hit with a board. I crawled out of bed and stumbled into the guest bathroom. God, I wish I was at home. After a slightly cold shower and a shave, I began feeling a bit better, but I needed some strong coffee.

I entered the kitchen slowly. Liz's mother worked at the stove. Liz was seated at the breakfast counter with two cups of coffee, one in front of her and one across her.

"I heard you coming, John, so I poured you a fresh cup of coffee."

"Thanks, Liz. Hi, Mom," I offered.

"You don't look like you're at your best this morning," Liz observed.

"I'm on the improve. Heineken and champagne don't mix well. I'm glad you were driving last night, lest I be in jail right now."

"Did you enjoy the party?"

"Yes, but I really enjoyed your company. You were really feisty with that Phil."

"John, don't' remind me of that ass. He really tried to destroy the party for us."

"Did he?"

"John, I cannot remember when I had a better time."

"That's good."

Mom spoke up, "Hey, what would you two like for breakfast?"

"Just some toast," I requested. "It smells like you're doing a beef roast?"

"Your nose doth not deceive you. We are having a prime rib roast. It was Elizabeth's Dad's favorite. Do you like prime rib?"

"Mom, you're a darling. You betcha I like prime rib."

"You know, it is traditional that prime rib be served on New Year's Day," Mom added.

"Well, I'll eat it just about any time."

I had my toast and coffee and felt a bit better. Liz and I retired to the living room. We sat together on the love seat, and the TV was on to *Rose Parade in Pasadena*. Carolyn was on the floor, entranced in the parade.

She said, "Hi, Uncle John. Do you like parades?"

"Yes, darling, I was at that parade a few years back."

"Really? I hope I can go there and see it someday."

"We'll try to make it a date someday, Carolyn," Liz inserted.

"Can you come too, Uncle John?"

"Sure, I hope so."

Dinner was absolutely great. The rib roast was perfect. Mom made spectacular double-baked potatoes, broccoli, a salad, and the desert was chocolate custard torte. This time Liz and I cleaned up, over Mom's objections, as she worked her butt off. Carolyn lent a hand and seemed to assume the role of director of the operation. We both followed orders.

New experiences present us with feelings of confusion and complexity. Once the experience has been conquered, it becomes simple and logical. Be patient and strive to learn quickly, and the complex and confusing becomes simple and logical.

It was time for Paul and me to take our annual trip to Mexico. Every year for the last three years, we traveled to Mexico right after the holidays for a week in the sun. This year we decided on a fishing resort near Cabo San Lucas. We were told that the fishing was great, and there was world-class marlin fishing.

Our itinerary involved flying from Minneapolis to Los Angeles, taking a Mexican airline to La Paz, Mexico, then a bus to the resort at Cabo San Lucas. We had problems from the beginning; our flight from Minneapolis to Los Angeles was delayed due to weather. We were scheduled to leave at eleven sixteen in the morning. At eleven o'clock, the inbound flight was yet to arrive.

At 1:30 p.m. we pushed away from the gate, then to the deicing area, and finally at 2:25 p.m. we lifted off. The four-hour-and-one-half flight was now scheduled to arrive at 4:50 Pacific time. Our flight to La Paz was scheduled to depart at 5:00 p.m. We needed lots of luck since we had to take a bus from one of the domestic terminals to the international terminal and had only ten minutes.

Once in the air, an infant two rows ahead of us began to scream. I was in the center seat, Paul had the window, and the fat lady who always sings to close the opera was next to me. I didn't feel it would be necessary to expound much on the pleasantness of the flight and, my thought went to how long four and one half hours really would be.

As expected, we did not make the Mexican connection. The counter people were very accommodating and booked us on the next outbound to La Paz at twelve eleven in the morning. Paul and I had six hours to kill.

"John, I have a coworker who I'm friends with. I'll give him a call and see if he has time to meet us," Paul suggested.

"Great. Give him a call."

Paul's coworker, Billy Haslick, picked us up in front of the international terminal at 7:30 p.m. He took us to a groovy fifties pub and restaurant not far from LAX. The food was typical: burgers, fries and sodas; and the music, loud fifties. It was something to kill time, but not terribly interesting.

When we reached the gate for our departing flight to La Paz, I thought I was about to board a flying third-world bus. The only thing missing were the chickens and pigs, but I was sure they were somewhere onboard that plane. The flight departed one and one half hours late. I surmised they had a problem loading the pigs.

The flight to La Paz was a topper: one-third of the plane was screaming, over-tired kids; one-third were fat ladies ignoring them as they slept; and the rest of us who were happy as punch to be on our final leg. At one point, I thought I heard a rooster crow, but that was probably just a fat lady snoring. I had the window, and Paul the center seat. A small man occupied the aisle seat.

Someone in the row in front of us must have loaded up on frijoles as the air became almost unbearable. I turned up the overhead air nozzle to full open. As I sat there, hand capped over my nose, I thought, *Why do other people's farts smell so much worse than my own?* The flight attendants handed out little bags of chips and some tomato salsa, and the air temporarily cleared. I thanked God there were no frijoles in the package. I promptly dribbled salsa over my yellow flowered shirt.

"Paul, how does this look?" I pointed to the dribble spot.

"Just like it was part of the shirt," Paul confirmed.

"Good."

After the chips and salsa, I dozed off.

"Fasten your seat belts in preparation for landing," woke me from my slumber. As we descended into the airport at La Paz, I could see the sun cracking through the curtain of night over the Sea of Cortez. A new day was about to begin.

We had no trouble with immigration then proceeded to baggage claim and customs. No one was even at the customs stations, and we walked into the main terminal. A medium-sized fellow stood at the exit from customs, holding a sign reading, "Castano/Greco, M/M Boothfield, and Phelps."

"I'm John Castano, and this is Paul Greco," I told the Mexican man holding the sign.

"Welcome to Mehico, Mestor Castano and Mestor Greeko. I am Felipe, I weel be your driver to de reesort. We must wait for tree more."

The Boothfields, an elderly couple who were on our flight and sat across the aisle from us, announced their presence. After several minutes, a twentysomething fellow in shorts, a tie-dye shirt, sandals, and a small backpack on his back came out. It was Phelps.

The Boothfields took the first bench seat in the van, Paul and I took the second, and Phelps flopped into the last, stretching out over the entire seat. We all slept most of the trip, which took three hours.

It was 10:30 a.m. when we reached the resort. The desk clerk was a very attractive Spanish-looking young lady, with large dark-brown eyes and short, black hair, who gave us a pleasant smile as we walked up.

"Good morning. My name is Mary. Are you Mr. Castano and Mr. Greco?"

"Yes, I'm John Castano, and this is my friend, Paul Greco."

"I'm sorry you were delayed in your arrival. We will do everything possible to make your stay with us a very pleasant one. Your casita is ready. We'll need you to register, and I'll need to see your passports."

"That sounds really good," Paul inserted.

"You speak English very well," I complimented.

"Thank you. I am from Southern California. My family moved there from Mexico when I was five. After college, I got this job at the resort."

"Here is your fishing itinerary," Mary said as she handed us an envelope. "You are scheduled for near-shore fishing tomorrow and Thursday. Wednesday, you are scheduled to go out for marlin. Saturday, you will go to a very nice beach where you'll be able to surf fish. You need to be here in the lobby by eight in the morning for transportation to the fishing piers. Your fishing licenses and marlin stamps are in the envelope. You'll need to sign them and give me the yellow copy. We encourage you to release the marlin unless you get a big one. The crew will take pictures of any you catch. The restaurant opens for breakfast at six. Do you have any questions?"

"Do we need to bring anything?" Paul asked.

"All fishing gear, food, and beverages are included. You should have a good hat, sunglasses, and suntan lotion."

We thanked Mary, and she directed us to our casita. After a quick breakfast, we planned to use the afternoon to catch up on some lost sleep. Our casita had two bedrooms, and I took one, and Paul, the other. I showered, shaved, and lay down on my bed. The room was small but well decorated in traditional Mexican style. A ceiling fan spun silently, and the breeze felt soothing. Next thing I realized, it was 4:30 p.m.

Paul left. A note indicated he was going to the lounge, and I should join him when I got up. The lounge was in the main building, just a short walk from our casita down a path lined with small palms, bougainvillea, and palmettos. When I arrived, the lounge was comfortably crowded. I looked around for Paul and spotted him at a table with two lovely, young ladies.

"Hi, Paul. See you found some company?"

"Hey, John, you finally woke up. You must have really been tired."

"I was. I'm feeling fine now."

"This is Susan Greenfield," Paul introduced the lady to his right. "And this is Gloria Cook." He nodded at the lady to his left.

"Sit down. You look like you're ready for an eye-opener," Paul said as he motioned the waitress to the table.

The waitress came over, and I ordered a margarita on the rocks, no salt. Then Susan, Gloria, and Paul ordered another round; the girls were drinking martinis, and Paul bourbon and soda.

Susan was a tall, thin blonde with green eyes and a flawless completion. She wore a tie-dye T-shirt, her nipples bulging distinctively, tan shorts, and saddles. Her arms and legs were as white as the new fallen snow. Gloria was shorter than Susan and had short, brown hair, blue eyes, and an olive completion. She wore a light-blue, low-cut blouse, and dark-blue shorts. She had low-cut sneakers with no socks. Her demeanor was much more conservative than Susan's. Both were in their mid to late twenties.

"Susan and Gloria are from Des Moines. They are sales representatives for Spitzer Pharmaceutical and are on, as the Europeans say, holiday," Paul informed me.

"They got here Sunday, as they had no problem with their flights. I told them about our fiasco. They are going fishing with us tomorrow."

"Great. I hope we are lucky enough to catch our supper," I followed.

"How will you cook any fish you catch?" Gloria asked.

"The restaurant here will cook anything we bring back as an entrée for dinner. The boat hands will fillet the fish we want, and we can drop them at the kitchen when we get back," Paul answered.

"That sounds super," Susan injected. "Let's hope we all get something good to eat."

We chatted for an hour or so, and I was able to see that Paul and Susan were hitting it off. Gloria and I held down the other side of the table. The girls agreed to join us for dinner. After dinner, Paul and Susan excused themselves and indicated they were going for a walk. I knew Paul wanted to be alone with Susan, and I suggested to Gloria that we retire to the lounge for a nightcap. She agreed.

Gloria ordered a Blue Canary, a lounge special made with gin, blue Curaçao, and lime juice. I had a double Drambuie in a snifter glass.

"As a lawyer, have you tried any medical malpractice cases?" Gloria questioned.

"No, I work in the family law area at our firm. I tend to stay away from litigation cases and refer them to others in the firm set up for that specific purpose."

"So what do you do in family law?"

"Oh, I do wills, trusts, real estate transactions, and of course, divorces."

"Divorces must be some kind of juicy stuff," Gloria offered.

"No, actually they are very sad. Marriage is the most important decision two people make in their entire lives, and to see one end because of making a bad decision is really sad."

"So how do you know if the person you love is the right one?" asked Gloria.

"You hit the nail right on the head. One does not marry just for love. Passionate love is an emotion, and emotions change. True love is far more than just passion. It's includes commonality, compatibility, complete honesty, and above all, a certain inner grit that forces you to work out your problems. Without those, marriages will fail."

"After all I had to eat and drink this evening, it'll take me a day or two to digest that."

I knew it was time to walk Gloria back to their casita. We talked for almost two hours, and it was getting late.

Susan and Gloria's casita was on the same path as ours, but another hundred yards farther down. As we passed ours, I commented to Gloria and noticed a light on. I hadn't left any lights on when I left. I also noticed the "Do Not Disturb" sign hanging on the handle.

Gloria invited me in when we got to her place. We sat an additional few minutes, talking about fishing and tomorrow. As I walked back, I confronted Paul and Susan hand in hand, slowly walking toward Susan's.

"Hi, guys, have a good walk?"

"Sure did," Paul replied. "I'm walking Susan home. See you in a few."

"You got it."

When I got to our place, I detected the faint scent of Susan's perfume. Paul's bedroom door was shut; it had not been when I left. I didn't want to make any assumptions and knew if Paul wanted to, he would tell me. I knew he wouldn't lie to me, as we were far too good of friends. I got ready for bed and was about to slide between the sheets when Paul came in.

"Hey, John, it seems like you and Gloria hit it off well."

"Ah, yes. Quite well. And so with you and Susan?"

"Like two bugs in a rug," Paul quipped.

"I'll see you in the morning. I have a wake-up call for six," and I slipped into bed.

I was up at 5:30 a.m. I made a pot of strong coffee, filled a cup, and sat in the common room, anticipating the coming day of fishing. The smell of the coffee aroused Paul, who staggered from his room into the kitchen only to emerge a second later.

"Where the hell are the coffee cups?" Paul grumped.

"Aren't we just bundles of joy this morning," I fired back. "The cups are in the cabinet to the right of the sink. Careful. The coffee is very hot."

I heard him mumbling something, sort of like "smart-ass," then he emerged a second time with a steaming cup of Jo.

"It's not fair, just not fair. We are on vacation and have to get up at this ungodly hour just to go fishing. Won't those damn things still be there at noon?" Paul grouched.

"Girls and late nights were not part of our itinerary when we booked this. Fishing was," I fired back.

"You're right, you're right!" Paul mumbled.

We got to breakfast at seven thirty, and Susan and Gloria were on the way out.

"Hi, guys, tough morning?" Susan quipped.

"No, we'll be ready as soon as we get some breakfast."

"See you in the lobby," Gloria responded.

We all gathered in the lobby at 8:00 a.m., Susan, Gloria, Rick Phelps, his friend Gustav, Scott and Sandy, and Paul and I. Felipe pulled the van in front of the door, opened the side door, and we loaded up. It took about fifteen minutes to reach the dock where Felipe directed us to the proper boat. It was a twenty-seven-foot, white boat with a center cabin, bridge on top, and a deck completely around. Several rigged fishing poles were in rod holders above the back of the cabin overhead.

As we approached, a burly, black fellow, about six feet, with a graying beard, no mustache, and wearing a hat that looked like it had been fished from the sea after several years afloat, greeted us.

"Good mornin'. I'm Capitan Nick and will be taking you to my best fishing spots today. This is my first mate"—he gestured to the man standing on the dock near the tie-up cleat—"Ishmael."

Capitan Nick had a Caribbean accent, probably Jamaican. Ishmael was short, about five feet six inches, with the classic Mayan look: slanted forehead, Romanesque nose, and dark completion. He smiled and nodded.

"Which of you are Castano and Greco?" Capitan Nick asked.

"We are," Paul said as he put his hand on my shoulder.

"Okay, me and Ishmael will be taking you two for marlin tomorrow, but on a different boat."

We left the dock promptly at nine. The boat followed the shoreline west for several miles, then turned south for a couple more, and anchored in about forty feet of water. Ishmael baited each pole and handed them out, instructing us to drop them to the bottom. Some poles had squid, some shrimp, and some chunks of fresh sardine. Before the last pole was baited and in the water, Phelps pulled up a catch; next was Scott. The fish were biting. Most of the morning we stayed in this area and caught pargo, a type of snapper and graybar grunt. Most were under a pound in weight. Scott and Sandy kept a few of the pargo, but all the rest were tossed back.

We had lunch then traveled a little farther out into a hundred-plus feet of water. This time we used bigger hooks and bait and fished near the surface. It was about 3:00 p.m. when Gloria let out a screech. The tip of her pole was almost in the water, and she was holding on with both hands. I walked behind her and grabbed the pole with my right hand. My left arm wrapped around her waist below the pole belt.

"Start reeling," I instructed her. "We'll pull the pole up, and you reel as we let it down. We'll keep doing this until we get the fish to the surface."

The combined effort took us a little over fifteen lovely minutes. I could see Gloria enjoyed every second of my assistance. Finally, the fish tired and surfaced. It was a blue fin tuna, a small one, about thirty pounds. Ishmael gaffed the tuna, and he and Capitan Nick hauled it aboard.

"Nice fesh," Ishmael remarked.

"Do you want to keep it? It is very good for eating" Capitan Nick asked.

"Sure," Gloria confirmed. "We'll have it tonight for dinner."

Everyone was gathered around, and Gloria invited them to share it with us. Scott and Sandy accepted. Phelps and Gustav respectfully declined.

Dinner was at seven o'clock in the restaurant. Paul and I met the girls in the lounge at six thirty.

"They called and asked if I had any special way to do the fish," Gloria said. "I told him to make it the chef's choice. I hope that's okay with you?"

"That's what I would have done," I affirmed.

We chatted about the day of fishing until seven o'clock. When we walked into the restaurant, Scott and Sandy were waiting. We were seated at a round table for six near the window overlooking the Pacific. Everyone was in good humor. Paul sat next to Susan, and I sat between Susan and Gloria. Scott and Sandy rounded out the table.

We began with fish chowder then a tropical salad of mixed greens and fresh fruits. The chef delivered the entrée personally: wood-fired grilled tuna with a mango, orange salsa, accompanied with a healthy serving of Spanish rice and black beans.

"Who caught dees wonderful fesh?" the chef inquired.

"Gloria caught it," I gestured toward her.

"Bery nice fesh," the chef followed.

"Well, John and I really caught it," Gloria chimed in.

"She really did all the work and did an excellent job. I just lent a hand."

When the chef and wait staff left, Paul raised a glass in toast to Gloria.

"Here's to Gloria, a super fisherwoman."

"Here, here," we all exclaimed.

"And here is to the great friendships we found today," I added.

"Here, here."

Dinner was excellent, and we all parted well satisfied and in a jolly humor. Paul, the girls, and I retired to the lounge after a "thanks" from Scott and Sandy.

Paul and Susan excused themselves about ten o'clock, as they wanted a little alone time together. Gloria and I chatted in the lounge until around 11:30 p.m.

"It's a glorious night. Would you like to take a stroll on the beach?" I proposed.

"Sure, that would be great," Gloria immediately replied.

The air was calm, and the temperature about seventy-five degrees. There was a half-moon just above us as we slowly walked on the hard-packed sand. Gloria slipped her arm into mine, and I pulled it into my side. The gentle lap of light surf was the only sound other than our conversation.

"Do you have a significant other at home?" I quizzed.

"Well, sort of. I have been dating this new physician, and he seems to be interested in a deeper relationship."

"Is it serious?"

"Ah, I think maybe, but it's still early. I'm not sure. I did have a goal of promotion into management, and that would require relocation. I don't know if I want to give that up, or if Doug would move if I were promoted."

"I understand completely. Marriage is the single biggest decision one will ever make, so taking your time is a very smart way to proceed."

"What about you, John. Do you have someone?"

"Well…maybe. It' a long and very complicated story."

"I'd like to hear about it. We have the night."

"When I was finishing up law school, I met this girl, Elizabeth. We all call her Liz. We became very good friends, but for whatever reason, it never developed into a romantic relationship. She eventually married, and I got engaged. My engagement failed due to my fiancé's parents. Liz and I remained good friends."

"Liz's husband died last September. I was their attorney. At first it was ruled an accident, but after some snooping of my own, we realized he was murdered. Since then I saw a lot of Liz and began to think I may have been suppressing my real feelings toward her. I warned you this was a long and complicated story."

"Keep going," Gloria asked.

"I'm not sure how Liz feels about me, and most of all, it is far too soon to expect her to have any kind of romantic feeling for anyone. I hired a private investigator to build some sort of case for murder before we take it to the police. I'm sure when they get it, both Liz and I will become suspects."

"Don't dismiss Liz's feelings. She may have been holding back to see where you're at. Either way, I don't think you need to rush anything," Gloria advised.

It was 1:00 a.m. when I got back to the casita. The scent of Susan was in the air. Paul retired. A note said, "Hope you had a good evening. See you at six." Tomorrow was the big day, marlin fishing.

We were on board the *Buccaneer* at 8:30 a.m. and headed for the open sea. Capitan Nick was at the helm, and Ishmael prepared the rigs. Paul and I sat in the cabin until we reached the marlin area. It was only twenty minutes or so, and sight of land was gone. About then Capitan Nick throttled back, and Ishmael popped his head into the cabin.

"Et's time to fesh."

We each strapped a rod-holding belt on and took a seat in the pedestal chairs at the stern of the *Buccaneer* and fastened our seat belts.

"A large fesh can pull you overboard if not strapped in," Ishmael explained.

He baited Paul's rod first and ran it out. He then did mine. We trolled at, I would guess, about five miles per hour.

"So I wonder what the poor people are doing," Paul cracked.

"Hoping to improve their lives, I would expect," I cracked back.

"I guess we're pretty lucky," Paul fired back.

"I don't think its luck. We worked hard to get here. We worked to get a good education so we could get a good job and worked hard at our job so we could afford this. It has nothing to do with luck, except maybe we were born into a good family who raised us to realize that to have a better life we had to work hard. Too many people grow up thinking that society owes them a good life, and all they need to do is ask for it from government."

"Gee, aren't you the scrooge," stabbed Paul.

"Let me be real clear on how I think about rich and poor. There are truly needy poor in this world and, given half a chance, would be good productive members of the society. It is our obligation to help them in every way we can."

"Then there are the lazy takers whose energy is devoted to how they can gain prosperity on the backs of others. Many of those realize the power of their democratic right to vote and use government as a tool, in which to maintain their votes, will take from the productive people of society and give it to them. These people are a drag and, if not properly denied, will bring down society."

"When too many citizens of a society use this tool, the productive members cease to be productive. The whole system will eventually fail. History is full of examples."

"I understand your point. So what do we do with the poor?" Paul inquired.

"The ones who are willing to work, we help. The ones who don't, there is not much we can do except to guard against government giving them too much at our expense. If they don't want to work to get what they want, then they have to be limited to the life they can afford. That sounds cruel, but that's reality. People do not like working hard to support people who choose not to work. That's just the way it is."

About then Paul's line snapped, and his pole bent to a ninety-degree angle as it sat on the rod holder.

"Fesh, Captain Nick, Fesh. Take de pole and put it into your belt," Ishmael instructed Paul.

Capitan Nick throttled back to a couple of miles per hour. Paul reached forward, grasped the rod, and inserted the butt into the holder on his belt. He then tightened the drag that was screaming out and was pulled forward by the strength of the fish. Suddenly, about one hundred feet behind the boat, a marlin surfaced, shaking its head, the line streaming from its mouth then crashing back into the sea.

The fish surfaced again and again. For the first twenty minutes, Paul made little headway, but the marlin tired after that and was slowly reeled into the boat. Capitan Nick throttled back more and came down from the bridge to assist Ishmael. The marlin, a modest size of between 90 to 110 pounds, glided next to the *Buccaneer*. Capitan Nick gently gaffed the marlin and pulled him onboard. Ishmael took a couple of pictures of the marlin, pulled the line up, reached over with pliers, grabbed the hook, and twisted it out.

Capitan Nick lowered the fish back into the sea and released the gaff. The marlin floated on the surface as the boat slowly pulled away, then there was a swirl, and he was gone. Capitan Nick throttled up, and Ishmael ran my line out again. He then replaced the hook and wire leader on Paul's rod, attached it to the downrigger, and let the rig out. It wasn't more than ten minutes, and my rod was bent over. Suddenly the same distance behind the boat as Paul's fish, a huge marlin, twice or three times the size of Paul's, plowed its head from the sea.

I fought this monster for thirty to forty minutes, making very little headway, when he emerged from the sea like a giant whale. Head shaking, he flipped his tail skyward and plunged back into the sea headfirst. The line tensed as it had not done before, then the sad sound of a twang as it snapped. My wall hanger was going to live and fight another day. We continued to fish for marlin for a couple of hours until some very dark clouds appeared on the southeastern horizon. Before we could blink, a storm bore down on us; the wind picked up; swells rolled in, and lightning sparkled about us. Capitan Nick asked us to don our life vests. He ordered us into the cabin.

Capitan Nick maneuvered us away from the center of the storm, but the seas were wild and frothy. I remembered I left my camera bag on deck and decided I would make a quick dash to retrieve it. Paul was in the head, and from the sound of it, he dismissed his lunch into the latrine.

I scrambled on deck and slipped between the gunwale and my stool. As I began to reach for my camera, the *Buccaneer* rolled on a swell and lurched over. Suddenly I was in the sea. As I rose on the top of a swell, I spotted the *Buccaneer* as it sailed away.

I was afloat, alone in the Pacific in a storm, and no one knew. The storm moved quickly to the north, and the sea began to quiet. Within two hours the sea became almost flat. As the sun approached the horizon, the clouds glowed red with a mixture of blue and gray, which crowded around the glowing red sphere. On the opposite horizon, I spotted a dot; it seemed to be getting closer, and finally in the dying sunlight, I realized it was the *Buccaneer.* They came back looking for me.

The closest it got was a couple of hundred yards. I began to holler and wave my hands, but in the dim sunlight, they didn't see me and continued slowly into the setting sun. After several minutes, they disappeared. I was alone again, more alone than I had ever been. It became very quiet, and the only sound was the soft lapping of water against my life vest. I began to shake as I realized that I would probably never be found, and I was going to die.

My thoughts went to the depths, *What was down there? Maybe a great white sizing me up as a possible dinner. Were there dolphins willing to give me some companionship?*

Then I realized the most spectacular sight—the entire universe, billions of stars, not blocked by the lights from humanity, in its full glory.

How could the universe just exist? In the blackness of eternal, endless space, a pinpoint of light appeared and exploded with a massive burst of light and energy, which congealed into suns, planets, and galaxies—the universe.

Then life on at least one planet developed and produced a creature who could contemplate its own existence.

How did all this happen. Just by chance? No, that could not be. There has to be something more, something deliberate, with intention and direction. We are not here due to mere chance.

At one time, I wondered just why the human species was so much more successful than other species and always dismissed the thought to the fact that we are so much more intelligent. Upon further reflection, I realized that our intelligence developed as a result of our diversity, and the real reason we are so successful is that we are able to adapt to our environment.

If you think of those species which have vanished or are in danger of vanishing, one thing stands out. They have very specific needs, be it diet, location, or other environmental restrictions; and when the need vanishes, the species vanish. Humans, on the other hand, began in a warm environment, as did most other primates. As need demanded, we moved into other environments more hostile to us and thrived because we were able to adapt our diets, protection, and shelter. We are the most adaptable species that ever existed. As a result, our intelligence grew, and we are now the dominate species on the planet.

There seems to be a feeling that human activity is an unnatural phenomenon and that we must abandon these unnatural behaviors in order to survive. Why people feel that our evolution would lead to a species that can behave unnaturally is ludicrous. We are all part of a natural evolutionary process, and we need to embrace that realization.

I feel that the evolutionary process is focused on achieving an intelligence that fully understands its environment and is able to control it. That means that the human species is a step in this process but will never, as a species, achieve that goal, as we do not have the capacity to do so. What we need to do is develop the next step, which will be capable to carry on the growth to complete understanding, then step aside, and allow that entity to grow, expand, and develop the next step.

I think about an hour or so passed when I saw the half-moon rising in the east. This was the same moon that lit the walk Gloria and I took just last night. All that seemed just so far away. Was this the end? Would those who loved me say, "He fell overboard in a storm while fishing and was never found"? Then I realized I was crying.

I began to contemplate my own death, alone, no one by my side, afloat in the Pacific Ocean. I have often thought of what it was going to be like. What was it going to be like on the other side? Was there another side, or are we just gone forever like a wisp of smoke in the breeze? Would anyone remember me ten, twenty, fifty years from now? Was that important?

I reflected on my concept of death. It is the one thing that is absolutely final; no second chance at it. When I was young, death was my greatest fear; but as I got older, the fear seemed to subside with acceptance of its eventuality. When it's time, will I be afraid and fight it, or lie back and accept it? Was death going to be a sunrise or a sunset? Right now I was ready.

My thoughts turned to Liz. There she was, in all her beauty, holding her hand out to me as if to say, "Come, John, I've been waiting for you." I thought back on New Year's Eve and the dances we had. The last dance was to *Mary in the Morning*. Would I ever see Liz again in the morning, glowing and soft, loving and kind? I began to dream about life with Liz and realized just how much she meant to me.

Floating there in the calm warm water of the Pacific, I realized I was completely relaxed. Suddenly I felt that I was lying there in the hand of God, and I was now ready for what God intended for me.

I must have dosed off, but I suddenly realized there was a seagull floating an arm's length off my right shoulder.

As we looked at each other, I realized it was getting light. It was bright, and I could see nothing but the seagull and the water around me.

Then I heard my name, "John." I saw no boat—no one.

Then the voice called out again, "John."

I responded, "Who are you?"

And the voice replied "I Am."

"Who?"

"I Am," came the reply.

"What do you want?"

"You, John."

"Am I going to die…God?"

"Yes, John, but not for many more years. I want you to finish your life, then we will meet again."

"But why have you come to me?"

"I am always with my people, all you have to do is look. I will stay with you, John. Now sleep."

I saw Liz. She held her hand out to me, and I took it.

"John, John Castano, are you okay?" I jerked awake. I realized I had fallen asleep. The sun was just rising. I had survived the night, and that glowing red ball returned in the east.

I looked right, and the white seagull was still there.

"John Castano." It was Ishmael.

"Mr. Castano, Mr. Castano."

The seagull rose from the sea and flew over a boat—the *Buccaneer*!

Nothing, except Liz, looked as great as the *Buccaneer* at this moment. I waved my hand, and as the boat approached, Paul leapt into the water and swam over to me.

"God, John, you look good."

He grabbed my life vest and pulled me to the boat, where Ishmael put a ladder over.

"Can you climb up?" Capitan Nick asked.

"You betcha," I responded.

Capitan Nick and Ishmael helped me aboard, followed by Paul, who gave me a big hug.

"You son of a bitch, you gave us a hell of a scare. We've been looking for you all night," Paul fired at me.

"Hey, guys, I just needed some alone time. Sorry I caused you such a fright."

"Smart-ass," was Paul's retort. "Why didn't you answer right away?"

"I was saying a prayer to God for leading you to me. It had to be divine intervention for you to find me after being out here all night."

Capitan Nick said, "I never lost anyone, and you were not going to be my first."

I shook Capitan Nick's hand hard then pulled him in and gave him a big hug.

"Thank you. I owe you my life. Thank you, thank you."

"Oh, dat's okay, mon. Just doing my job," I'm sure he was blushing, but being a black man, it was hard to confirm.

I looked for Ishmael to do the same, but he was up forward stowing some line.

"Hey, Ishmael, *thank you, thank you!*"

On the way to port, I went to the pilothouse and approached Capitan Nick. I touched him on his shoulder, and he turned his head.

"How did you find me? It's such a big ocean."

"We were looking all night, and we put out a man-overboard alert to other boats in the area and our coast guard. It was about two o'clock in the morning when I saw a light on the surface a long distance off. I thought it might be another search boat, so we slowly made for the light. It vanished a few minutes later, but we kept on the same heading, going slowly while searching the water. Just as it was getting to daybreak, we saw your orange life jacket with you in it."

We got back to the resort just after twelve. Susan and Gloria were waiting in the lobby. Both ran up to me. Susan gave me a hug, and Gloria followed with a giant hug and kiss on the cheek.

"You had us so worried," Gloria said. "How in the hell did you fall overboard?"

"I went to get my camera, and the boat did a big roll. The next thing I knew was, I was swimming."

"You're not hurt, are you?" Gloria asked.

"Only my pride, but I'm really very tried. I'm going to get some sleep, okay, guys?"

I showered and lay on my bed. When I woke, it was 6:30 p.m. I dressed and went into the common room. A note from Gloria was on the table and read, "We're at the pool. Join us."

I joined them at their palm-covered table near the pool. Susan and Gloria were in the pool; Paul was at the table. They all had adult beverages, and the waitress came over. I ordered a Mai Tai; I liked the pineapple.

When the girls saw me, they got out of the pool and walked over. Both had bodies of a beauty queen. Gloria's olive skin began to develop a milk-chocolate tan. She really looked delicious.

"No suit, John?" Gloria stung.

"I had enough swimming for a long, long time."

"I can understand that," chimed Susan.

After finishing our drinks, Paul and the girls returned to their casitas to change for dinner. I stayed at the pool and had another Mai Tai. They returned a half hour later, and we all went to the dining room.

After dinner, we spent the rest of the evening at the pool. Paul and Susan left for their stroll on the beach. Gloria and I chatted a bit longer, then I walked her to her casita. I excused myself when she asked me in. I just wanted go back to our place to reflect on what transpired the last two days.

Friday we all went to the beach to surf fish and swim. We met Capitan Nick and Ishmael on a catamaran at the beach in front of the resort. We were joined by Scott and Sandy, but Phelps and Gustav were not there.

"I hear you had a scary night," Scott directed to me.

"You know; it really wasn't scary. I never felt afraid, maybe because I'm naive. I did feel completely alone for a while until I began thinking of all my friends. Then I actually fell asleep."

"Well, you have quite the story to tell," Scott concluded.

Capitan Nick beached the catamaran on an isolated small beach. We waded ashore, and all the gear, food, and drinks were hauled to the beach by the capitan and Ishmael. Paul, Scott, and I fished for a few hours, while the girls took in some sun. Fishing ended when the three girls came crashing into the surf. We had a pleasant time and headed back to the resort at three o'clock. Upon return, we all retired to the pool, where we spent the evening eating burgers and fries at the pool for dinner. About seven thirty, Paul announced he and Susan were going for a sunset swim, and no invites were extended; none expected.

"John, would you walk me back to our place?" Gloria invited.

"More than happy to," was my response.

At the girls' casita, Gloria made us a drink. We sat and shared war stories about our jobs for about a half an hour.

I admired Gloria, as she was still in her bathing suit, a small bikini. Gloria got up, picked up her glass, and walked over to me. She sat the half-empty glass next to mine, then sat down on my lap. She placed her hands on the back of my neck and pushed my head up.

Looking into my eyes she said, "I think we could really make a great couple."

"I would not dispute that," I responded.

She lowered her head, and we embraced several times. I realized that both my hands were slowly moving up and down Gloria's smooth, soft, warm thighs. *Oh my!*

Back from Mexico, and it was back to the business of a new year. It seemed so refreshing to start anew, but the threads of last year still resided in the fabric of the new. So we begin with fresh goals and expiations. Monday morning I was in the office wide eyed and bushy-tailed, armed with a renewed desire to overcome the shortcomings of last year. My schedule was on my desk. Guess what? I had the sad duty to finalize the divorce settlement from last December. It was going to be just the average week, or so I thought, as averages can be the sum of two extremes.

Thursday evening I left the office about six o'clock and headed down the elevator to the P3 floor, where I had my parking space.

As I got to my car, someone grabbed me from behind in a stranglehold, stuck something hard into my upper back, and said, "Don't holler or try to fight, or I'll kill ya."

"Hey, man, I won't. What do you want?"

"We are going to take a drive. Get into your car. Open the door."

I got into the driver's seat, and once I closed the door, my guest rounded the car, opened the passenger-side door, popped the front passenger seat over, and slipped into the back seat.

"Drive out," he said.

"Where're we goin'?"

"Just drive out. Then I'll tell you where."

We got onto I-94 West. When we exited, I realized we were heading for Liz's."

"Are we going to the Danfurth's?"

"You got it, bub. But don't try anything because we have people there, and she'll get hurt."

"What in the hell do you want with us?"

"In due time. Drive."

We got to Liz's, and there were no cars in the drive. I parked in the driveway, and my guest exited the passenger side as I got out of the driver's side. We went to the, door and he knocked. The door was opened by another thug, who looked as if he had just been let go by the mob for being too assertive. We walked to the office, where Liz was seated at the desk with the asshole, Phil, behind her.

I immediately asked, "Where are Carolyn and Mom?"

"Don't worry, they're not here," injected Phil.

"They're at my brother's," Liz clarified.

"Don't worry about them. You need to worry about what's going to happen to you two."

Phil motioned me over to him and Liz. When I was face-to-face with the asshole, he lifted Liz from her chair and marched to the front of the desk. Liz was in front of him. The two thugs stood silent on each side of the desk.

"So what do you want?" I asked.

"You two have no idea?" Phil stabbed.

"No!" was my reply.

"You guys are either stupid or lying," Phil blasted.

"Okay, so tell me," I popped.

"Liz, your husband, Dan, was working on a project for the government. I know he had notes of this work. I want them."

"I don't know anything about any government work. This is the first I have heard of it," Liz offered.

Phil responded with an *"oh!"* of disbelief.

"You never talked with Dan about his trips to Washington?"

"He said he was on a special board to evaluate advances in his field."

"And you bought that shit?"

"Why would I doubt my husband?"

"I think you found the file and gave it to Sir Lancelot here."

There was a silence, Liz didn't know how to respond, and I wanted her to keep up the bluff.

The sound of crashing glass—Liz screamed, and I jumped about six feet. A muted *pop, pop, pop* broke the silence in a muffled way. The two thugs dropped to the floor. Phil grabbed Liz; she became his shield. He produced a pistol in the other hand and motioned me to come around the desk. I slid around one of the motionless thugs on the floor and followed him and Liz as they backed out of the room. Once we left the office, we went directly down the hall, into the garage, and out the side door. I thought, *This guy's been here before.*

We crossed the backyard of the next-door neighbor and two other backyards. I didn't know if I was thankful or disappointed there were no dogs or fences in these yards. We reached the side street, where a gray Jeep Cherokee was parked. Phil clicked the door release on his key chain and handed me the keys.

"You get in and drive."

He forced Liz into the front passenger seat, and he got in behind her. I started the jeep.

"Where to?"

"Just get us away from here. Don't speed or do anything funny, or you won't like what I do to Liz."

I accidently missed a Stop sign three blocks down, and the asshole slapped Liz aside the head with his pistol.

"Okay, I'm nervous and missed the Stop sign."

"Just don't screw up again. Get us to 94 West."

"Are you okay, Liz?"

"Yes, John," was her tearful reply.

We drove for about twenty minutes then exited on a road I had never been on.

"Turn right," Phil instructed.

We drove another ten minutes then turned left onto Stevenson Road. Another ten we reached a driveway, and Phil instructed me to turn in. After a couple of hundred yards, we reached a shabby old farmhouse. It was dark. Phil ordered us into the house, turned on the lights to a scantly furnished front room. He ordered us to sit together on the couch.

"I won't get fleas, will I?" I spit.

"Fuck you," he spit back. "Just sit, both of you."

He continued waving his pistol as if to signal the possibility he might use it. I didn't doubt he would.

"I know one of you has or knows where Dan's file is. If you two want to see a bright new tomorrow, you'll tell me where it is."

He walked over to me and said, "Open your mouth."

I just looked at him, and he hit me hard on the side of my head with the pistol.

"Last time. Open your mouth."

I did as instructed, and he stuck the barrel of the pistol into my mouth.

Phil turned to Liz and said, "I'm only going to say this once. If I don't get an answer, your lover boy will die. Where's Dan's file?"

Liz hesitated, and Phil cocked the hammer of the pistol.

"Okay, just take the gun out of John's mouth."

Phil did so.

"I gave the file to John. He gave it to this detective to find out what it was."

"A cop?"

"No," I said. "A PI I use at work."

"Call this guy and tell him to bring it here."

"Just like that? He's going to drop everything and bring the file here?"

"It's up to you to convince him to bring it. If not, its bye-bye for you two."

"So if we're dead, how you going to find it?"

"I will. We'll meet him at Use It Again junkyard."

I called Willie; this guy did have phone service in this shack.

"Willie, I need a really big favor. Don't ask any questions. Bring Dan's file to me ASAP."

"What's up, John?"

"No questions. A favor, please."

"Okay."

I gave Willie directions to a meeting place Phil gave me. We left immediately and drove back toward town. We arrived at the yard west of the Cities. Phil picked the lock, opened the gate, and we drove in, leaving the gate open.

We waited for about a half hour when we saw lights coming into the yard. Willie drove up in his black 1984 Cadillac. He got out and, briefcase in hand, walked over to us.

"You got the file?"

"Maybe," Willie answered. "But I want to make sure these two are okay before I give it to you."

Willie walked over to us, gave Liz a hug, and shook my hand. He then turned his back to me and, facing Phil, backed into me. I felt something hard in his belt. A gun. I shot before, but I never used a gun to kill something. *Could I do this? What if I missed? What if the gun didn't fire? God, what am I doing? I knew I had to do this.*

Knowing once Phil got the file we were toast, I slipped the gun from beneath Willie's coat and pulled the hammer back.

Willie said, "Here's the file," tossing the briefcase to Phil.

As Phil leaned over to pick it up, Willie turned sideways. Phil stood up as I raised the gun and pulled the trigger.

There was a flash in the darkness and a loud *crack* Phil dropped to his knees and fell backward. The bullet struck him just below the left eye and must have exited the back of his head as a pool of blood formed on the snow beneath his head.

"Oh my god! What have I done?" I shouted.

Liz stood but sort of curled up into herself and cried.

"It's okay," Willie assured us.

"What are we going to do?" I asked.

"I'll take care of it. Give me the gun, and both of you get into my car."

We walked to the Cadillac and got into the back seat. Willie went to retrieve his briefcase and got into the front seat.

"We're getting us out of here now! I'll call the shooting in anonymously when we get clear of here. I don't want us connected to this. This is very big, and I hope you two are not going to get in over your heads."

"Now what do we do?" Liz sheepishly asked Willie.

"This guy is not alone, and the others will be looking for you. You cannot go to either of your houses. For the time being, you can stay at my place. It's not the Ritz, but it is comfortable."

"Well, two of his pals are lying dead on the floor of Liz's den. Someone shot them through the window. Phil took us out of the house to a farmhouse west of here," I explained.

"Who the hell shot them?" quizzed Willie.

"We haven't the foggiest idea."

"What about work?" Liz asked.

"You'll have to take tomorrow off. Tell them you're sick or something. Over the weekend, we can come up with some sort of plan."

"My car is sitting in Liz's drive. What do we do about that?"

"It's fine there. We'll get it sometime over the weekend," Willie assured.

When we got to Willie's, it was almost midnight. He lived on the second floor of a four-unit apartment building.

Willie was right, it wasn't the Ritz. It was cluttered but clean. Willie gave Liz the guest bedroom, and I got the couch. Liz retired immediately, Willie said he had to leave; he had some urgent business. He said he didn't have a Heineken, but there were some Millers in the fridge, and I could help myself then began to leave.

"Is the file in the briefcase, Willie?" I stopped him.

"I have the file in a safe place. Best you don't know where it is for now. I knew that the dude was never going to let us go. He couldn't, but he wouldn't kill us until he had the file."

"When he found out the file wasn't in the briefcase he probably would have killed Liz and me and forced you to take him to the file," I speculated.

"I don't think so, as I would have stipulated that he wouldn't get the file if he killed either of you because that would tell me as soon as he got the file, he would have to kill me too."

"You going over to Liz's?"

"Best you not know," he said as he left.

It was about 3:00 a.m. when I woke with the feeling someone was in the room. The slight perfume smell was the kind Liz used. I sat up on the couch.

Liz's soft voice came through the darkness, "Did I wake you?"

"No."

"I couldn't sleep, John. What are we going to do? We killed Phil and saw two guys gunned down. We are on the run from god knows who. We cannot go to the police, home, or work. What's going to happen to us?"

"It seems that this dark night will last forever, but a new day always follows the night. In the morning we'll be able to see more clearly. Why don't you come over here?"

Without a word, I could see Liz's shadow rise, and she sat next to me. I put my arm over her shoulder and drew her close. She dropped her head on my shoulder, and we sat there silently for some time. When I woke in the morning, I slumped to my side, and Liz lay on my lap. I just looked at her glorious face and made no attempt to get up, as I didn't want to wake her. But, *boy,* I really had to pee.

Then I heard Willie clanking things in the kitchen. Liz jumped up and looked at me.

"John!"

"Yes, Liz."

"We slept here all night?"

"Well, it was only a couple of hours."

"Were you uncomfortable? Did you sleep?"

"Yes, Liz. But now I have to get to the head."

After I got back, Liz got up, and we followed the sound of pots and plates being slapped around, which ended in the kitchen. Willie was working away over the stove.

I said, "Mornin', Willie."

He turned. "So you guys are finally up? Have a seat. I'll get you some coffee."

We did, and he slapped two oversize mugs in front of us.

"The fixin's are on the table. Did you two sleep okay?"

"Sleep, what's that?" Liz replied.

"Didn't sleep well, hey. Well, I can understand that with what you two went through yesterday."

"No shit," I felt necessary to inject.

"Hope you two like scrambled eggs and ham. How do you like the toast, whole wheat?"

"I thought you said your place was not the Ritz. Where do I leave the tip?"

"Stick it, pal. You're paying."

After breakfast, Liz excused herself and went to her bedroom. Willie and I stayed at the table, sucking down the rest of the coffee.

"Who was this Phil? Why was he after Dan's file?" Willie asked.

"All I know about Phil is that he was some sort of playboy from Dan's club. Why he wanted Dan's file is beyond me."

"You say he had two thugs with him at Liz's, and someone shot both through the window?"

"That's what happened. He took us to some shabby farmhouse west of town. That's where I called you from."

"Why didn't the shooter shoot him?"

"He had Liz and me as shields. He knew the house. I think he may have been the one who broke in."

"So we got some fellow, now deceased, who knew of Dan's files, and now that Dan is dead, he wants them. Maybe this guy worked for the same fellows Dan worked for?"

"I don't think so as he said to Liz, 'Don't you know Dan was working for the government?'"

"Interesting," Willie injected. "And who did the shooting at Liz's?"

"It's a mystery to me."

"I'm going to call this friend I told you about and see if he'll look at the stuff today. Maybe things will become clearer if we know what Dan was working on."

"Sounds like a plan."

"You guys should get to your employers and excuse yourself for the day. Then stay put right here."

Willie called then left his apartment. I was in the living room when Liz came in.

"Willie left?"

"Yes, wants to check something out," I explained. "When do Mom and Carolyn come home?"

"That's right. They are driving back on Sunday."

"You should call your brother and see if they can stay another week."

"I'll do that," Liz agreed.

Liz called work and told Sandi that she had a family emergency and was going to her brother's in Duluth. She would let Sandi know on Monday when she thought she would be back. She then called Bill, telling him that he needed to have Mom and Carolyn stay for another week if that was possible. He and Toni would be happy to have them stay longer. She talked to Mom, and she agreed to stay. She then talked with Carolyn, and she was excited to stay with her cousin, Lana. She got up and went to the guest room to freshen up.

I called the office and explained to Celia that I thought I was coming down with the flu; flu season was in full swing.

"Well, you take care of yourself. Stay in bed and take lots of fluids," was her advice.

"Yes, doctor. If you need to get in touch with me and I don't answer, just leave a message."

"I'll have someone take your appointments. You have two, the Vermillions and Tom Galligar. Is that okay with you?"

"Yes, have Hank take them if he can. Thank you, Celia."

I then called my landlord, Ron Tomlinson, and explained I needed to be out of town for a few days and to just keep an eye on the place. Ron was fine with that.

Willie got back about 1:00 p.m. Liz and I were in the living room watching *The African Queen* on TV. Willie wanted to talk.

"This friend of mine spent about an hour looking at Dan's notes, and he concluded that he was working on the dynamics of a high-speed missile that changes course and altitude frequently. There was no reference to just what the missile was being used for, or why it needed to change course and altitude. This must be something he was doing for the government. The trips to Washington were probably to update whomever he was working for, maybe this Phillip Longhouse. Maybe that's who shot the two thugs?"

"Possibly, but he would have access to Dan's notes. Why would he care?"

"To keep them from getting into the wrong hands?"

"Good point."

"Liz, did you know Phil's last name?" Willie asked.

"I don't know. I think Dan began to dislike him, as he never seemed to hang around him or talk about him."

Willie indicated that we needed to go to Liz's after-dark tonight and retrieve my Beamer and Liz's car.

"What if these guys are waiting for us?" Liz questioned.

"We'll have to keep our eyes and ears open and stay alert," Willie responded. "We need to get John's and your cars out of there. John can help me with the bodies. We'll put them in my trunk. It's big enough. I've got a way of disposing of them."

"Why not just call the police? I was broken into," Liz reacted.

"As I told you yesterday, you're into something very big, and you're in over your heads. We don't need the police at this point to muddy up the whole thing and get you guys tossed into jail."

"Okay, you're right, Willie."

That evening the three of us went to dinner at a small Italian restaurant in a strip mall a short distance from Willie's apartment. After a pleasant family-style supper of salad, ravioli, and chicken parmesan, we headed to Liz's—about a half-hour drive. Willie circled the block and asked us if we saw anything unusual.

"No!"

"Do you have space for my car in your garage?"

"Yes, Mom has her car in Duluth."

"I'll back my car in. You go in and open the garage door."

"You think this tank will fit?" I popped.

"We'll make it fit, but you'll have to move your car, John."

Willie pulled in front, and Liz and I got out. She went in, and the garage door opened while I moved my car behind hers. I got out after Willie gingerly backed his car into the garage. I went in, and Willie had Liz lower the door. Everything looked good, and we were in without being noticed.

"You and John go into the office. I cannot look at those dead guys again," Liz asked.

"Okay."

I led the way. When we got to the office, the bodies were not there; no bodies, no blood, and no mess, and no broken glass.

"Did you guys dream all this up?"

"Hell, no, those thugs were lying on the floor, one on each side of the desk, and the center pane of glass was shattered."

Inspecting the glass, Willie observed, "It seems to have been replaced recently, as there are some small chips in the paint next to the glass."

I called Liz into the office. She hesitated but followed my request.

"*What!* Where are the bodies?"

"Someone took them and fixed the window. Probably the same guy who shot them," Willie explained. "Check the house quickly, pick up a few things you need, and get out of here ASAP."

"What the hell is happening?" screamed Liz.

"I don't know," I interjected. "But see if you can find out."

"Hold it, Willie," I interrupted. "I think this guy is looking out for us and has no interest in harming us. If he did, he would have done so when he had a chance."

Willie thought about it for a few seconds and then said, "Maybe he wanted you so he could get what Phil was after?"

"Then why did he remove the bodies, clean up, and fix the window?"

"So you wouldn't get busted by the cops before he got the file?"

"Wrong. It would have been obvious we didn't kill those guys but were victims. They certainly would have questioned us a lot, but we would not have been arrested."

"You certainly have a point there," Willie admitted. "But that would have brought in the cops, and that could have been a big obstacle."

Liz and I decided that we would risk it and not stay at Willie's. I offered to have Liz stay at my place until Mom and Carolyn came back. Liz agreed. Willie left, and we agreed to all meet for lunch at Murray's on Wednesday. Liz packed a few things, and we left together, her in her car, and I in mine.

Life is a series of events, many of which are new, and the way we handle them will have a huge impact on the rest of our lives.

Saturday and Sunday were quiet. Liz and I stayed inside the entire weekend as the weather was horrific. It snowed about twelve inches on Saturday, and Saturday night it turned cold, and the wind began to blow from the northwest. It was a classic Minnesota blizzard, which lasted all day Sunday. About three o'clock on Monday morning, the phone rang. As I scrambled to answer, I hoped it was just a crank caller or wrong number.

"Hello."

"John, it's James. Sorry to wake you at this hour, but I needed to talk with you now."

"Sure, James."

He never wanted to be called Jim, as he related to me once that all the kids in primary school used to tease him with "Little Jimmy," and he hated it.

"What's up?"

"Brett is dead. The police said he jumped from his fourth-floor apartment about one. Some people saw him lying in the snow."

"God, no! I knew he had some security problems, but never thought he would kill himself."

"Weather permitting, I am coming to Minneapolis in the morning to identify the body and make arrangements.

Would you meet me at the medical examiner's office?"

"Sure, James. Call me when you leave Rochester, and I'll be there."

"You're a really good friend, John."

I couldn't go back to sleep. I was responsible for his death, as I convinced him to plead out. I didn't think he would take it so hard as to commit suicide.

Then I heard Liz's sweet voice in the darkness say, "I heard the phone. Bad news, John?"

"Yes, James' brother-in-law, Deatra's brother, the one I was working with, killed himself."

"Oh no. Why?"

"Don't know, but he was really mixed up. He was in this radical animal rights group. He went against them under my advice. I hope that I didn't push him over the edge."

"John, that's something you can't control. Don't let it bother you."

James called at ten thirty and said the he was leaving, as the wind subsided and the roads looked okay. I told him I would meet him at the medical examiner's office at one o'clock. I was there at twelve thirty, and James arrived ten minutes later.

"Hello, James, the roads must have been pretty good. You made good time."

Snow removal from roadways in Minnesota is a well-perfected task, and crews are out early in force and work until the roads are passable with relative ease. I have often marveled at the ineptness of other cities a bit farther south at clearing snow from the roadways, but then why rush? When it snows, most everyone stays home.

"Hello, John. The roads were fine."

"Are you ready for this, or should we talk a little first?"

"Let's do it. We can talk later over some coffee."

We took the elevator down to the ME's office. I often wondered why morgues are always on the lowest level of a building. Maybe, as a society, we need to separate the living from the dead?

We pressed the bell, and a voice came over the intercom, "Can I help you?"

"Yes, this is James Boilen. We are here about Brett Malone."

"Okay."

The door latch buzzed, and we went in. It was a small waiting area with three chairs. We didn't sit, as a middleaged man, bald on the top and gray on the sides with dark-framed glasses and in a white lab coat, opened the inner door.

"James?"

"Yes. This is my friend, John."

"Okay, follow me."

We went into a large, well-lit room with several tables. One of which had a body covered with a sheet. It had several carts and some equipment around it and large lights above. We walked over to the cart, and the fellow pulled back the sheet, exposing Brett's head and bare shoulders. His head was covered with cuts and scrapes, and his nose pushed to one side. His jaw appeared broken and pushed in under his upper teeth.

"Is this Brett Malone?" the fellow asked.

"Yes," James answered then looked away.

"You're sure?" the fellow asked again.

James looked at Brett a second time. "Yes, that's Brett Malone."

The fellow looked at me. "Did you know Mr. Malone?"

"Yes, I had three meetings with him last month. That's Brett."

James asked what he needed to do to get the body back to Rochester for burial.

The fellow said, "Didn't the police tell you? We are keeping the body for a while. This doesn't seem to be a simple suicide. We need to do an autopsy. If you need additional information, talk with officer Kapinsky, Harold Kapinsky. Here is his card."

We left the ME's office and went to a small coffee shop just down the street. It had soft lighting, four high tables with three chairs each, and two soft lounge chairs sharing a small coffee table. We sat in the lounge chairs. Neither of us was hungry, so all we had was coffee. I suggested to James that we try to talk with the detective before James headed home. James agreed, and I called the number on the card from a phone booth in the back of the shop.

The operator answered and put my call through.

"Kapinsky."

"Yes, Detective, I'm John Castano. I was just at the ME's office with James Boilen to identify Brett Malone. The fellow there gave me your card and suggested we talk with you concerning Brett's death."

"Certainly, can you come to the precinct. The address is on the card."

"Yes, we'll be there in about a half hour."

We got to the precinct station at two o'clock. The desk sergeant called back to the officer, then he let us in.

"Straight back, then right. He is in the third office," we were instructed.

We got to the office and knocked on the open glass door. The detective spun his chair around.

"Yes."

"I called you a half hour ago. John Castano."

"Come in and have a seat. You are Mr. Boilen, I presume?"

"Yes, James."

"So how is it you two are IDing this Malone guy?"

"I'm his brother-in-law and live in Rochester, and John is a friend of mine who was helping him with a problem here in the Cities."

"So what sort of problem we talking about?"

"Brett was involved in an animal rights protest last fall and was arrested for disorderly conduct. I was helping him on that charge."

"And?" quizzed Harold.

"And I convinced him to plead guilty."

"So what?" Harold continued to quiz.

"This animal rights group, UFAC, wanted him to stand with the others as they held a very disruptive protest. The head of the local chapter was very upset that Brett pled out."

"I've heard something about this group. Who is the head honcho?"

"A guy named Albert Wertz."

"Hmm."

"So what is all the police interest in Brett's death?" I asked.

"Well, we don't think he jumped from that window. There was very little blood where he landed, which lends us to believe he may have already been dead and pushed out the window by someone. The autopsy will determine if our suspicions were correct."

"Oh no," James groaned.

"Well, let's just wait for the autopsy results," Harold asserted.

"When will that be?" I inquired.

"Tomorrow."

"Can I call you?"

"I'll call you," Harold assured. "And we may need to talk a bit more about Brett."

"That's fine."

We got up and left.

James headed back to Rochester, and I back home. When I walked into the duplex, I was greeted with the sweet garlic smell of tomato sauce simmering in the kitchen.

"Hello, John," came Liz's greeting.

I walked into the kitchen.

"Hi, Liz, the sauce smells fantastic. I didn't know you made red sauce."

"Every mother learns early in child-rearing how to make certain basic foods, and red sauce is one of those basics.

We are going to have it with gnocchi, steamed broccoli with garlic oil, and a Caesar salad. Some nice fresh Italian bread too. How did it go with James?"

"The police think that Brett may have been murdered."

Liz turned from the sink, where she was cleaning broccoli, facing me and said, "Oh, really, why do they think that?"

"Because he didn't bleed a lot after hitting the sidewalk, and that they feel may mean he was dead when he fell from the window."

"Do they have any suspects?"

"Well, they are not even sure it was murder. They are waiting for the autopsy results."

Dinner was just as delicious as it looked and smelled.

"You must have gone out for groceries? I certainly didn't have all this."

"Yes, I went to the grocery. That was it. I didn't want someone spotting me, if you know what I mean."

"I'm going into the office tomorrow, so you'll have the place to yourself."

"I like being here. Here with you."

"That's very flattering."

After dinner, I helped Liz with the dishes. I never liked doing dishes, but here with Liz, I somehow didn't mind.

In fact, I actually enjoyed it. My mind drifted back to Saturday before Christmas and Mom and Dad doing the dishes together.

Tuesday morning I woke up at six fifteen, fifteen minutes before the alarm was set to go off. I never woke up to the alarm, even if it is set at different times, but I always set the alarm because if I didn't, I would not wake up on time. I think it is psychological. I do not want to hear that blasted alarm so I wake up before it goes off. No alarm, no need to wake up. It was a normal weekday morning routine: make coffee, get the newspaper, coffee done, pour a cup, sit in front of the TV with the morning news on, and read the paper. A disruption to that routine could be disastrous, as my brain has yet to begin normal function.

Liz disrupted that routine. She came into the den so cheerful and bright I almost fell from my chair, and that's tough, considering I was in an overstuffed La-Z-Boy.

"Good morning, John. Sleep well?"

"Hell, I don't know. I'm still trying to wake up."

"Aw, come on, John."

She had a cup of coffee and sat on the love seat parallel to my chair and began to chatter like some pissed-off chipmunk. I couldn't gather my thoughts fast enough to follow her conversation, so I just kept nodding. Until I heard the words, "Okay, so that's what we will do."

"Do what?"

"John, weren't you listening?"

Then it struck me. We were getting just like married couples, and that is not what I intended with all my help and attention. I wanted to be a good friend, a helpful friend and a caring friend, but I didn't want Liz to think we were somehow destined to be together. I'm sure she felt the same way. Her husband, whom she loved dearly, has only been dead four months. I'm sure we were getting drawn into each other by the emotion from all that befell us. We cannot let that emotion force us into something that will not turn out right.

I would have to come up with a plan. I didn't want her to think I've tired of her. I haven't, just the opposite. But I needed her to understand our relationship was not romantic. We were just very, very good friends. But how? All this was just too hard to think about when I was only half awake.

I was in the office and had a sandwich for lunch when the intercom buzzed. It was Dorothy, one of our floating secretaries.

"You have a call on line three. She would not say who it was."

"Thanks, Dorothy."

"John Castano. Can I help you?"

"Hi, John, how have you been?"

The voice seemed very familiar, but I couldn't put a name to it.

"Fine!" I replied abruptly.

"It's Lynn. Lynn Williams."

It was my ex-fiancé, Lynn Markeson. We had not talked for over two years.

"How have you been, John? Married yet?"

"Still single. I have been very busy but had some time to travel with Paul to Mexico for our fishing excursion. Had a small problem though, fell overboard during a storm and floated in the Pacific overnight before they found me."

"God! That sounds very scary!"

"Well, at first I was scared, but after an hour or so, I accepted my situation, and it became quite pleasant. In fact, I even fell asleep for several hours."

"Thank God they found you. It makes me shudder to think about something like that. But to why I called. John, I think I have a serious problem, and I would like to see how you think I should handle it."

"Okay shoot."

"It is very personal, and I would rather not talk over the phone or come into your office. Could we meet sometime for a short time?"

"Of course. How about this afternoon? You name the place."

"I'm going to be visiting someone at Abbott Hospital at two. Could we meet in the coffee shop, say one?"

"That's good. One o'clock at the hospital coffee shop. Visiting anyone I know?"

"No, my husband's sister. She had a new baby."

I left the office at twelve thirty, as the hospital was not far from the office. When I arrived, I searched the room and saw Lynn waving at me from a corner table. I went to the table, and she got up. I gave her a long, strong hug.

"You're looking good, Lynn."

"Thanks, John, it's good to see you again. I picked up a sandwich for both of us. You still like roast beef with horseradish on a toasted Kaiser, don't you?"

"Sure do. Your memory is very good."

"I also got you some fries and a hot coffee, okay?"

"You got it just right."

"Tell me about this fishing trip."

"Well, not much to say. We were fishing marlin when this storm developed. Paul and I were ordered into the cabin, and we put on our life jackets. Then I realized I left my camera on deck, so I went out to get it when the boat did a roll and surged up. I fell over the side."

"And where was Paul?"

"In the head tossing his lunch. I screamed as the boat continued on, but no one could hear me. In a few minutes, they were gone. Sometime later I saw them pass by in the distance, but they never saw me. At least they were looking in the right area. It became a dead calm as night came, and I made my peace with God and myself. Then I fell asleep to be awakened by Paul and the deck hand at dawn. They found me. Do you remember my friends, Dan and Liz?"

"Yes, and how are they doing?"

"Not so well. It seems you have not heard?"

"No, what happened?"

"Dan was killed by what the police say was a falling tree last September."

"I'm so sorry. How is Liz doing?"

"Okay, but it is complicated. Some things are happening that are not good. We are just hanging on and hoping everything turns out okay."

"Sounds like you are not convinced that the tree killed him."

"What made you think that? Well, yes, but I can't talk about it right now. So what's happening with you?"

"This is going to be very hard for me, but here goes. Scott has been acting a little different lately, and I was not able to pin down just what was happening with him."

"So what do you mean by different?"

"He seems distant and is not as affectionate as he used to be. I have repeatedly asked him if anything was wrong, and he dismisses it by saying simply, 'No.' This seemed to begin about the time he and one of the neighbor boys started hanging out together."

"What do you mean by hanging out together?"

"Allen—he's the neighbor boy—comes over several evenings a week, and he and Scott go down to the rec room in the basement to watch sports. At first I thought nothing about, but it begins to seem more than just casual."

"How old is the boy?"

"About fourteen, but that's not all. A couple days ago I found a pair of the boy's underpants in the basement near the laundry area. That climaxed my suspicions that Scott may be having a relationship with the boy."

"I can understand your concern, and I agree that it does seem suspicious, but you need to handle this very delicately. To accuse or even think you suspect him of that could ruin your marriage. It could be nothing, and it is all completely innocent."

"So you don't think it was an accident?"

"We shouldn't make assumptions, as to assume implies a conclusion, and we are most often incorrect. That is because assumptions are full of biases and misconceptions. We can suspect, but then we must prove or disprove, but to assume usually makes an 'ass' out of 'u' and 'me.' Trusting a little grassroots philosophy is in order."

"That's why I came to you. Just how should I proceed?"

"Well, if it were me, I would just mention to Scott that you found the underpants in the laundry. Make sure it doesn't sound accusatory. He should respond with some sort of explanation. If he is open about it, you may have your answer. But if he is evasive, your suspicions may be justified."

"If so, then what?" Lynn demanded.

"Let's cross that bridge if we come to it."

We spent the next half hour catching up on our lives. I got the feeling that Lynn still had feelings for me, but I was not going down that road.

She agreed to let me know just what happened. I asked her to call me at home because it would be easier to talk.

Most people enter into marriage thinking it's going to be like driving over a flat, freshly paved highway. Instead they find they are on a potholed road, which has curves and hills that require the utmost attention. Too many quit because the road is too tough.

I was back in the office at 2:15 p.m. It was three thirty when Celia buzzed me on the intercom to inform me that a detective Kapinsky was on the phone.

"Hello. John Castano."

"Mr. Castano, this is Harold Kapinsky. We got the autopsy results on Mr. Malone, and it appears that he was indeed murdered. Cause of death was not the fall as we suspected, but severe, blunt-force trauma to the back of the skull caused by a round object approximately eight centimeters in diameter.

"There was nothing he could have struck in his fall that could have caused that injury," he continued. "It is estimated he was dead for fifteen to twenty minutes before the fall. We are sending investigators to his apartment in an evidence search. I have called James Boilen and informed him that the body may be claimed at the county morgue. We need to talk with the Boilens and would like you there also. Could you meet us at the precinct tomorrow at ten o'clock in the morning?"

"You bet I'll be there."

I no sooner hung up when Celia informed me that James was on the phone.

"Hello, James."

"John, did the detective, Kapinsky, call you?

"Yes, I'll be at the meeting tomorrow."

"Good, John. Deatra is not taking this well."

"I'm sorry, but I understand. It was her only brother. I'll help in any way I can."

"We are having Brett's body picked up by a local funeral home tomorrow. He'll be buried on Saturday."

"I'll be there," I assured James.

I called Liz at the duplex and advised her that Brett was indeed murdered. I also explained the funeral was Saturday in Rochester and asked if she wanted to accompany me there. She agreed but indicated that Mom and Carolyn were driving home from her brother's on Saturday, but she didn't need to be home.

"I'll be heading home in about an hour," I informed her.

"When would you like to eat, John?"

"Why don't we go out?"

"Fine, where would you like to go?"

"How about Mama D's?"

"Sounds good. See you in a couple hours."

Wednesday I was at the precinct station at 10:00 a.m. and was directed to an interrogation room. James, Deatra, Kapinsky, and another officer were already there.

"Have a seat, John. This is Detective Jacobsen, who is working this case with me. We're just trying to get some background on Brett. The Boilens said they knew very little about this organization, UFAC, which Brett was involved with. Can you help us there?"

"Yes, I had my legal tech at the office research the organization. Here are the results."

I handed over several pages of information I brought with me. Kapinsky took several minutes to read the report, handing each page to Jacobsen after he finished.

"This seems to be a very radical group, wouldn't you agree?"

"Definitely!" I agreed.

"This local guy, Wertz, what do you think of him?" quizzed Jacobsen.

"I saw him once, the day of Brett's hearing. He really didn't look too happy with Brett when he found out he pleaded out."

"Do you think he was pissed off enough to kill Brett?" Harold asked.

"Hell, I don't know. I just know he was really angry."

"Did you see Brett after his hearing?" asked Harold.

"No, it was the holidays, and I was out of town."

James injected, "Brett was with us at Christmas. We tried to get him to open up about the incident and the group he was with, but he was very closemouthed about the whole thing. He did seem very uncomfortable the whole time he was home."

"Well, if you guys think of anything else that's relevant, call us," Harold summed up.

James, Deatra, and I went to lunch after leaving the precinct. It was a nice diner just across the station. It was just before eleven o'clock, and James and Deatra ordered breakfast, and I ordered a house special, the Ruben with homemade chips and a quarter of a dill pickle. We discussed the possible motive that someone might have, but couldn't come up with anything. We departed after we finished our meal and agreed to keep in touch if anything came up. I headed back to the office.

Friday night after dinner I took Liz to her house. Everything was in order, and she decided to spend the night in her own bed. She thanked me profusely for the support and shelter during this time of disruption and trauma in her life. I wanted to be sure she felt comfortable at home alone, and she assured me she would. We spent an hour or so talking about nothing important before I headed home. She indicated she would meet me at my place at eight in the morning, as we were traveling together to Brett's funeral.

We got to the funeral home at 10:15 a.m. Visitation was from ten o'clock to eleven thirty with the funeral service to follow. Brett's body was to be cremated. The wake followed at a nearby restaurant. There were about forty people at the funeral and about thirty at the wake.

I didn't have time to talk with James and Deatra much, but then there was not much new. Liz and Deatra sat together and caught up on what they were doing. They haven't seen each other since Dan's funeral. Liz made no mention of the occurrences of the past couple of months concerning Dan's murder. At this point, that was just between Liz, Willie, and me, or so we thought.

We got back to my duplex at 5:30 p.m. Liz was going to head home, as Mom and Carolyn should be home. She invited me for dinner, but I declined because I just wanted to catch up on some reading. Liz understood and left for home.

It was a little after eight o'clock when my home phone rang. It was Lynn.

"Hi, John, how are you?" she sounded in good spirits.

"Just fine, Lynn. How did things go? I'm guessing that's what you're calling about."

"You're right. I did what you said last night at dinner. At first, Scott seemed a little confused then the light bulb went off. He said he and Allen were watching a basketball game, when Allen became very excited about a play and dirtied his underpants. Scott told him to rinse them out in the laundry sink. He forgot to take them with him when he went home. That's it!

"I did ask him why he was with him so much. He apologized for not telling me sooner, but it seems Scott saw Allen just hanging around the street alone sometime back and struck up a conversation. Scott realized Allen was lonesome, so he invited him to watch TV with him. That evening Allen confided in Scott why he was on the street.

"It seems," Lynn continued, "that Allen's mother is single, and he didn't have any idea who his father was. His mother would entertain male friends often, and when they came over, Allen was asked to leave for several hours. Scott offered to have him come over to our house during those times, and Allen agreed.

"I think Scott is missing having his own son, and Allen has become his surrogate son. We are not able to have children as Scott is sterile, and we don't want to adopt. That's the sum of it."

"Well, that has to be a relief," I commented.

"Yes, John, and I thank you for the advice."

"If I may be a bit intrusive, and you don't have to answer, why don't you two want to adopt? Scott seems to have welcomed this neighbor boy."

"I don't know," came back immediately.

"I would think this would be a perfect opportunity to revisit your position on adoption. If you decide to explore the opportunity, I could help you in the adoption process."

"We couldn't afford all that, as Scott doesn't make all that much."

"Not a problem. My expenses are very limited—just for you and old times—okay?"

"Well, I'll see how it goes, but thanks for the offer."

41

The next week was routine as possible, considering what happened to us. Liz and I talked several times by phone, but we had not seen each other. Liz was doing well, and it looked as if the impact of the events of the past couple of months started to fade. Her tax audit was scheduled for Friday.

I had a couple of phone conversations with Willie, and he made little progress in isolating someone who could have killed Dan, but he said he was getting close to what might be going on. He also had little news with regard to SIAIBM and Phillip Longhouse. I wondered just where we go from here.

On Friday I met Liz at the federal building for her audit at 1:15 p.m. Liz seemed cool and distant, but I thought she just had a case of the nerves. We entered the IRS office and told the receptionist we had an appointment with Joe Klink.

"Have a seat, and I'll let Mr. Klink know you are here."

We waited six or seven minutes, and the receptionist called us back. Joe had an office about halfway down a long hall.

"Mr. Klink, this is Elizabeth Danfurth and her attorney, John Castano."

"Thanks, Ilene." Joe motioned to us, "Please have a seat. This shouldn't take very long."

He opened a file on his desk and read it over for a minute or so.

"Mrs. Danfurth, your husband, Dan, indicated that he had an income of $13,700 from the Defense Department. Your husband, Dan, works for the university. Is he at work?"

"No, Dan had an accident in September and passed away."

"I sorry to hear that. You have my condolences."

"Thank you," Liz responded.

"We were not able to find a 1099-Misc. income form and the wages, which may be subject to a lower tax rate. Do you know whom he was working for at defense?"

"I have no idea. It wasn't until a few days ago that I found out he was doing some work for them. The only name I have is from some letters from a Phillip Longhouse. I don't know who he is or how to contact him."

"Hmm, nothing?"

"Really, that's it."

"Okay, I'll have to check into this further with Defense. If we determine the wages are subject to a lower rate, we'll issue a refund. Thank you, and both of you have a good day."

We left and had coffee at a coffee shop in the lobby. After analyzing what transpired during the audit, Liz turned personal.

"I saw your friend, Paul, at lunch today at Bill's Dinner. Why didn't you tell me about you being lost overboard and spending the night afloat in the sea?"

"I didn't want you to be worried if I ever took another fishing trip."

"Damn you, John. Our relationship is beyond that."

"I'm sorry, but that's how I felt when I got back. Only a few people know what happened. I'm still trying to sort it out in my mind."

"You could have died out there all alone. I would have been crushed. Two men, important in my life, dying within months."

"I know, but I never thought I would die. I just knew I would see you again. I apologize for being so secretive. It won't happen again."

"For god's sake, I hope not!"

"Paul seems to be totally overboard with this Susan you guys met on your fishing trip."

"Yes, we met a couple of unattached girls on vacation, and John really fell for Susan."

"And you got on quite well with a Gloria?"

"We connected, yes."

"So are you two an item?"

"Gloria was very nice, and I enjoyed her company. No, we are not an item. She has a doctor friend in Des Moines, who is single, and I think she is serious about him."

"You are not going to see Gloria again?"

"I don't know, but we left without making any plans. I can see this has you upset."

"No, John, just curious."

"Oh, okay, but we just enjoyed each other's company. That's all. When I was alone, in the dark, my thoughts were of you. I wished I was with you. I thought of all the great times we have had. I fell asleep thinking of you then had a dream that you were there, ready to pull me into your arms."

"Oh!"

On Wednesday of the next week, Willie called, "I've checked all the police reports in the Cities area, and there are no reports of murdered bodies being found, not even Phil."

"How can that be? I could see that whoever took the two bodies from Liz's disposed of them in a way that they haven't been found, but what about Phil? You reported it to the police, and they would have found the body, don't you think?"

"Seems logical, but there is no police report either on a body. Sometimes police think they may be able to draw out the perpetrators if they keep the whole thing under wraps. They hope the perps will start nosing around to find out why they haven't heard anything."

"You haven't been nosing around, have you?" I was worried.

"No, I'm not that stupid."

"So what do we do now?"

"Absolutely nothing, and don't say anything to Liz or anyone else, okay?"

"You got my word."

That night I had a searching dream again. I was searching for Liz, and no matter what I tried, I was unable to find her. I found myself walking down a long road until I reached her house. When I got there, someone else lived in it. They did not know Liz, so I began to search again in a hotel. I had her room number, but the elevator I was on did not stop at that floor; so I got off and tried the stairs, but all the doors were locked.

I woke in a sweat, my nightshirt damp. What did it all mean? I tried to think of something else, but the dream was branded into my brain. It was 2:22 a.m. I got up for a quick jaunt to the bathroom. Back in bed, my thoughts drifted back to my dream. Within a few minutes, I lapsed into sleep. I heard the doorbell, went to the front door, and looked through the side window; it was Phil. He was standing at my front door, his face mostly burnt away. I didn't answer. Then I saw two police officers standing behind him.

I awoke again, and it was 4:10 a.m. Hell, I couldn't get back to sleep after that. I lay there about twenty minutes then went to the kitchen and started my coffee. I flicked on the TV, but the only thing on were infomercials. I turned the TV off and went to the front door, opened it; no Phil, no police, and no newspaper. It was just too early for the newspaper. Coffee was done, and I retired to the den, full cup in hand, and grabbed a *US News & World Report* from two weeks ago.

A flash of sun swept over my eyes, and I jerked awake. My US News was in my lap, and a half cup of cold coffee was on the table. The clock on my desk glared 7:33 a.m. I realized I had fallen back to sleep in my La-Z-Boy and slept about three hours without a single dream. Maybe strong coffee was the key, or maybe it was sleeping in my La-Z-Boy; but whatever it was, I had the best three hours sleep I've had in the two months.

The coffee in the pot was still hot. I dumped the cold coffee in my cup and filled it with hot. I went to the front door, opened it, and the paper was here. I grabbed it and went back to the kitchen and unfolded the paper. The headline on the lower half of the front page read, "Two Bodies Found Floating in Mississippi River."

The articles said that two middle-aged males were found floating in the river just south of the I-35 bridge. Cause of death had not been determined, but foul play was suspected. Were these the two thugs from Liz's place? Highly probable. What was going to happen now?

I called Willie's house.

"Uh, who's this?"

"Hey, Willie, it's John."

"John? Oh, John! Waz up?"

"You've probably not seen the morning newspaper?"

"Nope."

"They found two guys floating in the river. They think foul play was involved."

"They do, hey? Probably the two guys from Liz's. It's really hard to dispose of two large dead guys. They usually come floating up somewhere."

"We need to have a meeting. Today?"

"Sure, lunch at Wanda's eleven o'clock?"

"See you there."

Wanda's was sort of a drive south of downtown, just off I-35W. Willie had the hots for the manager, Maggie. I think he shacked up with her for a week or so from time to time. I was there at 11:00 a.m. Willie was seated at the very end of the counter, both elbows on the counter, his hands surrounding his head, deep in conversation with Maggie. I walked over; I was sure I wasn't interrupting anything important.

"Hey, Durante."

"John, have a seat. Have you met Maggie?"

"Last time we met here."

"Okay."

Maggie left, and I sat next to Willie. The counter waitress came over to take our order. Willie ordered the special, an Italian hot beef on a Kaiser with German potato salad and a coke. Nothing like an Axis lunch special. I had a grease burger with the works and fries with an iced tea, not sweetened.

"So what do we need to talk about?" Willie inquired.

"I had a dream last night that Phil was knocking on my door, two policemen standing behind him."

"Oh, don't lay any dream shit on me. All that's crap. Phil is dead. Your shot went clean through his skull."

"Can we be sure?"

"I'm sure."

"Okay."

"The other thing is, do you think there is any way that they can tie those thugs to Liz?"

"Anyone who went to the extreme trouble to get them out of her house and clean up the mess the way they did isn't going to leave any evidence that would tie them to Liz. Trust me," assured Willie. "I'll very quietly try to find out anything I can about the discovery."

"That's good," I agreed. "But one other thing, will you see if there is anyone who fits what Phil would be like if he were still alive and in an ICU?"

"Come on, John, the guy is gone."

"Just for me, peace of mind and all that, you know."

"Okay, for your peace of mind."

The subconscious mind can deduce the correct answer sometimes better than the conscious mind, as it can focus more intensely on the situation, where the conscious mind is distracted with other stimuli at the same time. Dreams are the two minds reconciling the differences. Dreams should not be dismissed out of hand as inaccurate or trivial.

Our lunch came. The Italian hot beef was a bunch of thin, sliced processed beef soaked in mild garlic gravy. The burger was all it was supposed to be, as fat oozed from the patty with every bite. It tasted quite well. I thought that the real taste in a burger is not in the lean, but in the fat. The greaser the burger, the better it tasted. Same with the fries. My iced tea was made from instant and was just a trifle taster than plain water.

Back at the office a return-call note was on my desk. It was from Harold Kapinsky. I called the precinct and was transferred to him.

"Kapinsky."

"John Castano."

"Thanks for getting back to me, John. Could you come to the precinct? We need to talk a bit more."

I hesitated. Was this about Brett, or was it about those bodies in the river?

"Sure. Is this about Brett?"

"You got it."

I left the office and told Celia I would be out the rest of the day. I had an uneasy feeling, but it may have been due to misplaced paranoia, but then who wouldn't be paranoid after what happened?

Detective Kapinsky ushered me into another interrogation room.

"So tell me exactly what happened at the courthouse."

"It wasn't a lot. After pleading out, I was outside the courtroom while Brett settled up with the bailiff. Wertz was outside with three other UFAC people who were arrested along with Brett. When Brett came out, Wertz asked him what he was doing, and Brett told him he pleaded out. Wertz made some sort of comment, I don't remember exactly just how he said it, to the effect that Brett was a traitor. Brett said he thought that pleading out was best for him.

Wertz just glared with the look of intense hatred. We then got into the elevator and went down to the lobby, where we each went our own way."

"Who were the other three?"

"I have no idea. Wasn't introduced to them and didn't talk to them. Check with the court. Is Wertz a suspect?"

"Everyone who was in contact with Mr. Malone in the past few weeks is a suspect. Malone knew whoever killed him, as there was no forced entry, and he was comfortable enough to turn his back to the killer."

"That includes me."

"You said it," the detective assured.

I finished dinner of a broiled, rare rib steak, salad, tater tots, and a big chocolate-cream-filled Bavarian for desert and dozed in the den when the phone startled me fully awake.

"Hello. John here."

"John, it's Liz. How have you been?"

"So-so."

"Why's that?"

"I was interviewed by the police concerning Brett's murder, and I think they consider me a suspect."

"Oh, why do you think that?"

"Because they so much as said so."

"What motive would you have?"

"None, but they don't know that. Did you see they found two guys floating in the river, possibly the two from the other night?"

"Yes, that's what I called about. That and I missed talking to you."

"I'm flattered. I talked to Willie about that, and he is going to check and see if he can find any information about them without creating any suspicion. I'll keep you posted if I hear anything from him."

"Good, John. Do you really think those are the guys?"

"Yes."

Liz and I continued to talk mostly about what we've been doing. I got the feeling she felt I was trying to distance her. I couldn't tell if this upset her, but I tried to reassure her I was just busy, as it was the beginning of tax time. We agreed to meet at Murray's for a drink tomorrow after work.

We hung up, and I began to doze again when the phone rang again. It was Willie.

"John, the two dudes they pulled from the river were each struck by a single, .44-caliber bullet in the heart. That's all I could find out. They have not been IDed."

"So it looks like these are the guys?"

"Yep."

"So what do we do?"

"Not a goddamn thing!"

"Okay. Thanks, and have a good evening."

"One more thing, John. There was someone admitted to the University Hospital's burn unit the day after the Phil thing. He also had a gunshot wound to his head. He's listed as a John Doe, in very critical condition. I have a nurse friend there, but she couldn't get any information, as they have this guy under police guard. She's going to keep checking for me."

"*Burned!* How the hell did he get burned? He was lying in the ground next to his car when we left."

"Hold on, we don't know who this guy is."

"I just know it is him, a feeling in my bones."

I was at the office early, 7:30 a.m. I didn't sleep, so I had my coffee, grabbed a breakfast sandwich at McD's, and headed to the office.

Celia was at her desk and I said, "Good morning, Celia. What time do you get here? I thought I'd be the first here."

"No, sir, I usually get here around seven so I can get the daily schedule done and on your desk by eight."

"I had no idea."

"Yes, and Rudy is here too."

I was at my desk about ten fifty when Celia buzzed me, "Mr. Durante is on the phone."

"Hello, Willie."

"Mr. Castano, your intuition seems to be right on."

"How's that?"

"The guy in the U burn unit is named Phil Roland. He was shot. The bullet hit his left cheekbone. It did not penetrate the skull, but traveled along the skull and exited above and behind the left ear. Your shot knocked him out, but didn't kill him. The fire burned him over 70 percent of his body, and they don't expect him to live. The police are trying to get him lucid enough to give them information on the person or persons who did this to him."

"So what do we do now?"

"Can't do much except hope he kicks off before they get any info out of him."

"Shit, shit, shit, we're all going to jail."

"Stay cool, John."

"How can I stay cool, Willie?"

"Work at it."

I left the office for Murray's at four forty-five. I decided to walk, as it was only six blocks, and it was relatively mild, and I had lots of anxiety to walk off. Liz was not there yet, so I got a table in the lounge. The waitress took my order, a double Jack Daniels on the rocks. It came before Liz, and I sucked it down with due dispatch. Before the waitress got back, Liz arrived.

"Hi."

"Hi, John. It looks as if you got a good start on the night. Where's your Heineken?"

"This is not a Heineken night."

"Oh, what's happened?"

I explained the whole situation to Liz as carefully as I could, but she became noticeably disturbed. The waitress came over, and I ordered the same, and Liz had a coke. By the time we were finished, I had a couple more and was not able to drive. Liz took me to her house, where I slept it off. In the morning she had me at the office at seven forty-five. The whites of my eyes were as red as watermelon, and my head pounded as if some little bastard was trapped inside my skull and tried to chop his way out.

When I got to the office, I told Celia to hold my calls, and if anyone was looking for me to tell them I'm out. I pulled the shade on my window and curled up on the small love seat. It had to be about two hours when I woke to the knocking at my door. It was Celia.

"I think you need to talk with the two officers outside."

"Okay, show them in, but give me a couple minutes."

I opened the shade on the window, combed my hair, and straightened up my suit. There was a knock; it was Celia.

"Mr. Castano."

"Yes, Celia."

She opened the door. "Officers O'Riley and Stanford are here to speak with you."

"Yes, officers, how can I help you?" I said as they stood over me my desk. "Please have a seat."

"We are from Hennepin County Sherriff's Department. Do you know a Phil Roland?"

"Hmm, I'm not sure," I lied. "I meet a lot of people in my business, you know. What does he look like?"

Officer O'Riley described him.

"Yes, I think it is the fellow I met a couple times while with a client."

"We found your card in his wallet," O'Riley said as he pulled it out.

"Yes, I think I gave that to him the first time we met. He's in some sort of trouble?"

"Why do you ask?"

"Because you're here and went through his wallet."

"Yes, he was shot and set afire. He's in the burn unit at the University Hospital."

"Oh god."

"Who was the client you were with?"

Now what was I'm going to do? I would like to keep Liz out of this, but how could I?

"Elizabeth Danfurth."

"How can we get in touch with her?" quizzed O'Riley.

I gave them her office number. I felt it would be better for them to see her there than at home, where they could do some snooping. They asked where she was now, and I gave them her office address.

The officer's parting word was, "We'll want to talk to you again."

"Today?" I asked.

"Maybe."

As soon as they left, I called Liz and gave her a heads-up. I explained what I told the officers and tried to ease her nervousness. She promised she would call me after they left. I then called Willie, but he was not in his office. I called his house, and no answer there either, leaving urgent messages on both answering machines.

It wasn't ten minutes, and Willie called back, "What's so urgent?"

"Two detectives were here asking me about Phil."

"How did they get your name?"

"He had my card in his wallet. I gave one to him the first time we met at Liz's club."

"Don't panic," Willie responded. "The card doesn't mean you had anything to do with his accident."

"No, but it ties me to him, and who knows what else will turn up."

Liz called after the police left. She told them the truth but said nothing about the incident at the house and junkyard. They seemed satisfied and left after a few minutes. I thought, *Good job, Liz.*

I learned early on in my legal education that if you are going to be misleading when explaining something, be as close to the truth as possible. Complete fabrications almost always fail.

I was up at six o'clock Saturday morning. I certainly felt much better than yesterday. I had tickets to the Timberwolves game this evening and was meeting Paul. Tonight was going to be a soft-drink-only night. I sipped my coffee and went through the morning paper when the phone rang.

"John, Willie here. Just thought you would like you know that Phil expired overnight."

"Did he say anything?"

"Don't know?"

"We all thought he was dead. So what now?" I asked.

"If Phil talked to the cops, they should be around to see you any time now. If you don't hear from them today, he probably didn't say anything."

Nothing much happened over the weekend, so by Monday morning I was feeling somewhat safe. I got to the office at 8:45. Celia told me the police were in my office; O'Riley and Stanford were waiting for me.

"Mr. Castano, we need you to come with us to the police station," O'Riley said.

"What's the problem? Is this about Phil Roland?"

"No problem, we need to talk. And yes, it is about Phil Roland," O'Riley answered.

"How long do you think this will take?"

"You may be gone a while," Stanford informed me.

On the way out, I told Celia I may be gone for the rest of the day, and she should reschedule my appointments.

The police car was parked in front in the loading zone. They asked me to get in the back. It took about ten minutes to get to the sheriff's department in the County building. They drove into the basement garage, and we took the elevators to the third floor. We entered an office at the end of the hall, and three other people were waiting.

"John, this is Robert Jerome and Joe Foley of the Government Bureau of Investigation," O'Riley pointed to the two men standing behind the desk. "And this is Captain Robertson of Hennepin County Sheriff's Department," he said as he gestured to the man seated behind the desk.

"It's my understanding you knew Phil Roland," the captain asked.

"Not really, we met twice, once at a restaurant, that's when he asked me for a card. The next time was at the New Year's Eve party. He was intoxicated and a bit of an ass. That's the extent of it."

"Phil Roland was not his real name. It was Garson Petroff. He was one bad dude. He was Romanian who illegally snuck into the US about three years ago. He has been tied to several murders, and we have been looking for him for the last two years," GBI agent Foley informed me.

"So you can see why we are interested in talking to people who knew him," chimed in Agent Jerome. "How well does this Elizabeth Danfurth know him?"

"Not much better than I do. He was an acquaintance of her late husband, Dan. They met at Dan's athletic club.

She only met him a few times herself," I explained.

"What happened to her husband?" the capitan asked.

"A tree he was cutting fell on him."

"When was that?"

"Last September. I handled the estate."

"Petroff had a gun, and it was in his hand when police found him, so he was probably about to do someone who must have beat him to the draw. The bullet hit him in the face, knocking him out, then they poured gas over him and the car, probably to get rid of any evidence," Foley illuminated. "What we are really interested in is what Petroff was up to. Do you have any idea?"

"Not the slightest," I lied.

He was obviously after Dan's notes, but I didn't feel further police involvement, even the GBI, at this point was a good thing. Then I thought, *I sure hope I'm right.* Except lying to a federal officer is a felony, but I was willing to take the chance.

"If you think of anything, let us know. We are going to talk to Mrs. Danfurth about this also," O'Riley finished.

I was waiting for the elevator. *Ding,* and the door opened, and there was Liz with two other officers.

I held back and said, "Hi."

"Hello, John, do you know what this is all about?"

"They are going to ask you some questions about Phil Roland."

"Phil, why?"

The officers quickly shuffled her down the hall, as they didn't want me to tell her anything more.

"Call me when you're done, I'll be at home."

I no more got into my duplex, and Liz called.

"John, do you think they suspect us?"

"Yes, they think we are involved somewhere in this whole mess," I affirmed. "What did you say to the officers?"

"I didn't say anything about the incident with Phil two weeks ago. I told them I didn't know him well and didn't think much of him. I didn't think Dan liked him much either, but he kept forcing his presence on Dan. They really asked a lot of questions about Dan and his accident. Do you think Phil killed Dan?"

"That's a good possibility. I thought that since our first brush with Phil. We may never know for sure now that he died. The only thing that confuses me is why would Phil kill Dan before he had his research?"

I called Willie and filled him in on the investigation. He seemed concerned but was not in a panic. He seemed to think that they did not consider us serious suspects.

Tuesday and Wednesday were uneventful. Thursday I reached the office at the usual time. There was a return-call note on my desk from Liz, and it was marked, "Urgent." I called her at home.

"John, you need to come to my place immediately!"

"What's up, Liz, trouble?"

"I don't know; just come!"

When I got to Liz's, there was a black Suburban parked in front. Liz answered the door, and I followed her to the office. To my surprise, Alexi Antonoff was there with GBI agents, Jerome and Foley. My thoughts were swimming.

"What's going on?'

"Hello, John," Alexi opened the conversation.

I met him at Dan's funeral, but had not seen him since.

"You two are probably totally confused about all that is going on. That's surely understandable."

"Now why in the hell would you think that?" was my sarcastic reply.

"Why don't you sit next to Liz, and I'll try to explain."

"You know Bob and Joe. I'm a special agent of the GBI assigned to the Defense Department," Alex explained.

"The president initiated a project to develop an Anti-Ballistic Missile defense system. The Defense Department is carrying out the project. Dan was recruited, along with many others in the civilian population who had specific expertise in areas of research for the project. This is what Dan was working on when he had his accident."

"We are almost sure Dan was murdered, and we think Phil may have been responsible," I injected.

"Oh, we had no idea it was more than an accident," Alexi commented. "Why do you feel he was murdered?"

"Because Dan was far too experienced a woodsman to allow a tree to fall on him where it did. Plus the killing blow could not have been made by a tree branch. The killer placed Dan there after he was dead and finished the tree cutting so it would fall on him and cover his act. We suspected Phil."

"Good conclusion, but I know it wasn't Phil. We had Phil under surveillance, and he was nowhere near the cabin when Dan died. I'll have to explain," Alexi continued.

"My assignment was to insure Phil and any others were not able to access any of the research Dan was doing for the Defense Department. We had Phil and his enforcers under surveillance almost from the beginning. We followed them here the night he was trying to get the file from you. I will check into the possibility Dan was murdered."

"When they came here that Thursday night, I had to do something, as I knew as soon as Phil got what he wanted, you were dead. I shot the two knuckle guys, but I wanted Phil alive so I could find out who his go-to contact was. I followed you to Phil's place then to the junkyard. When that PI you hired, Willie Durante, showed up with Dan's file, I knew you three were history," Alexi continued.

"Who set him on fire and why?"

"I don't know. We left after you."

"Then how did you know Phil was still alive and in the burn unit?"

"We heard the police unit call for an ambulance and checked it out with various hospitals until we found him. I was able to access him, as he was under tight security, but he was not conscious. We wanted to find out who his contact was, but he died before regaining consciousness."

"We came back to Liz's later that evening, picked up the bodies, and cleaned up. We had the windowpane replaced next morning. We didn't want the local police involved in this."

"Then you have been shadowing us all along?" I speculated. "Then why did you drop the bodies in the river?"

"As I said, we don't want the locals involved. This thing is top secret, and we don't need locals meddling in the case."

Alexi continued, "Dan's trips to Washington a couple times a year were to meet with the others doing similar research. SIAIBM was the Defense Department's cover name for Dan's group. Phillip Longhouse is the operational name for the group leader. The vacation inn is employed by the Defense Department as a cover for the meetings.

They have a very secure room in the basement where these meetings are held. *And,* none of this can leave this room, *understand!*"

I was very suspicious at Alexi's explanation. If what he said was true, he and his pals committed numerous illegal acts even as federal agents, including murder. I don't believe that the GBI would approve of what he was saying.

Why was he telling us this, as he knows it is illegal?

"Yes," both of us answered.

"We need to secure Dan's notes. Does Durante still have them?" demanded Alexi.

"Yes, but I don't know where he has them."

"Call him and have him bring them here ASAP," Alexi advised.

I called Willie's office and asked for him. The receptionist said Willie hasn't been in the office since Monday. He left in the morning, and no one has seen him since. When I explained this to Alexi, he looked very disturbed.

"Call his house. Maybe he's sick," he requested.

I did so, but no answer, and the answering machine was off.

"John, come with me. We need to get to Willie's. Jerome and Foley will stay with Liz."

We headed to Willie's apartment. The door was unlocked, and we went in to a stifling smell of death and rot. I choked and placed my hand over my mouth; Alexi did the same. We found Willie in his bedroom across the bed.

His throat had been slashed, and he fell onto the bed. He was stabbed multiple times in the back. The knife lay on the pillow at the head of the bed.

"We'll have to call the locals in on this one," Alexi conceded.

The apartment had been ransacked. Alexi called the police, identified himself, and reported the murder. We opened as many windows as we could to relieve the smell then waited for the police to arrive. When they came, Alexi explained that they were trying to reach Willie with regards to a GBI investigation. and when we found out he had not been in his office for three days, we came here. They seemed to buy it, but then, how much choice did they have?

The police took the investigation from there, poor bastards, and we returned to Liz's. Alexi suggested on the way to Liz's that Jerome stay with Liz, and Foley would stay with me, as someone else could be looking for the file. I agreed. Liz was shattered by the news of Willie. I was worried about her, hoping the weight of all this didn't damage her psychologically or physically. The human body has defense mechanisms to prevent such damage in most stressful situations, but our almost-demise and now a fourth death could be overwhelming.

When I told Liz, she started to shake, then completely broke down. I supported her for some time.

"One of the GBI officers will stay with you until they are sure you are free from danger," I assured her.

Liz retired to her mother's quarters, where she was with Carolyn through the day's trauma. I and the agents sat for a bit in the office.

Alexi commented, "I don't think this was a professional job on Willie. This was someone who was really pissed at him. A professional doesn't fatally slit someone's throat and then stab him multiple times. Whoever did this was angry with Willie. We'll keep Jerome and Foley with you guys for a couple days to play it safe, and if nothing turns up, we'll free you up."

"Sounds like a plan," I agreed.

"I'm going back to Willie's tonight, very late tonight, and see if I can find Dan's file," Alexi planned. "Do you have any idea at all where he could have stashed it, John?"

"All he told me was that it was in a safe place."

A search by Alexi yielded nothing. He also searched Willie's Cadillac and came up empty. Saturday and Sunday were uneventful. Monday morning Foley and I parted company with the understanding I see anything suspicious, I would immediately call. Jerome and Foley said they would take a lower profile, and we were free to do what we wanted, if that were possible with all that's happened.

I was in the office by nine o'clock Monday morning. Shortly after arriving, there was a knock at the door, and Greg Steinman stuck his head in.

"John, can I talk with you?"

"Sure, come in, Greg," I indicated. Greg was a founding partner in the firm.

"Are you in some sort of trouble, John? The police here and all that."

"No, I don't think so, Greg."

"Can you talk about it?"

"Sure, this fellow of a friend of mine and client was murdered in a rather gruesome fashion. I met him on a couple of occasions, and he asked for my card. They found the card in his wallet and contacted me while investigating. That's the extent of it."

"I heard on the news that Willie Durante, the PI we've used from time to time, was murdered also."

"Yes, I was the one who found him. He was doing some personal work for me, and when I couldn't reach him, I went to his apartment and found him dead."

"That's shocking! Seems like murder is all around you these days. May I ask what Willie was doing for you?"

"As I said, it was a personal job, and I can't talk about it just yet. In no way does it involve the firm, and I was paying him myself. No firm money was used."

"If we can help in any way, feel free to ask us," Greg offered.

I didn't mention Brett's murder. I didn't feel Greg needed to know at this time, but I forgot about Rudy, who did the research on Brett, UFAC, and the two thugs who were off the radar screen.

"I hope all this goes away soon, Greg, but I will come to the firm if I need some help."

The rest of Monday and Tuesday were business as usual. When I got to the office on Wednesday, Greg was waiting for me in my office.

"Good morning, Greg."

"John, John, John, this is much more than you have led me to believe," he began.

"Yesterday afternoon I had a talk with Rudy. He told me you had him research a fellow named Brett Malone, who was later murdered. This morning I was talking with Celia, and she said you thought someone was into your safe. John, just what's going on?"

I was in a corner. I needed to let Greg know some of what was happening, but I couldn't tell him the whole story. I had to do this in a convincing way.

"Greg," I began, "this is very complicated, and I need to begin at the beginning."

I sat at my desk and leaned forward toward Greg.

"I don't know if you remember Dan and Liz Danfurth?"

"Yes, John, I do. They are clients of the firm."

"Right, and they were also my good friends. Liz still is. I knew Liz from my university days. Then you probably know Dan died in an accident last year."

Greg nodded in the affirmative.

"I handled his estate and visited Liz in December to settle everything. After that meeting, I began to doubt that Dan's death was an accident, so I began to do some snooping. It looked very likely that Dan was murdered, and I hired Willie on a personal basis to look into it in more depth."

"He came up with the same conclusions and possible suspects, but no motive. We didn't think we had enough to go to the police yet, so he continued to investigate. Maybe he got too close, and Dan's killer killed Willie. The police are now doing the investigating."

I continued, "As far as Phil Roland, I first met him at a restaurant in December while dinning with Liz, her mother, and daughter. He knew

Dan from the athletic club that Dan belonged to. During the introduction and following conversation, he found out I was Liz's lawyer and asked me for my card. That's how it got into his wallet and brought the police here during the investigation.

"There was a third death, Brett Malone. Brett was completely unrelated," I explained. "He was the brother-in-law of my good friend, James Boilen."

"I know him. He's a lawyer in Rochester, right?" questioned Greg.

"Yes. Brett was his wife's brother. Brett got involved with an animal rights organization, United Front against Animal Cruelty, and got arrested for disorderly conduct and trespassing at a protest. The group was going to use the legal hearing to continue their protest in an effort to get more publicity for their cause. James wanted me to talk Brett into pleading guilty and taking the fine."

I continued, "I had Rudy research the group and used that information to convince Brett to plead guilty. His pals were not happy with Brett. Initially they thought Brett committed suicide by jumping from his apartment, but it didn't take long to realize someone killed him in the apartment and pushed him out the window to make it look like suicide."

"Did someone from the animal rights group kill him?" Greg quizzed.

"Don't know. The police are still investigating," I answered. "But that's the story."

"You're right. It's hard to believe that all this is circumstantial. Are the police looking into Dan's accident?"

"Yes, sort of."

"What do you mean, 'Sort of'?"

"Well, they were not completely convinced it was murder, but are looking into the situation," I deflected Greg's question.

"So then it's probable that we'll see the police around here again?"

"Probably."

Before Greg left, Celia informed me that Officer O'Riley was on the phone. I motioned to Greg to stay and put the phone on speaker.

"Hello. John here."

"Yes, John, this is Officer Sean O'Riley. I wanted to let you know that we arrested two individuals in the murder of Brett Malone. It's Albert

Wertz and Brett's significant other, Hillary Holden. We have a confession from Hillary.

She didn't actually kill Brett. Wertz did that, but she helped Wertz push him out the window sometime after the killing. We have a bunch of evidence and expect them held without bail."

"Do you have a motive?" I asked.

"Ms. Holden said it was revenge. Wertz did not want his people breaking away from the group. Brett was viewed by Wertz as a traitor."

"Thanks for letting me know, Sean. Did you let the family know?"

"That's my next call, John."

"Do you have the murder weapon?"

"Yes, we believe so. It appears to be a crude ax made from a yoked tree branch with an oblong rock laced to it with rawhide. There was blood and hair stuck to it. It was found in Wertz's apartment. Very simple but very lethal and easy to get rid of. Wertz just kept it too long."

"I would like to attend the arraignment and preliminary hearing," I demanded.

"Sure, John, we'll let you know when they are scheduled."

I hung up and looked at Greg, who, before this conversation, I thought was very suspicious of my involvement in these murders.

"It looks like Brett's murderer is in the bag," I directed to Greg.

"Good, John. Keep me in the loop," Greg responded as he left my office.

I called Liz at her office and told her the news of Brett. Just one of these solved seemed to relieve her tension a little. We talked about twenty minutes.

Liz asked, "Could you stop over tonight? Have dinner with us?"

I couldn't refuse. "My schedule is open."

I haven't said much about the GBI protection, as they were almost invisible. They would follow us to work in the morning, be there to follow home, and spend the evening in front of the house. I didn't know how long this would last, but if there was anyone still trying to get to us, these boys knew what they were doing.

I followed my call to Liz with a call to James. Officer O'Riley talked with him prior to my call. James seemed relieved at the arrest of the person everyone was sure killed Brett. I told James I would attend the arraignment and preliminary hearings and would keep him informed.

Dinner at Liz's was excellent as usual, pork roast with mashed potatoes and buttered green beans. We said nothing of our continuing saga with Carolyn and Mom, as Liz had not told them what befell us while they were in Duluth. After dinner we sat alone in Dan's office, and I mentioned that the firm knows much of what we have experienced the past months.

"Is this going to be a serious problem for you at work?" Liz asked.

"Being involved in murder is always a serious concern of an employer, but much more so with us because we cannot be perceived as having shady employees. Good law firms need to have impeccable reputations."

"Do you think this will affect your job?"

"I sure hope not."

Thursday morning O'Riley called to inform me that the arraignment of Wertz and Holden was scheduled for one o'clock that afternoon in the county courthouse. I indicated I would be there. I did ask if it would be possible to talk with Hillary after the arraignment. O'Riley said he would arrange it.

The arraignment was routine, as persons charged with Murder One had to accept a not-guilty plea. A flight risk was established, and bail was denied. I left and waited for O'Riley outside the courtroom. He came down the hall and asked me to follow him. We went into a side room adjacent to the courtroom, where Hillary was seated at a small table. She was in shackles. I recognized her as the defendant outside the courtroom when Brett had his hearing.

"Hi, Hillary, I'm John Castano. I don't know if you know who I am?"

"Yes, you're the lawyer who talked Brett into pleading guilty. Why did you do that?"

"Because it was best for Brett."

"Yeah, and it got him killed!"

"Excuse me! Murdered!"

"We had to do that."

"Why?"

"Because he was a traitor, and traitors are killed."

Hillary was obviously under the influence of Wertz. I followed that with a hard truth.

"Traitors are people who desert their country in a time of war and consort with the enemy."

"Yes, this is war, and you are the enemy."

"And who told you that?"

"Al. He says that we are at war with all animal abusers."

"I'm an animal abuser?"

"Yes, all you pigs. You eat meat, right? An animal was killed for you just so you could have your steak. That makes you an animal abuser."

"And the very animals you propose to protect eat each other. The lion eats the gazelle. The tiger eats the buffalo, and the wolf eats the deer. So then why are we considered animal abusers?"

"You are still an animal abuser because you should know better."

"Hooo, we are above our animal brethren?"

"You got it!"

"Then killing Brett is far less serious than killing a steer, right?"

"You're an asshole. Take me away," she said to O'Riley.

O'Riley took Hillary back to her cell, and I sat in the room and reflected on just what transpired. I trapped her. Did I really want to do that? Maybe I would have gotten more had I been conciliatory? Then what did I want? I thought that would never have worked, as Hillary was programmed.

We human beings have a grace and a flaw, and they are the same; we are trusting beings. We believe what others tell us is true, and in most situations, it is indeed. But a little paranoia can be a good thing. There are many people who will take advantage of our trusting nature and deal us something less than the truth. With these people, their self-interest trumps the truth. Be particularly cautious of people who say, "God wants you to do it," or invokes God's name as a reason to do something. These can be dangerous people. Question people who use some sort of cause for the better good of humanity in order to get you into their fold or people who overuse the word "fair."

There were all those souls who perished at Waco. There was Stalin, who killed millions of Russians to achieve his ends; there was Hitler, who killed millions of Jews to achieve his purpose; and there was the Inquisition in the fifteenth century, in which thousands were killed for sake of a slight difference with the order of things. History is littered with hundreds of examples, but then, who puts any credence in history's relevance today?

What does this have to do with trust? These events were accomplished because the perpetrators were told and believed that what they were doing was right and just. It wasn't until later that they realized they were misled.

So how do we keep from getting duped? It's tough. Mostly it depends on good judgment and the ability to question what others tell us. We cannot accept statements on blind faith from people we don't know very, very well.

Under those circumstances, we must question and demand proof and facts before committing. There is an element called a "gut feeling" used often by the police. Gut feeling—it's a combination of good judgment, observation, and experience; and it's the lack of experience that makes young people like Hillary so vulnerable.

And so, was Hillary a soldier in the UFAC army, sold a bill of goods of semi-truths and plain untruths, outdoing the fighting, while the generals sat, by watching the out come and expecting the results they intended? Would I be able to get through to her? Probably not, but then I had no real goal to do so except as a mission of my humanity. On that, I left the room and departed the courthouse.

I didn't return to the office but drove directly home, Foley close behind. Foley and I had pizza for dinner and spent the evening watching basketball on the TV. Liz called, and I updated her of the arraignment. She wondered just how long Alexi felt we needed our shadows. I said I would call him and solicit his thoughts and get back to her.

I asked Foley to contact Alexi, as I wanted to talk with him. An hour hadn't passed, and he called.

"Alex, John here. Liz and I were wondering how much longer you felt it necessary to have Foley and Jerome with us?"

"Are you two feeling a bit restrained?"

"Well, sort of."

"I would have liked to keep them around until we found Dan's file, but we can ease up on you two, I guess."

"So what's happening with the search?"

"Everything has been a dead end. I'm following up on a few other possibilities."

"Good luck," I offered.

"My guys will be gone tomorrow. If you spot anyone suspicious, call us immediately."

Sunday morning was the usual: coffee, toast, and the newspaper. I lectured at the ten-o'-clock mass. The gospel was the parable of the prodigal son, and Father's sermon was devoted to the grace of forgiveness, something with which I have struggled. Somehow I feel forgiveness without repentance is a useless expression. The key is how we know if the repentant truly repented or just uses repentance as a deception. I figure God is the only one who knows that, other than the repentant.

After mass, I went to brunch at my usual diner with my usual grumpy waitress. I feel this is a good sign of forgiveness, as most would not be so faithful to the diner. I felt relaxed when I got home. The answering machine blinked with a message. I hit the Play button; it was Mom.

"John, your dad had a heart attack this morning. They took him to the emergency room. I'm with him. Call me…"

She gave me the number of the emergency room. I called immediately.

"Emergency, can I help you?" the feminine voice answered.

"Yes, this is John Castano. I am calling about my father, Paul Castano, who was taken there this morning."

"He is no longer here. He's been taken to CICU. Can I transfer you there?"

"Please. Thank you."

The phone rang several times before a second feminine voice answered, "Cardiac Intensive Care, can I help you?"

"Yes, John Castano. My father, Paul, was transferred there from emergency. I would like to speak with my mother, Isabel."

"One moment."

It may have been only a couple of minutes, but it seemed like it was hours.

"John, your dad is being worked on right now. All I know is he's still with us."

"I'll leave now and should be there in a couple hours."

"Thanks, John. Beth and Terry are here."

I grabbed a few essentials and tossed them into an old suitcase, my briefcase and my personal phonebook, and piled into the Beamer. The drive would take all of two long, long hours. My memories of Dad rolled through my thoughts. I most enjoyed the days when Dad and I went hunting, just he and I. He would wake me well before dawn, and we would pile into the Chevy and head to a favorite rabbit plot.

Dad loved rabbit, as he grew up with it as a staple during hunting season. We didn't hunt as often as he and Grandpa, but we made an every-Saturday trip into the wild during hunting season. I can remember the smell of dry leaves as we marched through the local wood lot and the crunch of those leaves under our boots. The small shrubs made a scraping sound on my trousers as I brushed through the shrubs, and the golden rays of fall sunshine filtered through the trees, forming hazy beams that softly touched the ground.

When least expecting it, a rabbit would dart from a small pile of dead branches, its white tail popping up and down as it ran from shade though a beam of sunlight and back into shade. Then the pop of my twenty-gauge shotgun. Dad would have rabbit to eat this week. I can remember the pride as I walked from the woodlot, holding the rabbit and seeing the look of approval in Dad's face.

My thoughts drifted to the warm, sunny summer days when Dad and I took the boat to the river to fish walleye.

We baited a minnow on a three-way swivel rig in the slues and backwaters of the Mississippi. Dad found one of his favorite spots, and we anchored the boat. He fished one side, and I the other. I remembered the tap, tap of a bite, and Dad said, "Wait until he takes it." The key to walleye fishing was knowing just when to set the hook. Try too soon, and the fish was gone with the minnow; wait too long, and the fish would feel the hook in the minnow and spit it out.I remember the warm sunshine and soft breezes of a clear summer morning. A bald eagle circled overhead, looking for an unaware fish swimming near the surface. Spotting one, the eagle plunged downward, pulling upward to slow its plunge and extending its talons as it neared the surface. With a precision one could only marvel at, the eagle penetrated the surface, plucked a fish from the water, and soared off with its meal.

My reminiscing led me to recognition—death is an inseparable part of life. All living things strive to extend life as long as possible, but life will inevitably surrender to death. So how do we deal with that inevitability? Am I going to be dealing with another death, my father's? How am I going to handle that? Can I manage that under the situations that have intruded into my life the past couple months? Suddenly I realized I was very warm and rolled down the driver-side window, the cold air splashing against my face.

Because of its inevitability, why not surrender to death at the earliest opportunity? All living things are born for a purpose and they strive to achieve as much of that purpose as possible before death overtakes them. That is the meaning of life. In the rabbit or the fish, the purpose was simple: the continuation of the species. With people, God endowed us with compassion, understanding, and the ability to achieve wisdom so that our purpose is not only preservation of the race, but improvement of humankind.

Suddenly I felt the Beamer slide on a patch of ice. I tried everything I was taught to bring the car under control, but nothing worked. The car spun several rotations, and time seemed to slow to a crawl before the car came to a crunching halt in the snowbank alongside the road. I sighed in relief that today was not my time to meet God.

I was stuck. The front wheels were on the shoulder of the road, but the ice did not give me enough traction to pull the rear wheels free. I did not have a shovel, sand, and salt, which could have gotten me out. I'm a city boy. I was sitting there for about twenty minutes when a compassionate trucker pulled over.

"Got yourself stuck?"

This could have been a great opening for a smart-ass comment, but under the circumstances, I felt it would be to my advantage to play this one humbly.

"I sure did."

"City boy, right? No shovel, no sand, no salt, right?"

"You got it."

"Okay, I'll get you out."

The driver went back to his truck and set out several flares in the right traffic lane. He then drove the truck into the traffic lane up to the front of the car. He climbed out of the cab, got a chain out of the utility box, and attached it to the frame under the front of my car then to the frame of his truck.

"Get in your car and start it. Put it in neutral. When I pull you out, give me a chance to unhook the chain, then pull the car onto the shoulder."

"Okay, thank you."

The chain tightened, the front of the car jerked, and the truck slowly pulled the Beamer free. After pulling me out, I pulled over behind the truck. The driver went back and kicked the flares off the road into the snowbank. I walked over to the truck as the driver came up.

"Thank you so very much. What do I owe you?"

"Nothing, just a promise that you'll get some winter survival gear in that car before you hit the open road again in winter."

"Well, thank you. Those flares cost you some money. I don't know how much they cost to replace, but here is thirty dollars."

I didn't want to lessen his good will gesture, but I did know he used four of his flares.

"Hey, ten bucks will cover it."

I gave him ten and thanked him several times before getting back on my way. It was still forty-five minutes to the hospital. I realized I needed to keep my attention on the road and not on thoughts of the past.

When I got to the CICU, Mom, Betty, Terry, and Nancy were in the waiting room. Mom jumped up and gave me a long, sorrowful hug. I kissed her on the neck. She began crying.

"How's Dad?" were my first words.

"Still hanging in there," Terry injected.

"Hi, Terry, that's good. Hi, Betty. Hi, Nancy."

"They only let one of us in there every half an hour. Next time, you go in," Mom suggested.

We are occasionally confronted with a situation that requires us to react in a manner not consistent with our true nature. Forced to react, we must always do so with a strong sense of rationality. To act irrationally in such a situation is asking for disaster.

Gilson was on the leading edge of medical care, so I knew Dad was in the best of hands. Was that going to be enough? I sure hoped so. I wanted to go fishing with Dad again. The nurse came out.

"One of you can go in now."

Dad was lying flat in his bed. There were tubes and wires everywhere. I looked at the nurse who came in with me. "Can I talk with him?"

"Sure, he's sedated, but if you talk loud enough, he'll hear you."

What do you say at a time like this? The usual "How are you?" or "You're looking good" doesn't work well, nor does, "You look like hell."

"Hi, Dad."

His eyes opened, and he looked at me for a long time. "John, you're here. Why did you come all that way?"

"Dad, that was nothing. I came to see you. How are you feeling?"

"I had the big one, John. I'm not coming home."

"Dad, you don't know that."

"John, you take care of your mother. She is going to need you."

"Dad, stop talking that way. You don't know what's going to happen."

"Just do as I ask, John."

"I love you, Dad."

"I know, John."

Many people know when they are at the gates. I didn't want to believe Dad was one of them.

When I returned to the waiting room, Dad's doctor was there, and Mom introduced us.

"Dr. Chandy, what are Dad's prospects?" I asked.

"We are doing all we can for him. He had a massive heart attack. This is his second one. The first did some damage to the heart muscle, and this one did a great deal of damage. We need to stabilize him right now. It's going to be touch-and-go for the next couple of days. After that, we'll have to evaluate the true extent of heart damage and determine a long-term course of therapy."

"Thank you, Doctor," I commented.

"Why don't all of you go home and rest. You cannot see him, and he is under sedation. If there is any change in his condition, we'll immediately call."

We looked at each other, and all seemed in agreement.

"Okay," I said.

Mom put up some resistance, but we finally got her agreement. We headed to Mom and Dad's.

We all gathered in the kitchen. Nancy ordered Chinese carryout from Fong's for dinner.

I picked up the order. We sat most of the night in the kitchen, talking about the past, the present, and the future with Dad in it all the way. About ten, Betty and Terry left for home. Nancy was staying at Mom's; Josh and their two sons returned to Madison. Nancy took her old bedroom, and I went to mine. Mom wanted to stay up for a while.

I was asleep in a flash. It was about 3:00 a.m. when I was wakened by someone shaking me. It was Mom.

"John, the hospital called and wants me to go there as soon as possible."

"Sure, Mom, I'll get dressed. Wake Nancy and call Betty."

We got to the hospital at three forty-five and went to CICU. The nurse indicated that Dr. Chandy would be out in a bit. Betty arrived a few minutes after us. I knew in my heart what Dr. Chandy was going to say, but my mind kept saying Dad was still going to be okay. Dr. Chandy walked into the waiting room, and I knew.

"I'm sorry to get all of you down here so early, but Paul had a cardiac arrest about an hour ago. We tried several times to restart his heart. He did not respond. I'm sorry, but Paul expired at 2:46. Would you like to see him?"

We went into his room. Dad lay on his bed; all the tubes and wires were gone. A sheet covered him to just below his shoulders. Except for the ashen, gray color, Dad looked as if he was just taking a nap. Mom walked to his side and looked at him for a few seconds. She then bent over and kissed him on his lips then collapsed over him, both arms grasping his lifeless body; she let out a loud cry then began to sob. Nancy and I went to her side and rubbed her back and shoulders. Finally, after several minutes, we gently lifted her from Dad. Betty was curled into the corner of the room, crying uncontrollably. I went to Betty and lifted her to a standing position and wrapped her up in my arms.

It was several minutes before she stopped sobbing.

Monday morning I first called the office to inform them that my father died, and it would be a few days before I got back. Celia offered her sincere condolences and asked that I relay the funeral arrangements as soon as they were set, and I said I would. Next, I called Liz at her office.

"Good morning. Elizabeth Danfurth."

"Hi, Liz, it's John. Have some bad news. I'm in La Crosse. Dad died this morning."

"Oh, no! John. I'm so sorry. How are you doing?"

"I'm okay, Liz, but I don't know if the reality of it all has sunk in yet."

"I'll come down. What happened?"

"Dad had a massive heart attack. He was still alive when I got here. All of us were able to talk with him. He died at three o'clock this morning."

"I'll be there tonight. Do you have room for me?"

"Sure do. Thanks, Liz. See you tonight."

I called Gilson's Mortuary—I thought a health organization owning a mortuary was a conflict of interest—and made an appointment for eleven o'clock. They said they would pick up Dad's body at the hospital. Next, I contacted Father Petrosi at St. Mary's Church and informed him of Dad's passing. He seemed truly sorry, as Mom and Dad were pillars of that church for years. Mom wanted a mass for Paul probably on Wednesday, with internment in the Church cemetery. I indicated that Gilson's was going to be handling the arrangements and would be contacting him.

Monday evening Mom made her special lasagna dinner. Josh came over with the boys, and Betty and Terry came over. Mom's lasagna consisted of one layer of Italian sausage and cheese, a second layer of ricotta with spinach, and a third layer of meatballs and cheese. Each layer was ladled with her rich hamburger red sauce and topped by a generous layer of shredded mozzarella, and don't forget the sliced hard-boiled eggs mixed in each layer. She made several loaves of her special Italian bread. Served with the lasagna was her hearts-of-romaine salad, with her special Caesar dressing. Desert was Mom's own tiramisu.

It was obvious what such a production accomplished, other than feeding nine hungry souls; it kept Mom's mind from dwelling on the loss of her lifelong companion and best friend. This was a feast to soften the sorrow, which lingered just under the surface in each of us, a winning hand that helped us forget, if just temporarily, the bad hand we were just dealt.

Liz arrived at five thirty in the afternoon. She looked gorgeous in her black, full-length alpaca coat with lightgray fur cuffs and lapel. Her pink cheeks and nose glowed against the darkness of the late afternoon framed by the opened front door. She stepped in and smothered me with her hug, which lasted for a minute, yet seemed only seconds.

"John, I so sorry. How's the family handling it?"

"As well as possible with something as sudden as this."

"I certainly understand, John. It hurts a lot now, but the memories of all the good times will eventually let us ignore the hurt."

"I hope so. Let me take your coat. The family is in the kitchen. Mom made us a feast."

Dinner was spectacular. Mom could have been the head chef at the swankiest New York restaurant. All of us ate until we were stuffed then had a big slice of Mom's tiramisu. Dinner conversation focused on the earlier years and the fun we all had when we did family things. I recalled the trip to Madison one holiday season to attend *The Nutcracker*, and Betty snored through the entire second half. Betty became playfully defensive in response to our teasing. Liz seemed to fit well into our family, as she participated well to the single-sided reminiscing.

Visitation was from 10:00 a.m. to 12:00 p.m. on Wednesday at the mortuary, with a funeral mass at St. Mary's at one o'clock. Internment was to follow mass in the church cemetery just behind the church. A reception was to follow in the church hall, which we were having catered by Ruffalo's, Dad's favorite restaurant.

Celia and all three partners in the firm, plus several others, arrived at eleven o'clock. Celia said they closed the office for the day. They stayed for the mass, internment, and reception. At noon, the mortuary closed visitation except for the immediate family. We looked upon Dad's cold, stiff face for the last time. Mom broke down for the first time since the hospital, and Liz and I had to support her. She didn't kiss Dad, but kissed her fingers and placed them on Dad's lips.

"Goodbye, darling. I'm missing you so much," were her final words. She stared at him, as if expecting a reply, then she smiled, turned, and we left the room.

The mass was a eulogy on Dad's life and the need to remember him even though he was no longer among us. Father Petrosi knew Dad for many, many years and delivered his sermon in superlative fashion that put most of those who knew Dad into tears.

"God considers only one thing in judging us all, and it is not how many times we missed church, or how much we gave to the church and charities, but did that come from the heart? Paul had the biggest heart I have ever known."

"We must never forget Paul as his life was a lesson on humanity. He was not a man of pride, but one of humility. He never turned away from the needy, always extending a helping hand. Paul Castano was an example we should all remember," was the essence of Father's eulogy.

The reception was mostly a social gathering, where old friends caught up on each other's current news. Liz and I spent much of the time with Celia, the partners, and the office staff. Greg told me to take as much time as I needed to take care of family business. I thanked them, but felt a bit uneasy with the offer.

Liz was leaving for her home shortly after the reception ended.

"John, anything I can help you with, don't hesitate to ask."

"I will, Liz, thank you. You're such a good friend."

"When will you head back?' she asked.

"I'm not sure. I want to be sure Mom is okay before I leave. It might be a day or two."

"Call me," Liz demanded.

"I will."

The next two days, Betty and I helped Mom get her affairs together. Nancy, Josh, and the kids returned to Madison. Mom wanted to leave Dad's clothes and personal items where they are for now due to some deeply hidden hope that somehow, he would come walking through the door, and everything would be back to normal, the denial of the finality of Dad's death. Sunday, Mom and I attended church together, the eight-o'-clock mass, which was their usually attended service. Father announced Dad's passing to the shock of many. Dozens offered Mom their sympathy and support after mass.

Is it not a comfort looking out there as the real world goes about its business with all its uncertainty then pulling down the shades and retiring into you own secure cocoon?

Monday morning began as a normal day. When I arrived at the office, Celia said that Greg wanted to talk with me, and I was to go to his office. I dropped my coat in my office and went to Greg's office. Greg was on the phone, so I knocked on the doorframe of the open door. He signaled that I come in, and I sat in one of the chairs in front of his desk. It wasn't more than a minute before he finished with his call.

"Good morning, John. How are you and the family doing?"

"It's been hard, but things are getting easier. Mom seems to be okay."

"That's good, John. Jim, Mat, and I had a meeting on Friday, and we decided to place you on a leave of absence for a couple of months. We agreed with all that's happened the past couple months, you could use a little time to get your affairs in order. Take the rest of today to wrap things up here. We'll continue your salary during the leave of absence."

"Boy, that's a shocker, Greg. I really didn't expect it."

"We thought this would be best for you and for the firm. I hope you understand."

"Oh, I understand, Greg. I'll wrap things up today."

Back in my office, I realized what just happened; I just got fired. The whole leave-of-absence thing was just a legal way of easing me out. The salary continuation was my severance. At the end of the two months, I would not be asked back, and my salary would cease. I understood that the firm needed to protect its reputation; and while my involvement in the murders has not gone public, just the fact that police are coming to the office to speak with me is a bit of a fright to them. Some people do not value loyalty!

So that's the way it's going to be. There are several events in one's life which can be classified as traumatic, and being fired is definitely one. It's not the potential for economic loss, but the rejection that produces the trauma. You realize that your superiors feel you are no longer worthy of being part of the family. It is much the same as if your mother and father came to you and said, "Get out. You're not our son." Rejection is a major negative-emotion builder, and that's where I'm at right now.

I thought, *Is there something I could do to make them change their mind?* Then I answered the question, *No! It's done. It's over and accept it.*

I asked Celia if she could find a cardboard box for me.

"Sure, John, how big?"

"Ah, one of those the reams of paper come in."

She brought the box into my office and noticed that my personal items were piled on the desk.

"Are you going somewhere?"

"Sit down, Celia. I am being given a two-month leave of absence. The partners feel I needed the time, and the firm didn't need to be associated with the mess I'm currently buried in."

"You'll be back in two months?"

"No, Celia, I won't be back. This is the way I'm being told the firm doesn't want me."

"I'm so sad for you. What will you do?"

"Just fade away, I guess."

I packed my personals in the box. Then I used some time to contact my very best clients and informed them of my leave of absence. I indicated that the other lawyers here would handle them until I returned. All asked why I was taking a leave of absence. My reply was that my father died, and other family problems necessitated my leave. After completing that, I visited with each of the others in the office to inform them of the situation.

On my way out, I stopped at Celia's desk. She stood up, and I gave her a big hug and all my best for her in the future. I could see a tear well up in each eye. I told her I would keep in touch. She was happy to hear that and wished me good luck. I ended with, "I'll need some good luck soon, as all I've had for the past couple months was very poor luck."

It was about ten o'clock in the morning on Saturday when the doorbell rang. At first, I didn't get up from bed, but it kept ringing, so I struggled from my sanctuary, put on my robe, and opened the front door. It was Liz.

"God, John, I've been so worried. I called your office on Thursday, and Celia told me about your leave of absence. I have called here and left messages since."

"I really didn't want to talk to anyone the past few days."

"Not even me? I'm very hurt!"

"I'm really sorry. Please forgive me."

"Come on, John. Get out of this stupid-ass mood. So you lost your job and been having some tough breaks, but life goes on."

Liz came in and closed the door. We went to the kitchen, which was a total mess.

"Jesus, John. this place is a pigsty. Where's the coffee?"

I pointed to the refrigerator. Liz started a pot of coffee.

The lecture continued, "I thought you were a bigger man than this. Self-pity won't get you anywhere."

"I know, Liz, I just couldn't help myself. Something just snapped when I got home Monday."

"Snap my ass!" Liz shot back.

"You do have a nice ass, Liz," I quipped.

"Damn you, John, I'm serious. You need to get your shit together now."

"Okay, okay, Ms. Landers. Is the coffee ready?"

Liz removed the old dishes from the table and wiped it off with plenty of soap and hot water. She poured two cups of coffee, slapping one down in front of me. She sat opposite me with the other. The coffee was just as I liked it, strong and hot.

"You plan to spend the rest of your life locked up here?"

"Don't know. Probably have to go out to get some supplies?"

"You're still not being serious. Why don't you go and take a nice, hot shower. You look like hell and smell a little too."

The shower was soothing, and I had a chance to think about my situation. I thought how stupid I was being for sulking all this time. Liz was right. I'm a better man than that. I don't know why I behaved the way I did, as I can't stand stupid behavior. Stupidity is when someone does something dumb even though they should know better. It seems to be rooted in emotion, not logic. In fact, it is the absence of logic. Einstein said insanity is when a person keeps repeating a particular action expecting a different outcome. I disagree; I think they're just stupid. Maybe insanity and stupidity are synonymous.

Suddenly my thoughts were interrupted when the shower turned cold. It was Liz starting the dishwasher. Just as well, I needed to get out anyway. I finished, dressed, and walked to the kitchen. Liz had it in perfect condition.

"You look much better. You need to get out of this house. Let's go out and get a bite to eat."

"Sure. Sounds good." My appetite was returning.

"When we're done, we'll do some grocery shopping, okay?"

"Sure, whatever you say."

We had lunch at a small family restaurant in a strip mall a short way from my duplex. I had a Ruben basket, and Liz ordered a burger and fries and a strawberry shake. It felt good to get something solid in my stomach. Our conversation revolved around our families. All the mayhem of the past few weeks seemed so distant.

"Have you talked with your mother this past week?"

"Yes, I called her every day. She seems to be getting along well. Betty and Terry have been keeping her busy."

"Good, she's such a nice lady."

"Liz, I'm so lucky to have you as my friend. I don't know what I would have done had you not come over."

"I was so concerned that something bad happened to you. I thought maybe those bad guys came over, and I would find you—god, I was shaking when I reached your duplex. When you opened that door, well, you looked like shit. But to me, you really looked good. I thought it was going to have to take a lawn mower to get your beard off, but I really wanted to just grab you and squeeze, then I got so pissed. You were overwhelmed with your own selfpity."

"You're right, Liz, but I'm thinking clearer now, thanks to you."

"I hope so, John, but if the depressed feelings begin taking over again, call me."

We went to the grocery and picked up most of the essentials I used up during the past few days. We returned with Liz's trunk full of paper bags. After putting the stuff away, Liz and I used the rest of the afternoon to clean the duplex. Liz called her mother and said she would be having dinner at my place and would ring her in the evening when she was on her way home.

Liz pulled two porterhouse steaks, both about an inch and a half thick, from the fridge. She also started baking two large baking potatoes. She swished me from the kitchen.

"If I can't find something or need your help, I'll call you. Just go and watch some basketball or something."

"Yes, ma'am."

She broiled the steaks just as I liked them. The potatoes were double-baked, and green beans and a salad completed dinner. She snuck two éclairs into the groceries, and we consumed them for desert. After dinner, Liz washed the dishes, and I dried and put them away. I thought back to Christmas when Mom and Dad did the dishes my first night there. It was a good feeling, one of great security and serenity. *Only if this could last,* I thought.

It was Tuesday, and I was working with some of my files when a thought popped into my mind. Officer Kapinsky mentioned that the crude hammer that Wertz used to kill Brett had hair and blood from both Brett and someone else. Could it be? For some wild reason, I thought of the possibility that Wertz also killed Dan. I decided to talk with Kapinsky about that possibility.

I drove to the precinct police station. Kapinsky was there, and I asked to talk with him. The desk sergeant took me to an interrogation room. After a few minutes, Kapinsky walked in.

"Good afternoon. John Castano, right?"

"Yes."

"So what did you want to talk about? Is it the Malone murder?"

"Sort of. You said that there was hair and blood from a second person on the weapon he used, right?"

"Yes, why do you ask?"

I explained my suspicions that Dan Danfurth, a friend of mine and client, was murdered in September. It was ruled an accidental death, but things didn't add up, so I hired Willie Durante to check into it."

"Wasn't this Willie Durante murdered just a few days ago?" quizzed Kapinsky.

"Yes."

"Interesting. It seems associates of yours are turning up murdered all over the place."

"No shit. I don't know if they have something in common."

"Durante had his throat cut and stabbed multiple times. That doesn't fit Wertz's MO."

"I don't know if there is any relationship there, but my friend Dan was killed by a blow very similar in size and placement to Brett's, a round blunt instrument to the back of the head. The coroner attributed it to the blow from the limb of the tree as it fell on Dan. I don't think that a tree limb did that."

"So why come to me?"

"You told me that the rock hammer that Wertz used had hair and blood from both Brett and someone else. Is it possible to check the other sample against my friend's hair and blood?"

"Sure, if you can get his full blood type and a sample of his hair. We had the blood of both samples typed, and the hair of one of the samples matched Mr. Malone."

"I'll do that. Just give me a day or so."

"Fine, call me when you have the blood type and a hair sample."

I left and went immediately to Liz's.

Mom answered the door, "Hello, John. Liz is not here. She's still at work."

"I know. Do you mind if I wait for her? It's very important."

"No. Come in. You can wait in the office."

Carolyn came into the office. "Hi, John, are you here to see Mommy?"

"Yes, but I came to see all of you."

Liz arrived home about five thirty.

"John, I saw your car parked out front. How are you?"

"Okay, Liz. I need you to get some information for me as soon as possible."

"Oh, what?"

"I think that the stone ax that Albert Wertz used to kill Brett may have been used to kill Dan."

"How? Why? What reason would he have? I don't think Dan even knew him."

"I know it sounds crazy, but I have this feeling, and I can't let it go."

"Okay, what do you need?"

"Call Dan's doctor's office and see if you can get his full blood type. Do you have something that might have Dan's hair on it, like a comb?"

The combs were cleaned probably by Mom. All of Dan's clothes were donated to the St. Vincent DePaul Society.

We searched the entire house for any remnants of Dan's hair. We sat in the office trying to think of any place we could find hair.

"Dan's hunting clothes at the cabin," Liz suggested.

"Hey, that's a thought. I'll go up there tomorrow."

Liz gave me the key.

"All his hunting clothes are in the closet near the back door."

I was on the road by 8:00 a.m. and arrived at the cabin at ten thirty, parking in the same spot as I did in December when I came up to settle Dan's estate. The snow in the drive was cleared several days ago, and a light dusting covered the tire tracks of the plow vehicle. Liz told me that the neighbor, George Hansen, plowed the drive when it was needed. I thought so much has happened since then. I opened the front door and stepped in. My mind drifted back to that weekend and how simple things were. It was cold as the heat was reduced to fifty degrees.

I went to the back door and opened the closet. There were all of Dan's hunting clothes. On the top shelf were two hats, one a pullover sheepskin with ear flaps, the typical Norske hat. I took it from the shelf and went over to the light from the kitchen window. Sure enough, a tuft of hair was stuck to the fur in the inside back of the hat. I got a plastic food bag and carefully removed all the hair I could find, placing it in the bag.

After returning the hat to the shelf, I wandered into the great room, where I sunk into the overstuffed chair near the now cold, dark fireplace. Again my thoughts drifted back to that December weekend and how striking Liz looked when she walked through the door after her morning walk. It was then that the realization struck me; I was in love with Liz. I probably loved her since the first night we met in the Big Ten, but I never realized it until just now. How could such a profound feeling go unnoticed until this moment?

What was I going to do? I didn't expect Liz to feel the same, as the husband she so dearly loved was not yet completely cold in his grave. I couldn't let her know. But what if she already knew? My thoughts raced. How was I going to face her now that I realized my love for her? I began to think maybe I was just making Dan's murder into something just to be near Liz. My life just became far more complicated.

On the drive back to the Cities, my only thoughts were of Liz. Up until now, things were pretty much black and white, but now I have shades of all kinds creeping into my life. When I got to the duplex, my answering machine blinked a message. It was from Liz, and I should call her as soon as possible. I knew she was probably on her way home from work, as it was 5:15 p.m., so I waited a bit to call.

"Liz, it's John, what's up?"

"I got Dan's blood type. His doctor didn't have it, but they suggested that I contact the U hospital blood bank, as Dan regularly gave blood. They had his whole profile. He was AB positive."

"Good, I was able to get some hair from one of his hats, the Norske one."

"Oh, that thing. I hated that hat. It made Dan look like a frump."

"Well, it had plenty of hair. I'll get the hair and blood type to Kapinsky tomorrow."

Thursday morning I called the precinct and talked with Kapinsky. He took down the blood type and asked me to drop the hair off as soon as I could. I had it to him by late morning. After leaving the precinct, I spotted a dark-blue Chevy with one person in it half a block down. I knew I saw that car before.

I got into my Beamer and drove past the now-empty blue Chevy. Something didn't seem just right, but I couldn't quite put my finger on it.

I talked with Paul last evening, and we made plans to meet for a late lunch. I drove to Harries BBQ on the west side, getting there about one o'clock. Paul had something important to tell me. He was seated near the side window.

"Hey, Paul, how are things going today?"

"Very well. Made a big sale this morning. That's really going to help my bottom line. I have to really start saving."

"Oh, what's up? A new car?"

"No, this's my big news. Susan and I are getting married, and I would like you to be my best man."

"Hey, congratulations! I'll be honored to be your best man. When and where's the wedding going to be?"

"June 16 in Des Moines. Gloria is going to be the maid of honor. You two will have a chance to catch up with each other."

"That reminds me. You saw Liz a bit ago and mentioned Gloria. She really seemed—I don't know—sort of upset about our relationship and really pissed that I didn't tell her about my little swim."

"Yeah, I remember. So what's with you and Liz?"

"I'm in love with her. I think I have always loved her but would never let myself admit it. I just realized that this week. I'm just not sure how she feels about me. We're friends, very good friends, but I don't know if her feelings are any deeper than that. Plus, she is just coming off the death of her husband."

"Seems to me her reaction to Gloria may be a very good clue," Paul intimated.

"Well, we'll see."

Friday I was at home, watching TV, when Kapinsky called.

"John here."

"This is Officer Kapinsky. We got the results back from our crime lab. There is a 95 percent chance that the other blood and hair came from Mr. Danfurth."

"So I was right."

"Looks that way."

"So what happens now?" I asked.

"We'll confront Wertz and his accomplice. We may be able to pry the motive for Danfurth's murder from one of them. We'll keep you posted."

"Okay."

"We would like you and Mrs. Danfurth to come to the precinct station and make a formal statement as soon as possible. Bring whatever evidence you have with you. Did this private eye, Durante, was it, give you anything?"

"Not much. He ruled out a few people as suspects and did say he was getting close to something big but was murdered before he let me know what it was."

"I'll contact Liz and see when we can get down there."

I called Liz and filled her in. She said she could get free this afternoon. I picked Liz up at work. We arrived at the station and were escorted into the large interrogation room. Kapinsky and Jacobsen were waiting for us. Liz gave them background on Dan and his activities at the university.

"I don't have the notes and copies of the death certificate and police reports, as I gave them to Willie Durante, who was looking into the murder for me. I was not able to find those items since his murder."

"Is it possible that his murder is related to Mr. Danfurth's, and they took the notes?"

"I don't know. Possibly."

"We'll contact the officers investigating Mr. Durante's murder and see if they have come up with anything. We'll also check with the police and coroner upstate and get the reports directly from them."

We left and decided to end the week at Murray's. It was crowded as usual. We had a drink and some appetizers.

We agreed to do something this weekend. I was feeling apprehensive because of my feelings for Liz. We left in good spirits.

It was about nine o'clock Saturday morning. I finished up the morning newspaper and my last cup of coffee, which long cooled from hot to room temperature, when the phone rang.

"Hello."

"John, James here. Officer Kapinsky called me this morning with a complicated development. Hillary Holden is pregnant, and she claims Brett's the father. She wants an abortion, but since she is a ward of the county, they won't pay for it. She asked the officers to contact us as next of kin and see if we would ante up the money."

"Great. What can I do?"

"We don't believe in abortion. Plus, it's Brett's child. Could you talk to her and see if you can talk her out of it. We would take the child."

"Sure, I'll be happy to try. No guarantee."

"I understand, but give it your best."

I previously informed James of the murder of Dan, and that it was Wertz who killed him. We chatted a few minutes, catching up-to-date, except I didn't mention my dismissal from the firm. I had not yet come to complete grips with reality. I wasn't going to be able to do anything about Hillary until Monday.

I no more than hung up when Liz called.

"Good morning, John. Let's do something tomorrow."

"Yes, I am the lector at church at the ten-o'-clock mass. Would you come to church with me?"

Liz was not Catholic. I guess she really didn't belong to any organized religious belief, so I felt I would not be imposing by asking her to attend with me.

"Sure, that would be great. Can I bring Carolyn?"

"Definitely. After mass I know of a nice place we can go for brunch."

"Sounds great, John. Where and when should we meet?"

"Be at my duplex at nine o'clock. We'll drive together."

It only takes ten minutes to get from the duplex to church, but my experience tells me that when you're dealing with concrete times, you build in a buffer.

At nine ten Sunday morning, the doorbell rang. I opened the door, and Liz and Carolyn stood before me. Carolyn was in a red coat and black patent-leather shoes, and Liz was cloaked in her black coat with the fur trim.

"Sorry I'm late."

"Hi, John," Carolyn greeted.

"We have plenty of time."

At church, Liz and Carolyn sat with me in the special section for lectors and Eucharistic ministers and their families. We sat in the front row. I felt that the entire parish was looking at me, wondering if this was a family member or significant other. I avoided that thought as much as possible. The mass centered on the need to love others as you love yourself.

Carolyn said, "John, I love you."

I smiled at her then looked into Liz's eyes. She was smiling.

We went to brunch at Alice's. After brunch, we went to the mall and did a little window-shopping. Shopping is a means to an end. If you want to listen to music on a radio but don't have one, you go shopping for one. This is not true for a segment of our population. Shopping is an end in itself. A shopper has no specific need they are attempting to fill; they just like shopping. It's a form of entertainment. I am not a shopper. In fact, I hate shopping unless I have a specific need for something. Liz is a shopper, and I put up with shopping in order to be with her. Liz saw a sweater and thought it was me, so she purchased it on my behalf. We had a great family time.

Monday morning, I called the precinct station and asked for Kapinsky.

"Yes. Kapinsky."

"Harold. Castano. I got a call from my friend James Boilen, and he said that Hillary Holden was pregnant with Brett Malone's baby and wanted an abortion."

"You got it right. What can I do for you?"

"James asked me to talk with her. They want the baby."

"Well, I can get you in there, but she is a very hard nut."

"When and where?"

"I'll get back to ya."

Monday evening Kapinsky called, "I got you in to see Ms. Holden. Go to the county jail at 10:00 a.m. tomorrow and ask for Officer Bronson. It's not visiting hours, but he'll be letting you talk with her without any distraction."

"Thanks, Harold."

Tuesday morning I left my place at nine o'clock and arrived at the county jail at nine thirty-five. I told the receptionist I would like to speak with Officer Bronson. She made a call, and I was asked to be seated. About ten minutes passed, and a big, dark, brute of a man opened the door.

"John Castano?"

"Yes."

"Follow me."

I was taken to the empty visiting room and sat on one side of the table. After a few minutes alone, Hillary was escorted in by a uniformed female officer and was told to seat across me.

"So what do you want?"

"James Boilen called me and asked if I would talk with you."

"Yeah, about what?"

"About your pregnancy and wanting an abortion."

"So what business is it of yours?"

"The Boilens asked me to talk with you."

"So what do you want to talk about?"

"The county and state will not pay for an abortion. The Boilens are not either. If you don't want the baby, and that seems obvious, they would like to take the baby as they are relatives of Brett."

"Tough shit!"

"Well, the state will take it when you give birth. The Boilens will probably be chosen to adopt it, as they are relatives."

"I'll do the abortion myself."

"That's very dangerous."

"I don't care. I'm going to be in jail most of my life anyway."

"I don't understand. You protest against people who you feel harm animals. Yet you're willing to kill your unborn child? That doesn't make any sense."

"Fuck you! Fuck the Boilens! Brett fucked me and got me pregnant, then he got fucked himself."

Hillary motioned to the officer to take her back.

"Call me if you have a change of heart," I challenged her.

Wednesday afternoon I just walked into the duplex after shoveling about four inches of fluffy snow from our drive and walks. My landlord usually does it, but I had little to do during the day except read and watch TV. The phone rang; it was Hillary.

"Mr. Castano, I've reflected much on what you said on Monday, and you're right. I can't abort my baby and would be willing to let the Boilens take him. Do you think I might be able to see him occasionally?"

"That's a very sensible thing to do, Hillary, and I think the Boilens would be happy to let you visit him."

"I didn't want Brett killed. Al came over late, and Brett let him in. I didn't know Al was going to do that. Brett and I were standing in his living room talking when Al walked up behind him and hit him with his club. I screamed when Brett fell to the floor facedown. Then I saw the blood running from his head, and I started crying. I asked Al why he did that, and he said the organization couldn't tolerate any traitors.

"After sitting there for a long time, Al said we needed to clean up the blood. So we pulled Brett's body over to the window. We then cleaned up the blood on the floor. It wasn't hard because it was wood. Then Al said we needed to push Brett out the window to make it look like a suicide, so we turned off the lights, opened the window—it didn't have a screen—and we lifted him into it and Al flipped Brett's head and shoulders over and pushed him out. I heard the thud and began crying again. Al pulled me from the apartment after making sure the door would lock."

"It's sad you got tangled in all this, but it shows how easy it can happen if you pick the wrong friends," I sympathized.

"So how do we handle this?" Hillary quizzed.

"I will have the appropriate papers drawn up. You will have to go over them with your lawyer. If anything needs to be clarified or changed, we will do that. Then we'll have a meeting with you, your lawyer, the Boilens, me, two witnesses, and a notary. Once the papers are signed, witnessed, and notarized, you will get a copy, the Boilens a copy, and a copy will be filed with the court. When you have the baby, the court will execute the agreement, and the Boilens will be awarded custody. It will be up to them to apply for adoption. Are you sure that's what you want?"

"Yes, yes. Please do that."

"It will take me a couple days to get the paperwork drawn up. I will then get a copy to your lawyer, and he can go over it with you. Once it is finalized, we'll arrange the meeting."

I called Celia after hanging up with Hillary and asked her if she would do me a favor and prepare the necessary documents. She agreed, and we planned to meet tomorrow after work at Murray's. I then called James. I had not called him after my first meeting with Hillary, as I thought there was still some opportunity. The receptionist put me through to James.

"James Boilen."

"James, John here. I got some good news. Hillary Holden agreed to give up the child."

"Oh, that's great! Deatra will be so happy."

"You think you two will be able to handle two newborns in a couple months, as Hillary is due to deliver in June?"

"U-bet-cha."

"I'll have the documents to Hillary's lawyer on Friday morning. Provided there are not a lot of changes, we should be able to finalize this sometime next week. You and Deatra will have to meet with Hillary up here."

"That'll be hard, meeting with Brett's killer."

"Well, John, she really was just a bystander. She and Brett were in the apartment when Wertz came over. While Brett and she were talking, Wertz came up behind Brett and hit and killed him. She didn't suspect anything, but she did help Wertz clean up the blood and helped push his body out the window to make it look like suicide."

"I didn't know that," James clarified.

"Wertz has been tied to Dan's death also. Dan's blood and hair were found on the same club Wertz used to kill Brett."

"What reason did he have to kill Dan?"

"We don't know, but the police are working on a motive."

"Boy, this whole thing is really getting complicated."

"Yes, James." I always wanted to say that.

Thursday at four thirty, I met Celia at Murray's. She gave me the documents in an unmarked ten-by-fourteen white envelope.

"There are six sets, John. Is that enough?"

"Plenty. Thank you so much."

"We all miss you at the office, John."

"Well, that's so nice of you to say that."

"But it's true."

"Well, I don't think the partners miss me."

"What can I say, John?"

I talked Celia into having dinner with me. We shared memories of the good times. She offered to help me if she could. I really appreciated that and told her that she and the others were like family.

That evening at home, I reviewed the documents. They provided an avenue so that the Boilens could pursue adoption of the yet unnamed baby. Naming rights would be by agreement between the Boilens and Hillary. Hillary would have visitation rights, as determined by the court after the baby was born. I felt that this would be acceptable to both the Boilens and Hillary.

Friday morning I went to the public defender's office. They directed me to a Mr. Ronald Ziegler's office. He was handling Hillary's case.

"Hello, I'm John Castano. I am representing James and Deatra Boilen in a custody proceeding for Hillary Holden's unborn child."

"Oh, this is the first I've heard of a custody proceeding."

"Hillary's pregnant with Brett Malone's baby, who was the brother of Deatra Boilen. The Boilens have indicated they would like to gain custody of the child when it's born. Hillary has agreed. I have the necessary documents and told Hillary you would go over them with her. If she has no problem, we'll need to set a legal signing."

"Okay, I'll get back to you after I talk with Ms. Holden."

I got a call on Monday morning from Ziegler.

"Ms. Holden has no objection to the agreement. When would you like to have the signing?"

"Let me call the Boilens and see when they can be here. I'll get back to you in a few minutes. What's your number?"

I called James, and they said that Wednesday afternoon would be fine. I called Ziegler, and he agreed to Wednesday at two o'clock. I indicated I would get the notary if he could round up two witnesses. Ziegler was agreeable.

I met the Boilens for lunch at Dave's Diner at eleven thirty on Wednesday. We discussed just how the signing should proceed. They seemed very excited about the prospect of having Brett's child as their own. I told them that until the birth and official court transfer of custody, Hillary could change her mind. While we could challenge that in court, the county would take custody until the matter was resolved by the courts. I impressed on them the need to be sympathetic and cordial to Hillary. They should be supportive to her plight.

The signing went without a hitch. The Boilens seemed to really connect with Hillary and were as pleasant as anyone could expect. I got the real feeling that they liked her. They offered to help her in any way they could. Ziegler asked if they would be willing to testify as a character witness if needed, and the Boilens said they would.

I left the Boilens with Hillary and headed down. On the way out of the jail, I felt a hand grasp my shoulder. I turned, and it was Kapinsky.

"Mr. Castano, just the fellow I wanted to talk to."

"Hey, Harold, what do you need?"

"We cracked Wertz. It took a lot of prodding, but he finally fessed up."

"Oh, so what did he have to say?"

"You remember this guy, Garson Petroff? You knew him as Phil Roland, who turned up partially barbecued about a month ago, right?"

"Yes," I said with anticipation. Did they connect Liz, Willie, or me to that incident?

"Well, it seems Wertz was employed by this creep to spy on Mr. Danfurth."

"What was he looking for?"

"Scraps of paper, notes, anything Danfurth had written down."

"It was back in September that Petroff asked Wertz to kill Danfurth. Wertz found out that Danfurth was going to his cabin on Friday morning for the weekend, so he followed him there. After parking his van in a neighbor's drive, he took his club and went to the Danfurth cabin. He saw Mr. Danfurth with his chainsaw heading out behind the cabin, so he circled around through the edge of the woods.

"By the time he reached Danfurth, he was making his final cut on this dead tree. Danfurth couldn't hear Wertz, so he walked up behind him while he was bent over cutting the tree and slammed the club into his skull. After a few minutes, he dragged Danfurth to a spot where he figured the tree would fall on him. He wanted to make it look as if it was an accident.

He then went back to the tree, where the chainsaw was still running and sitting in the alreadymade cut. He continued the cut and the tree fell on Danfurth."

"But why did Petroff want Dan killed?"

"Wertz has no idea, just that he got paid five hundred for the job, so he didn't care."

"Since Petroff is dead, we may never know the reason. Thanks, Harold. I hope you'll keep me posted if anything else turns up?"

"Sure will, John."

I felt Liz needed to know this development right away. I waited for her outside her office. About 5:15 p.m. she came out with several colleagues.

"Liz."

"John, what are you doing here?"

"I just came from the county jail and have some news. I saw Harold Kapinsky when I was leaving. Albert Wertz confessed to killing Dan. The hair and blood on his ax was Dan's. They pressed him until he confessed."

We walked together to her car.

"Why, what reason did he have to kill Dan?"

"Well, this is where it gets twisted. Phil Roland paid Wertz to kill Dan. Do you have any idea just why Phil wanted Dan dead? You know his real name was Garson Petroff?"

"No! Why was he using an alias?"

"They have no idea. The police said that Petroff paid Wertz to spy on Dan."

"Spy. What was he looking for?"

"Dan's notes."

"So that's why he wanted Dan's file. But why?"

"It must have something to do with the missile defense work he was doing for the government."

"A spy?"

"Most likely."

We reached Liz's car.

"Can you come over tonight?" Liz asked.

"Sure. As you know, I don't have many commitments these days."

"Great. I'm sure Mom will have something good for dinner."

Mom made roasted chicken with dressing, gravy, and beans. It was great as usual. After dinner, Liz and I continued the conversation in the office.

"Have you found Dan's file?"

"No, Alexi and I have searched everywhere—no file."

"It's lost?"

"I'm still hoping it'll turn up."

"Have you heard anything from Alexi?"

"Not a peep."

Saturday morning I was doing some reading when a call came in.

I answered, and a young male voice asked, "Are you John Castano?"

"Yes, and to whom am I talking?"

"My name is Bill Fabiano. I run a small used car lot in Bloomington. A couple weeks ago, I picked up a black Cadillac at an estate sale. The car belonged to a William Durante. Yesterday I began cleaning it up to sell. One of the things I do is remove the bottom cushion of the back seat, as I have found this a repository for all sorts of trash.

Under this seat was a brown file folder. It had lots of notes and other things in it. It also had your name and phone number. It looked important. Would you like it back?"

"Definitely."

"I'll be here until five o'clock. Come down any time and pick it up."

"I'll be there in about an hour."

I got his address. It was just off of I-35W. I was there in forty-five minutes. As Bill said, it was a small lot, only fifteen cars or so. There was a small office at the rear of the lot. A thirtysomething, well-shaven man wearing a bright-yellow coat, gray Norske hat with the ear flaps tied up, and black leather gloves came out as I got out of my car. "Don't see many customers driving BMWs in my lot, so you must be John Castano."

"Yes, and you're Bill Fabiano?"

"In person. Come into my office."

I knew why he was wearing a coat and hat, as the temperature inside was around fifty degrees. It was sparsely furnished with a small desk and desk chair, two simple cushioned chairs in front of the desk, a file cabinet in the corner, and a small electric heater behind the desk. On the desk was a phone, a few scattered papers, a half-eaten what looked like a ham and cheese sandwich, an opened thermos with steam rising from the mouth, and a half-full thermos cup with what looked like cold coffee.

"Caught you at lunch?" I speculated.

"Yeah, but that's fine. I like a little company. Business is really slow this time of year. Things will pick up when people start getting their tax refunds."

"That's understandable."

He reached down and opened a desk drawer, pulling out the brown file folder.

Holding it in front of me, he asked, "Is this it?"

"It sure looks like it."

"Are you some sort of a scientist? The stuff in here is really high-tech."

"No, I'm a lawyer. This belongs to a client of mine. He's the scientist."

"Well, here it is," he said as he handed it to me.

"Thank you so much." I reached into my pocket with my other hand and offered him a twenty. "For going through the trouble of calling me."

"Hey, man, that's not necessary," he said as he made no effort to take the money.

"Please, it'll make me feel better." I placed the twenty on the desk.

"Thanks, man. By the way, Durante's car is on the side of the office. It's just about ready for sale. You interested?"

"No, one car is enough for me."

"I didn't think so. BMW guys don't usually dig Cadillacs. Well, that one will sell fast around here."

I thanked Bill again, got into my Beamer, and headed for home. As I left, I circled past Willie's car. He really liked that boat. I hope the next owner would take care of it as well as Willie.

On the way back home, I began to think about the whole situation revolving around this file. Dan was dead, two thugs were dead, and Phil and Willie were dead, all centering on this file. Why was Alexi so interested in retrieving it? He was not involved in the research. His job was to provide Dan with security—something he failed to do adequately. The people who should want the file are SIAIBM and Longhouse. They should have most of Dan's research except for the latest entries.

What was I going to do with the file now? Because of some lingering doubts and some kind of gut feeling, I didn't think I should just turn it over to Alexi just yet. At home, I parked my car in the garage. I took the files into the den and opened the folder. The research notes were clipped together and looked intact. Willie made a second copy of the research notes, and they had handwritten notes in the margin at various points. The letters from Longhouse were in the folder. Also, there were all the copies and notes I gave to Willie. There was a three-by-five spiral notebook in the folder, which was not there before.

I opened the notebook; it was Willie's handwriting. The first page had my name and phone number. The following twelve pages were notes detailing his investigation. First were the notes of his interview with Liz. The following several pages detailed his work up until the junkyard incident. The remaining entries exposed a suspected connection between Phil and a one Albert Wertz. It didn't say much except that Phil used Wertz to spy on Dan. The final entry made a single comment, "It appears Phil Roland is reporting to someone unknown to me at this time, but I have a good idea who it might be and will follow up on the suspicion in the next couple of days."

Where to put the file where it would be safe was my next concern. I took out the original notes and Willie's notebook. Then it dawned on me. Willie had the greatest place—under the back seat of his car. Whoever looks under there except someone cleaning a car for resale? I went to the garage and opened the back door. How do I get the back seat cushion up? I couldn't find anything in the owner's manual. It was early, so I thought of calling my BMW dealer.

It was Saturday afternoon, and service was closed. I told the receptionist that my wallet slipped under the back seat of my car, and I needed to know how to dislodge the seat so I could get it. I was on hold for several minutes when a male voice picked up.

"Mr. Castano, I understand you lost your wallet under the back seat of your BMW Coupe and need to get it out?"

"That's right."

"Okay, here's how you do it," and he proceeded to give me detailed instructions on how to remove the back seat cushion.

I went to the garage, and it worked—the seat popped out. I took the file and laid it on the floor under the seat and reinstalled it. I checked it several times to be sure it was secure and wouldn't pop loose while I was driving. I placed the second set of notes and Willie's notebook in a large plastic bag, popped the top of my Shop-Vac, dropped the notes in the bin, and replaced the top.

I decided not to say anything to Liz about finding the file; not that I suspected her intentions, but I thought she would be safer not knowing. I didn't want a repeat of that horrible night at her house.

It now came to the critical question, What should I do now? I knew there were others who wanted the file. Who were they? How do I expose them? Do I go to the police? Will they even believe me? Kapinsky. I could tell Kapinsky.

I called the precinct, but Kapinsky was not in. I indicated to the desk sergeant that it was urgent police business, and I needed to talk with him. The sergeant said he would try to get in touch with him. He took my name and phone number. It wasn't ten minutes, and Kapinsky called.

"John, I got a call you needed to talk to me."

"Yes, Harold,"—we were now on a first name basis—"I have some new information regarding Dan's murder."

"Okay, let's have it."

"I found Willie Durante's notes on his investigation into Dan's murder. He tied Petroff to Wertz long before you got Wertz to confess. Willie was on to something. He indicated that Petroff was reporting to someone else, whom he did not identify. This all revolves around the research Dan was doing for the government. Apparently, he was working on some top-secret stuff, and Petroff was after it."

"This is sounding very interesting. Do you have any idea who this other guy is?"

"No."

"Well, I'll check out Petroff in more depth. Maybe I can come up with someone."

"That's just what I was hoping you would say. How can I help?"

"Just let me know if you find out anything else."

"I have his notebook if you would be interested?"

"Do you have some time now? I would like to see the stuff you have."

Kapinsky and Jacobsen came to my place, where I gave them Willie's notebook and the letters and charge cards that were with the file. They asked to see the file, but I refused, as it belonged to a client of mine, and I could get into some legal tangle if I did so without permission.

They did not persist but indicated, "If the sheriff in the county where Dan was murdered wants to continue a further investigation, he may get a court order forcing you to turn them over."

"Keep them in a safe place and do not tell anyone that you have them until we have time to check into this whole matter more deeply," he warned.

Sunday was quiet. I didn't go to church. I felt I needed the time just to hibernate for a few hours. I didn't even shower and shave. I was not going to answer the phone. If someone came over and pounded on the door, I might answer. The phone didn't ring, and no one pounded on the door. I enjoyed just vegging out and doing nothing to tax my brain. I retired early.

It was dark and late when I suddenly woke to the sound of a door latch snapping closed. My awareness went from a sleepy stupor to full adrenalin rush in a second. Someone was in my house, in the den. I had no weapon handy; I didn't own a hand gun. My shotgun was in the storage cage in the basement. I would have to get to the kitchen in order to arm myself with a knife, but I would have to walk past the den.

The loudest noise in the room was my heart pushing blood through my carotid arteries. I slowly slipped out of bed as silently as possible and slowly shuffled to the open bedroom door. I looked to my left down the hall, past the now shut den door to the living room. The light from the streetlight dimly illuminated the front room. I decided my best tactic would be to work my way in the opposite direction down the hall to the garage. I had all sorts of tools there which I could use to defend myself.

I exited the bedroom and slowly shuffled, barefoot, into the darkness, where I knew I would reach the door to the garage. About halfway down, my uninvited guest knocked something over, and it made a slap; it sounded like the picture of Mom and Dad, which sits on the back of the end table next to my La-Z-Boy, then silence. I continued to move in almost total darkness toward the garage door, my arm extended toward it. Suddenly there it was, my fingertips firmly against the door. I positioned myself against the knob side of the door and slowly turned the knob.

The door gave way, and a thought went through my head. Did I WD-40 the hinges, or were they going to squeak? Oh god, here goes. It opened, and I slid through the door, taking a step down into the shadowy garage. Streetlight seeped into the garage through the small overhead door windows. I partially closed the door and walked to the workbench in the back of the garage. I reached the bench, and the light from a flashlight swished past me. I picked the hammer, whirled and with all my might, and flung the hammer at the light.

I heard a thud, and the light was gone. I picked up the hatchet, which was next to the hammer, and slowly but deliberately walked toward the open door. I was almost there, my heart pounding so hard it seemed as if it could burst from my chest, and I heard the front door slam. I turned on the garage lights and hit the door-open button. The garage door slowly opened, and I caught a glimpse of a dark sedan turning the corner.

I turned to the open garage door, where the flashlight lay just inches from the hammer. There was a smear of blood in the wall where whomever I hit must have rubbed his hand. I walked down the hall to the kitchen and called MPD.

"Someone just broke into my home. I hit him with a hammer, and he left bleeding."

The dispatcher responded, "I'll have a unit there in five minutes."

I walked back to the den and noticed the third drawer of my file cabinet was open, and Mom and Dad's picture lay facedown, partially over the *US News & World Report* magazine I read earlier. I saw a squad, no siren, but redlight flashing pulled into my drive. I opened the front door and noticed what looked like drops of blood down the walk.

"That looks like his blood," I pointed to the officers as they came up the walk.

"Did you shoot him?"

"No, hit him with a hammer."

I explained to the two officers—the oldest looked like he was in his early twenties—the sequence of events. I showed them the hammer and flashlight. Their questioning took on a tack of my being suspected of doing something to a friend or visitor.

"Officers, it seems like you don't believe the story and think I knew this person, beat the hell out of them, and they ran off in self-defense."

"Well, we have to cover all the bases, and that's certainly one," the youngest piped.

These were rookies, new officers; they usually get the graveyard shifts. But they need to learn a few things, one of which is you don't give the victim the thought you don't believe them.

"You must think I'm stupid. If I beat the crap out of someone whom I invited into my house, why would I call the police?"

"That isn't as strange as you think," the older officer offered.

"Well, that may be true, but I live alone, and there was no one in this house at my invitation."

"Okay, we'll need to call in the detectives on this," the older officer informed. He asked his partner to go to the squad and call in the "Dicks."

The officers finished and waited in the squad until the detectives arrived. The detectives took several minutes to get briefed by the uniformed officers. They left after the briefing, and the detectives came in.

"So this guy woke you up after he busted into your house?"

"Correct."

"Do you have any idea what he was after?"

"Not a clue. He was in my file cabinet. I'm a lawyer and have information relating to my clients in there. Maybe he was after that?"

"Was any information missing?"

"I don't think so. I think he heard me before he found what he came for."

The detectives had a lab guy gather some evidence, and they all left. It was getting light. It was 6:46 a.m.

I made some coffee and went to the den with my cup. Sitting in my La-Z-Boy, I didn't tell the officers the whole truth. I think whoever it was, he was after Dan's file. But how did he know I had the file? I told no one. The only three people who knew I had it were Bill, the used car dealer, Kapinsky, and me. That was it. Bill must have told someone after he gave it to me. I needed to go to his business first thing.

It was Monday morning. I hadn't had a full night's sleep. At 9:30 a.m., I left for Fabiano's. When I got there, he had not yet arrived, so I parked in front of the office to wait. Willie's car still sat at the side of the office, not yet for sale. Fabiano got to the lot at ten fifteen.

"Mr. Castano, right?"

"Yes, could I talk with you?"

"Sure." He pulled a lunch bag and thermos from the car. "Come into the office."

I sat in the same chair as Saturday. Bill dumped his thermos and lunch in a drawer of the file cabinet and turned on the space heater. He sat at his desk.

"Did you tell anyone else about the file?" I queried.

"Yes, some guy came in here about an hour after you left. He said he was a friend of Willie and that Willie had some papers of his. He asked if I found anything in his car. I said, yes, a brown file folder. I thought he was your client, so I told him I found your name, called you, and you came and got it. You gave me twenty bucks for just calling him. He didn't leave me even a dime."

"What did this guy look like?"

"This dude wasn't your client."

"No, my client is dead."

"So why did you want his files?"

"Dead or alive, he's still my client." I asked again, "What did this guy look like?"

"He was your height, average build, clean shaven, and almost bald on top. What hair he had left was light brown.

That's all I remember."

No one came to mind. I decided to bounce this off Kapinsky and let him know what happened. While he knew nothing about Dan's research, he was looking into both Willie's and Dan's murder.

I went directly to Kapinsky's precinct. He was in, and by now, the desk sergeant knew me and just let me go back to his desk. He saw me coming and waved me on. Kapinsky and Jacobsen were seated at the desk, sipping coffee and munching sweet rolls, a half-empty box sat on the desk.

"John, how can I help you?"

"Hey, Harold. Morning, Ron. Someone broke into my home last night, say about 3:00 a.m. I was wakened by his rustling in the den. I snuck into the garage, but he must have heard and followed me. He shined his flashlight at me, and I grabbed a hammer and flung it at the light. It must have hit him in the hand, as he dropped the light and ran down the hall and out the front door, leaving a blood trail."

"So let me guess, the guy was after the file? I told you to keep your head down and not tell anyone about the file," Kapinsky fired back.

"I didn't tell anyone, but as you know on Saturday, that used car salesman called me. He had Willie's car he was cleaning up for resale. He found Willie's notebook. That's how I got it. Someone talked to him after I left, and he gave him my name. I think that's related to the break-in—that's what he was looking for."

"Interesting, John. Did you call the department?"

"Yes, the officers were from the third precinct. They investigated, took evidence, and left."

"Did you get a description of the guy?" Jacobsen queried.

"Yes, just an average type, not enough for me to know who it might be."

"Give me the name of the salesman. We'll check into this. Oh, by the way, I'd like to see the notes."

"Sure. It's at home. If you can stop by this afternoon, I'll show it to you."

"We'll try, John," Kapinsky responded.

I left the station and returned home, entering cautiously in the event the intruder returned to try to complete his search. No one was there. Should I stay here tonight? Yes, I decided, but I'll put noise producers on the doors to the outside should anyone try to open one. I went to the storage closet and located my trusty double-barrel, twentygauge shotgun. As I held it, the thoughts of rabbit hunts with Dad flashed in my memory. If I had to use this tonight, it would be a far larger animal.

It took me fifteen or twenty minutes to locate my shells. I had a partial box, left over since the last hunt; they were three-inch shells with number six shot. I went upstairs with the gun and shells, sat in the La-Z-Boy, and loaded the gun. I checked the safety—it was on. I leaned the gun against the arm of the couch. That's where I planned to sleep tonight.

I returned to the basement and found my stash of Christmas decorations. I knew I had three red Santa socks, you know, the kind you put candy in for St. Nick's Day with bells on the toes. I would use them on the front, garage and kitchen doors, pinching them in the door to hold them in place near the top. If the door were opened, the sock would fall, and the bells jingle.

I checked all the windows, making sure they were locked. Everything was ready should the mystery person return. I relaxed in the La-Z-Boy, feeling a sense of security. I'm ready. The phone rang.

"Hello."

"Hi, John, it's Liz. How are you doing?" Liz questioned.

"Okay, I guess." Should I tell her about the break-in? No, she would worry. Plus I would then have to get into the details of the file, something Liz best not know just yet.

"What have you been doing?" she asked.

"Not much, catching up on a lot of reading I've been accumulating. How are things going there?"

"Carolyn has the flu and has been really sick. I'm afraid Mom might get it."

"Didn't you and Mom get the flu vaccine?"

"Yes, but I'm not convinced that they work."

We talked for fifteen minutes or so. I went back to my *US News*. The phone rang again.

"Hello. John here."

"John, this is Frank." He was my landlord and lived in the other side of the duplex.

"Millie noticed there were police over last night. Was there some kind of problem?"

"Well, yes, I was awakened by someone who had broken in. I was able to chase him off, but felt it was best to call the cops."

"Was it robbery?"

"Probably, but he was scared off before getting anything."

"This is really going to make Millie afraid."

"Tell her the cops doubted he would be back. If caught in the act, burglars usually steer clear of the place, as they know the cops will be looking for suspicious people in the area."

Harold and Ron arrived at the duplex about four o'clock in the afternoon. I produced the copy of Dan's notes. Harold took a few minutes to browse the dozen-or-so pages and handed it to Jacobsen who did the same.

"This is very high-tech stuff, John. We would like to take this with us."

"I would prefer you not, Harold. As I said, without permission, it could cause some real legal problems for me."

"Okay, but we need to check a few things out."

"Fine."

They left about 4:30 p.m., and I put my sock back up.

I reflected on how violated I felt that some uninvited individual entered my home. These are personal hallows, and to have someone violate the sacred space is intensely emotional. I retired about ten o'clock, sleeping on the couch in the den. I slipped the shotgun, loaded and ready for any potential invader under the couch. I slept very badly, waking frequently with every crack or squeak houses made in winter as they shrank and expanded. Morning arrived without incident.

I had plans that evening with Paul to go to the T-Wolves game. I considered canceling, but on second consideration, I realized I needed some relaxation time. I met Paul at six o'clock at Lewis's, a small downtown restaurant for dinner. We both ordered steak and reminisced over our Mexican vacation.

The conversation quickly turned to Paul and Susan's plans for a summer wedding.

After a few minutes, Paul remarked, "I'm sure this marriage will last."

"Paul," I responded, "half of all divorces result because people enter marriage as a test, not being really sure this is the person they want to live the rest of their lives with. I don't think this is how you feel."

"I know so," Paul responded.

"That brings to mind an incident that happened last fall when this fellow came into the office to consult me on a divorce. I asked him why he wanted to divorce his wife of sixteen years. He told me that she liked to 'do it with a mechanical device.'

"I asked him if she was refusing to have sex with him. He told me that she never refused him. So I asked just why he was so intent on getting a divorce. His answer was, 'How would you feel to wake up and hear this groaning and moaning coming from the bathroom? I thought my wife was sick, and I went to the door, asking if she was okay.

She said sure. So later that day when she was shopping, I went to the bathroom to snoop around. I found this mechanical device. Since then I have heard her frequently.'

"I asked him again just why he wanted a divorce. His answer was that he felt inferior and that he obviously couldn't satisfy his wife. I quizzed, 'Why do you feel inferior?' I remember his answer to this day, 'Obviously, Mr. Winky was no match for this device.'

"I told him that I was not a marriage counselor but thought that would be the route to go rather than a divorce.

'Sure, your wife needed something you were not providing, but that's not grounds for divorce. Work it out.'"

"So how did it work out?" Paul inquired.

"They got divorced."

We finished dinner and went to the game. The T-wolves lost, but we had a great time.

The next two days were uneventful. I hadn't heard anything from Kapinsky. I continued to sleep in the den next to my shotgun, but all was quiet. Thursday night I got a call about seven thirty.

"John." I recognized the voice. It was Alexi. "You have something I want."

"Yes, and what might that be?"

"Dan's research notes. I know you have them."

"And just how did you find that out?"

I suddenly realized that it was probably Alexi who talked to Fabiano. It was probably him or someone working for him who broke into my home.

"It's no concern of yours. I just want that file."

"And why? You are not involved with the research. You were only to provide protection. So why do you want the research?"

"That, John, is none of your business. I didn't want it to come to this. I wanted to spare you, but I was unable to get the file through clandestine means. You made that impossible. So now we have to do this the hard way. I have something of yours, which I will trade for that file."

"And what might that be?"

"Your friend, Elizabeth Danfurth. You give me that file, and I'll let her go. If you don't, the next time you see her, she will be in a coffin."

The thought sent a chill through me. Would he really do it? I cannot take the chance. I realized that instant that Alexi was the one in charge of the quest for Dan's research. Wertz and Petroff were just the grunts, and my suspicions were correct.

"So how do we play this?"

"Do you remember where the junkyard is that Phil took you to?"

"How could I forget!"

"Bring the file and meet us there in one hour."

"Then what?"

"We take the file and let Liz go, as she doesn't know what's happening."

"Somehow I don't believe you, and what's going to happen to me?"

"Well, that's how it is going to shake out. We'll discuss just what's going to happen to you, and don't call the cops, or Liz is history."

On the way to the junkyard, I thought of Liz lying in a pool of blood, motionless. I couldn't stand the thought.

This is going to be a chess match, and Alexi will have to work for a checkmate. I'll try the bluff first and see if I can lead them out of the junkyard—that would improve our chances. If that didn't work, I would insist on the release of Liz before turning the file over. The plan was to say I didn't have it with me but would give up its location if the proper conditions were met. If Alexi thought I would just drive in there with file in hand, he was more stupid than I thought.

I got to the entrance of the junkyard and hesitated. Am I ready to pull this off? Hell, go for it. I drove in and just past the office building I saw Alex's and Liz's cars. They were parked near where Phil's car was. I pulled alongside, and the driver-side door of Alexi's car opened. Officer Foley got out, his right hand fully bandaged. It was then I realized it was Foley who broke into my home!

"John, do you have the file?"

"Yes."

"Bring it and follow me."

"No, I'll follow you, but not with the file."

"Alexi won't be happy."

"So you think I should give a fuck."

"I guess if I were in your pickle, I would be as big a prick as I could too."

We walked about fifty yards, weaving around stacks of crushed cars. There was a thin layer of crusty snow covering the ground. It was as if we were walking in a forest of dark, huge stacks of cars.

For an instant I thought of all the stories behind each of these derelicts, each unique. Finally, we rounded a stack, and ahead I saw, standing in a junkyard clearing, three shadowy figures, illuminated by the blue-gray light of an almost full moon. We approached, and I recognized Liz, Alexi, and Jerome.

"John, oh John!" Liz shouted and started toward me. Alexi grabbed her arm and pulled her back to his side.

"John, what's happening?"

"I'm not sure, Liz. Just do what Alexi tells you. You'll be all right."

"I don't see a file folder." Alexi broke the silence.

"You insult me. Do you think I'm just going to walk in here, folder in hand, and then get on my knees so you can shoot me in the back of the head? If that's the case, you're more stupid than I thought."

"Okay, John, so how do we play this?"

"Well, the file is somewhere, but before you get it, you need to let Liz go. Then I'll tell you where it is."

"If we let Liz go, she'll tell the cops."

"Well, that's your problem. You'll have to figure out how to deal with it. But if Liz isn't out of here, you'll never get the file. By the way, I left a message for Officer Kapinsky and filled him in on this whole thing. You kill us, he'll be looking for you, asshole."

"You're a piece of shit, John."

"No Alexi. The bad smell is coming from your direction."

"Call it, John!"

"Let Liz go to her car by herself and drive out. When she's out of here, she'll blow her horn several times. Foley and Jerome will stay here with us. Then I will take you to the file."

"And I'm supposed to trust you?"

"Shit, Alexi, I don't see any other way. Either you kill us, don't get the file, and get hunted for the whole thing by the Minneapolis police, or you let Liz go, and when I know she is safe, I will get the file, and you take your chances.

So what is it?"

"Well, John, this move is yours. Liz, go and do as John said."

I said, "Liz, don't run, just walk over to your car, get in, and drive out. Blow your horn several times when you are out of the gate."

"I cannot let you do this John. When they get the file, they'll kill you."

"You have to, or they'll kill us both. Maybe I can work something out with them."

Liz shrugged and shook her head no; but I insisted, and she turned, didn't hurry, but walked swiftly into the darkness. We waited about five minutes. It seemed like an eternity, and not hearing Liz's horn, Alexi dispatched Foley to check out the situation.

"Joe, find out if Liz has left."

We waited an additional five minutes, and Alex dispatched Jerome.

"Bob, find out what's happening and pronto."

I asked Alexi after Jerome left, "What is so important about the file?"

"I have some clients who will pay handsomely for that information."

"So it's all about money?"

"Come on, John, everything in this world is all about the money."

"No, Alexi, you're wrong. There's much more in life than just the money."

"Okay, John, have it your way."

Alexi turned in the direction of where the cars were parked and peered into the darkness, trying to focus on something in the darkness. It was my chance. I spun and started running like hell toward the back of the yard. I heard two pops. Alexi shot at me. I didn't feel as if I were hit and kept running.

Suddenly I tripped over something and fell facedown into the snow. I gathered my thoughts, rolled over, and got up.

Alexi's voice pierced the darkness, "Run, John, run. But I'll find you, then I'll kill you."

I zigged and zagged through outcroppings of car piles. I turned around the last pile and found myself in a dead end. I backed against a pile of junked cars and knew Alexi would not be far behind. I felt like a cobra locked into a cage with a mongoose. I looked around for something I could defend myself with, but what could I do against a gun?

Then I spotted it. An old six-foot-long two-by-four, one end sharpened to a point, the other end knurled over, as if it had been pounded by a sledgehammer. It must be a large stake used to keep the piles of junked cars from toppling.

I picked it up and positioned myself just inside the pile of cars. Could I do this? My thoughts went back to the confrontation with Phil. I shot then. I was able to defend myself then, and I must do so now. I wondered why Liz had not sounded the car horn. Was she all right? My heart was pounding so loud I was sure Alexi could hear it.

Then I heard him approaching, his feet breaking through the crusty snow. *Crunch, crunch, crunch, crunch,* then a pause followed by *crunch, crunch,* followed by another pause that seemed to last for an hour, then crunch. Suddenly Alexi's shadowy profile appeared around the end of the pile of cars merely three feet to my side. Grasping the two-by-four like a bat, I swung it with all the force I could muster. The narrow edge struck Alex across the crown of his forehead. There was a loud slap and the crunch of bone.

His arms flew into the air, and the pistol he had in his right hand flipped up and landed at my feet. Alexi plunged backward, as if a falling tree and crashed to the snow. His face peered skyward, his eyes half open. Blood poured from his nose and from a large gash in his forehead, running down both sides of his face, staining the white snow. Oh god, I killed him! How could I do that?

I leaned back against the junked cars, my heart still pounding, mouth dry as a saltine, and my face feeling as it was on fire. About the time I regained some sense of reality, I heard it—footsteps in the snow. They approached faster—*crunch, crunch, crunch.* It was probably Jerome, since Foley's right hand was unable to hold a gun. He came to finish the job.

What was I going to use to defend myself this round? Then my eyes caught the sight of Alexi's gun lying in the snow a few inches from my feet. I bent down and snatched the gun from the snow. I quickly wiped it off and looked for the safety. It was off.

I raised the gun and pointed in the direction of the edge of the pile of junked cars. As soon as Jerome saw Alexi, he would come fast. The footsteps grew louder. Then just as Jerome caught sight of Alexi, they stopped. My hand began to shake.

"John, John Castano?" It was Kapinsky. "Are you all right?"

"Harold, thank God it's you. Yes, I'm okay. A bit shaken. What are you doing here?"

"That's a bit of a story. The question here is, just what's going on?"

"I'll explain everything—that's a bit of a story also."

"Well, you sure put the fix to Alexi. I'll have the locals take care of wrapping this up. Let's walk back to the cars.

Tell me about all this. Give me the gun—is it Alexi's?"

"Yes."

"My friend, Dan, who was a professor of physics, was recruited by the Defense Department to work on a new, highly secret project to develop a missile system, which could be used to intercept and destroy incoming hostile missiles. Alexi was working for someone willing to pay him to obtain the research. Petroff and Wertz were his soldiers."

"So why did Petroff have Wertz kill Dan?"

"Well, we may never know for sure, but I think that he killed Dan because he was getting suspicious of Phil."

"Next question, who killed Petroff?"

"I don't know. So what happened to Foley and Jerome?" I asked.

"Well, when Liz got to her car, we were there and stopped her. She filled us in on what was happening. We took Jerome and Foley into custody when they came back to check on Liz. Then we heard two gunshots, Liz screamed you name, and I took off in that direction."

We reached the cars. There had to be six or seven cops. Liz was standing next to them with several officers.

When she saw me walking up, she ran, grabbed me with such a hug Samson could have given, and began crying, "Oh, John, you're alive. I thought Alexi killed you. I was devastated." Tears poured from her beautiful brown eyes.

After a bit, she said, "John, I love you so. I didn't know what I was going to do if I lost you too. I've loved you from the first time I saw you at the Big Ten."

I whispered in her ear, "And I love you too."

"John, Liz, get into the back seat of my car," Kapinsky ordered.

He and Jacobsen talked with the uniformed officers for several minutes, then he walked to the car and got into the front.

"You'll need to come to the station with us, as we need to get a statement, then you'll be able to go."

"What about our cars?" Liz asked.

"Give me the keys. The uniforms will drive them to the station."

Jacobsen rolled down his window, flagged a uniform over, and told them to drive my car to the station. We departed the yard, turning left.

"Okay, Harold, how did you know we were at the junkyard?"

As we left, the ambulance came in, lights flashing.

"After you left the station on Monday, Ron and I drove down to see Fabiano. You know, those used cars he's selling are just a key turn away from the junkyard themselves."

"True," I agreed. "But he's just trying to eke out a living like the rest of us."

"That's true. Anyway, we got the description you got, but one additional bit of information. He said the guy was driving a dark-blue 1989 Impala, and here's the key to this—he noticed it had a federal government license plate, and he gave me a partial number. So our next stop was the Feds' motor pool office at the federal building. We had the secretary check to see if it was one of their cars. Sure enough, it was assigned to the local GBI office, specifically to a Robert Jerome and Joe Foley.

"Hey, by the way, were you running a bluff with these guys and didn't have the file? We looked through your car and didn't see it."

"I could have produced it, but not while they were still holding Liz."

"Where is it? It is going to have to be material evidence in their prosecution."

"I'll give it to the you if the Defense Department gives me the okay, as it is classified government property."

"Okay, John, I'll contact the GBI and let them know. They will undoubtedly want to talk with their agents we now have in custody.

"Well, anyway, we decided to tail the two and see if we could determine if they were involved with your breakin.

I noticed Foley's right hand was wrapped in a bandage, which would be consistent with being hit by a hammer.

Tonight we followed them to the garage where Ms. Danfurth parks. They waited until she approached her car, then Foley got out and talked with her, both got in and drove out. We decided to follow Ms. Danfurth, Jerome, and Foley; and they came right to the junkyard. A few minutes later, Alexi drove in. We didn't like the smell of this, so we put in a call for a silent backup. Then you drove in, and we knew something was going down. That's the whole story."

At the station, we were asked to give our statements. Kapinsky indicated that Jerome and Foley were going to be turned over to the feds, and they will want our statements. After giving our statements, he gave us the keys to our cars, and we were free to go. Two agents from the GBI arrived as we were leaving, and they were being directed to an interrogation room. My guess, they were here for Jerome and Foley. I followed Liz home.

She invited me in, and the first thing she said was, "Exactly how did you find Dan's file? Who is this Fabiano?"

"He has a small used-car lot in Bloomington. He purchased Willie's car at his estate sale, and while cleaning it up, he found the file under the back seat. Willie had notes in the file and my name and number. He called and asked if I wanted it, and that's how it came back into my possession."

"And what was all this about the hammer?"

"I didn't tell you about the file as I thought it would protect you. I didn't want to worry you, so I said nothing about the break-in."

"Break-in, what break-in?"

"Monday morning about three o'clock, I was wakened by someone in my duplex. He was in the den, looking for the file. I snuck into the garage, but he heard me and followed. When he opened the door, I picked up a hammer and threw it at him. It hit him in the hand, and he ran out the front door. It was Foley. That's why he had his hand bandaged. Foley followed me to the used car lot and found out I had the file."

"Damn you, John! You could have been killed."

"I had no idea, Liz. I did call the police. Later I talked with Harold about the break-in, and that's when he and Jacobsen got involved."

"And you stayed home the entire time? Weren't you worried he would come back?"

"Yes, so I slept with my loaded shotgun. He never did. Any other questions?"

"I really meant what I said at the junkyard. I never planned on saying anything, but I was so emotional it just slipped out. I love Dan. Also, he was a great husband and father, and this is not rebound from his death. I loved you both so much."

I felt she was testing the waters, and they were flowing in her direction.

"And I meant what I said. I never admitted it, not even to myself, but I've always been in love with you. I realized just how much as I was driving to the junkyard. I couldn't stand the thought of you being hurt."

"So what do we do now?" Liz questioned, hoping for some kind for answer from me.

"Let's keep it between us now. We need to let things level out. We've been through a lot the past couple of months."

"That's good thinking, John."

At home I had some time to reflect on what just happened between Liz and me. I thought, *Is it possible for a person to love two others in exactly the same way?* I wasn't thinking the love we have for family and friends, but the love a man and woman share. Men of the Mormon faith have taken multiple wives. Polygamy has been written of since man could put his actions and feelings to paper and probably before. Did these men have the same feeling for each of their wives and the wives for them? I thought, Most certainly. Our capacity to love is far greater than we can even imagine.

We live in a monogamous society since the purposes of marriage are first, the raising of a family, and secondly, the fulfillment of our sexual and companionship needs. Raising a family necessitates the singularity of the relationship between a man and women. Polygamous relationships have rarely succeeded when family outcome was the determining criteria.

I probably never fought to try to salvage my relationship with Lynn because my subconscious feeling for Liz inhibited it. Liz, being more pragmatic than me, realized any relationship closer than good friends was not going to happen. She met Dan, allowed herself to fall in love, and married him. It was a good marriage, which ended far too soon through no fault of theirs. Had Dan not met an early demise, they would probably have been happily married until natural causes separated them.

All this was far too taxing on my brain after having being almost killed, almost killing another man, and discovering that Liz and I shared the same feeling for each other all in a single day. That was more than most people experience is an entire lifetime. One might think that after all that, that I would be seated in the receiving room of a psychiatric hospital babbling to myself. The human brain has far more capacity to deal with stress, provided we allow it, than most everyone gives it credit for.

I remembered the book, *Clear and Present Danger* by Tom Clancy, which I purchased the other day and stuck into my coat pocket. I went to the coat closet and found the pocket, pulled out my gloves, then removed the book. It looked different, but I thought nothing until I opened it. In the center of the book was a lead bullet, mushroomed over and tangled among shards of paper.

It was one of the bullets Alex fired at me. It passed through my coat, both gloves and three quarters the way through *Clear and Present Danger.* How ironic! Had that bullet traveled just three inches to the right, it would have struck me in the hip. I would have fallen, and my end would have come by way of another bullet into my head. I realized we travel through life only mere inches from death, and the slightest wrong move at the wrong time could be the end of our mortal life. The book was unreadable. I closed it, bullet intact, placed it in a plastic bag, and put it into the memorabilia drawer of my file cabinet.

Sleep overtook me while I sat in the La-Z-Boy. It was three fifteen in the morning when I woke after a dream. I was looking for Liz but had a very difficult time finding her. The girl, cured of CP by an act of God, appeared and, without saying a word, extended her hand. I took it then realized Liz was holding the other. We smiled, and the girl was gone.

At eight o'clock in the morning, the phone rang. It was the GBI and Special Agent Henry Gomez.

"Mr. Castano?"

"Yes."

"This is Special Agent Gomez from the GBI. We have been working with Harold Kapinsky and Ron Johnson on the incident last night involving Antonoff, Jerome, and Foley."

"Okay, and what can I help you with?"

"It seems all this involves one research file of Dan Danfurth's, and you have the file. Could you provide us with the file?"

"Sure, but how do I know you're not involved with Antonoff and the others? They were GBI."

"I understand your concern. How would it be if I bring Harold Kapinsky and Ron Jacobsen along?"

"I think that would be fine. When?"

"In an hour if that's okay?"

"Sure, one hour."

At nine o'clock, a black Suburban pulled in front, and four men got out. Two were Kapinsky and Jacobsen. The other two I figured were Gomez and another agent. I let them in. Harold introduced me to Gomez and Agent Winston.

"I have the file in the garage, in my car."

All of us went to the garage. I opened the back door of the Beamer and popped up the back seat cushion.

"Here, this is the file." I handed the brown folder to Gomez. "It's just as I got it from Mrs. Danfurth."

"Thank you so much. Harold has provided me with Willie Durante's notebook also. Was there other related material?"

"Yes, Willie made a copy of the research and used it to have some expert review the material as part of his investigation. I have that copy also."

"May we have it?"

"Sure."

I went to the Shop-Vac and popped the top. I pulled the copy, wrapped in plastic from the bin, and dusted it off.

"Here. That's all of it."

"There is one additional matter. We are expecting a phone call from Washington at nine thirty. It'll be for you."

"Okay, let's go to the den."

I couldn't imagine who from Washington would want to speak with me.

At exactly nine thirty, the phone rang.

"May I answer it?" Gomez requested.

"Sure."

He talked with someone for a few minutes then asked me if I would take the phone. I answered, and the voice said, "John Castano this is Dick Clancy. The president would like to speak with you."

"Okay?" I forced out over my immense surprise.

"John, this is Bill. I hope you are doing well. I understand you had been through a great deal the past few weeks."

I recognized the voice of President William Ryan.

"Yes, Mr. President, you could say I lived a lifetime and more in the last four months."

"I spoke with an Elizabeth Danfurth, the widow of Dan, who I've been told lost his life while helping to defend our country. I invited her to the White House in a month or so to receive the Presidential Medal of Freedom posthumously for her husband, Dan. I would like you to accompany her to the presentation."

"Of course, Mr. President, I would be extremely honored."

"Congratulations," Kapinsky offered.

"Yes," said Gomez, "when we found out just what went down here, I placed a call to the director. He called the Defense Department, and the whole thing hit the President's desk at two in the morning. First thing this morning the secretary of defense recommended to the President that he issue a Medal of Freedom to Dan, and he agreed. Both felt that would enforce the importance of the project to all the others involved and that their efforts would not go unrecognized."

"I understand."

As soon as they all left, I placed a call to Liz.

She answered, "So, John, did you accept the President's offer?"

"How could anyone refuse the President?"

"Good. I'm looking forward to that day," Liz said with excitement. "Did you think about our conversation last night?"

"Sure did, even dreamt about it. We need to talk again soon."

"What did you have in mind, John?"

"How about dinner tonight at LaBreeze's?" (An upscale continental restaurant in St. Paul.)

"Sounds good. What time?"

"I'll pick you up at six."

I picked up Liz at six o'clock. She wore a long emerald-colored form-fitting dress with white lapels and cuffs.

Her hair was wrapped on the top and back of her head. She wore a simple emerald pendant and earrings. Her face glistened, and her brown eyes sparkled; she was simply stunning, finished by her black leather high-heeled shoes.

Liz ordered one of specials of the night, cioppino, and I had the boneless, sixteen-ounce grilled rib-eye steak with demi-glace sauce and double-baked potato. We each had soup and a salad. For wine, we ordered a French pink Chablis. As usual, dinner was superb.

"How do we deal with our feelings?" Liz sheepishly questioned.

"That's a hard question. First, we must not let our emotions cloud our good judgment."

"This may be overly presumptuous. If so, please excuse me, but do you think we'll ever be more than just good friends?"

"I certainly hope so. But right now, I think we need to take it slow. You're still dealing with Dan's death and probably not over grieving yet. We'll need to work you through that before we can consider the next step," I suggested.

"I understand and agree. I hope you understand that Dan will always be a part of me."

"Yes, I would not expect anything else, and please don't take this wrongly, I hope you don't feel I can be a replacement for Dan?"

"Heavens no, John. Remember, I actually loved you before meeting Dan."

"That's what I thought, but I needed to hear it from you."

For dessert, we ordered cherries jubilee for two. Liz glowed with all her radiance in the light from the flaming cherries. It was the capper to one delightful dinner. After returning to Liz's, I parked in the drive and turned off the engine. We walked to the door and stepped inside. She turned and looked through my eyes, into my very soul. I took her in my arms and brought her face near mine. We looked at each other for a few seconds, then we passionately embraced, then again, and finally a third time. Tears welled in Liz's eyes, and I softly brushed them away.

"Those are because I'm happy," Liz explained.

60

Three weeks later I returned home from a short trip to La Crosse to visit mom. I pushed the garage door opener as I entered the drive and waited as the door slowly rose. I drove the Beamer into the garage and closed the door, exited the car, and opened the door into the duplex. As I stepped into the side hall, something cold and hard slammed into the left side of my face.

The next thing I remember is the sound of pots rattling. The sound didn't hurt half as much as my head—a pounding, stabbing pain that felt as if the side of my head had been ripped off. I opened my eyes and raised my head, and the pain intensified to almost unbearable. As my eyes sort of focused, I realized I was in my den. There were no lights on in the den, but some light streamed through the partially opened door.

I realized my hands were bound behind the chair and secured to the back support of my desk chair. I was seated, but the casters had been removed so I could not move it. My feet were tied together. I realized there was drying, sticky blood that ran down my cheek, onto my neck, and upper arm from a wound to the top left side on my head.

Someone was in my kitchen, cooking what smelled like a steak. The cooking seemed to stop, and there was silence. Whoever it was must be eating. I looked around my den. I was in the center of the room facing the door. My desk was on my right in the corner—triangled—so I was able to see out the window onto the street. To my left in the opposite corner from the desk was my La-Z-Boy, and next to that were an end table and the couch, which I slept on after the break-in.

Then a very disgusting feeling overtook me. Why is all this not ended? What more can happen? Am I going to die? Just then the door swung fully open, and the light from the kitchen blasted into my eyes. It hurt. In the doorway I saw the silhouette of a person.

His deep voice blurted out, “So, finally awake. Good. Now we can begin.”

An average-sized fellow with scruffy black hair and a dirty mustache walked in and stood about three feet in front of me.

“I’m sure you want to know what this is all about, right?”

I nodded yes.

“We know you gave Professor Danfurth’s research folder to the GBI, but we also know a copy was made by Dr. Cumson when he was asked to analyze the research for the PI you hired. We think you have that copy, and we want it.”

“I don’t have a copy,” I mumbled.

“Awe, come on, we know you have it.”

“Who are you and who are we?” I asked in a slow, soft voice.

“I’m Al Reitbrock, and I am the organizer of the United Front against Animal Cruelty.”

“And why does UFAC want Danfurth’s research? You guys are into animal cruelty.”

“UFAC is just our cover. We round up a bunch of stupid students who are all sickened by animal cruelty, and we sell them on our animal cause. They go out and get us money and attention. They are our soldiers. They are everywhere in the university, and that is how we know there was a copy—Cumson had one of his TAs, our soldier, make the copy.”

“But our real intention is to destroy the huge, evil, capitalist pig country called the United States of America!

That is why we joined forces with Alexi Antonoff, but now it’s up to me to finish the project.”

“So why didn’t the TA just make two and take the extra?” I quizzed.

“Because at that time, he didn’t know just what it was, but our soldiers report any curious activity to their cell leader, and that’s when we realized what it was.”

It was then I realized it. He was being so informative only because when he leaves my home, I will not be alive.

A chill came over me, and I began to wonder how I was going to get out of this mess.

I realized blood had run down my left arm and soaked into the rope tying my hands. It was enough to lubricate the rope, and I could probably slip my hand out. I couldn't do it while Reitbrock was in the room. I put the copy in my Shop-Vac in the garage, but after giving it to the police, I moved the Shop-Vac to the basement. My plan was forming up.

"Any other questions?" spit Reitbrock.

"No, but I know you have no plan to leave this house until I'm dead!" I shot back. "So why should I cooperate?"

"True, but I can make your last hour alive very, very, very painful, or dispatch you painlessly. The choice is yours. Tell me where the copy is."

I took some time in apparent deliberation, but my plan was sent, and I needed Reitbrock to believe me—at least temporarily.

After what I thought was a couple of minutes, I responded, "Okay, okay, I'll tell you if you let me live."

"I can't do that!" Reitbrock fired back.

"Then you'll have to try to find it after I'm dead, but you won't find it."

Reitbrock turned and left the room. I could hear him doing something in the kitchen. After several minutes, he walked back into the room carrying a small pot.

"You asked for this!"

He walked over to me and dumped the pot, which contained hot water, onto my legs. I screamed. My head exploded with pain, and I passed out. Then I remember the splash of cold water on my head.

"Let's go, John. Let's wake up."

I rolled my eyes and slowly raised my head. Reitbrock was there in my face.

"Let's go, John. I need to know where that copy is. If you don't tell me, this is just the beginning."

I looked at him, but my eyes didn't focus well.

"Could I have some water?" I said in a barely audible, graveled voice.

"Sure, I'll be right back."

Reitbrock returned with a coffee cup filled with water. He placed it to my mouth, and I drank the entire cup less a few slops, which ended up on my chest. After a few minutes, I regained some sense of reality. My abdomen and legs felt as if they were on fire. I looked at him with defeated eyes.

"Okay, John, will you tell me now?"

"Yes. The copy is in the collection bin of my Shop-Vac."

"And where is your Shop-Vac?"

"I think it is in the garage. I'm not sure."

"Okay, I'll be back." Reitbrock headed to the garage.

I think about ten minutes passed, and Reitbrock returned.

"I didn't find a Shop-Vac. Are you fucking with me?"

"No, I said I wasn't sure. If it is not there, it is in the basement locked in my locker."

"Well, tell me where the key is and how to get to the basement."

"The locker has a combination lock, and I don't exactly know what the combination is at this point. If you let me go down there with you, I may be able to open the lock."

"You're shitting me!"

"You slammed me in the head with something, knocking me out for I have no idea how long, then you burn me with boiling water, and I'm supposed to remember a combination I use only a couple times a year. No, you're fucking with me!"

I guess I was convincing, as Reitbrock left the room for a couple of minutes. He returned with one of my Wüsthof knives. I knew it wasn't to kill me, as he still didn't have the file.

He approached me, bent down, and cut the ropes that bound my feet. He then cut the ropes that bound me to the chair. At that instant, I slipped my hands free of their binding, lurched forward with every bit of strength I could muster, and shoved Reitbrock as hard as I could.

Surprised, he flailed backward, crashing into and flipping over my desk, disappearing over the back. I knew my loaded shotgun was still on the floor under the flap of the couch where I slept those post break-in nights. I lurched onto the floor in front of the couch, pulled out the shotgun, and flipped off the safety.

I knew Reitbrock would be up and at me in seconds. He got up from behind the desk and looked at me lying on the floor. I fired. The blast hit him in the right arm sending a splattering of blood and flesh onto the back wall. He spun around and dropped behind the desk. I got up and waited for what I thought was several minutes, but probably only a several seconds.

Was he dead—from an arm wound? I didn't think so. I slowly approached the desk, gun raised. When I was about four feet from the edge of the desk, Reitbrock lunged up toward me, Wusthof in hand. I fired the second shot, striking him center chest.

Reitbrock collapsed to the floor. He was dead. This time I really killed a person! I dropped the gun and grabbed the edge of the desk. I remembered intense pain in my head.

I felt warm, soft skin next to my face and a perfume smell I recognized. Then I heard the soft, familiar voice say, "John, I love you so much."

My eyes snapped open and began to focus on the most beautiful face I have ever seen. It was Elizabeth. I tried to say, "I love you too," but the words would not come out, so I told her with my eyes. She looked into them and understood. Liz bent over me and grasped my face in her soft, gentle hands and bent down, giving me a kiss on my lips. Tears welled in her eyes, and some dropped onto my face. She gently swept them from my cheeks with her fingers. I tried to say, "Leave them," but all I could do was muster a weak attempt at a smile. She kissed me again, then I noticed several hospital staff surrounding my bed. Liz got up, and they took over.

The doctor leaned over me and asked, "John, can you hear me?"

I struggled to answer, and a weak "yes" popped out.

"Good, John. It's going to be a little hard to talk and move for a while, but we will get speech and physical therapy up here today to begin working with you. You are in the university hospital. You've been here for three weeks in a coma. Do you understand?"

"Y-y-ye-es," I squeezed out.

"I'm your primary physician, Raheid Mohabid. All your vitals look very good. The blow to your head fractured your skull and produced a severe concussion, which caused your brain to swell, and that caused you to lapse into a coma. Luckily, you were found quickly and brought immediately here, where we took steps to reverse the swelling.

"You also had third-degree burns to both legs. The burns are on the mend, but it will take some time for them to completely heal. I understand that someone poured hot water on you while you were seated, and that certainly would do it, but the good news is that it produced a clean burn, which reduced the chances for infection."

"Okay."

I looked around the room for Liz and spotted her standing at the foot of my bed. She was smiling, but I could see the moisture from her tears on her face. She smiled weakly and squeezed my toes.

Two weeks of intense therapy followed, and I was able to talk almost normally. Walking was a bit difficult, particularly with the burns and bandages, but I was making progress. Liz visited me daily and brought Carolyn to visit one day this past week. When she walked into the room, she ran to my side and gave me a great, big arm hug.

"Oh, John. You got to get well fast so we can all go to the zoo soon."

"I will, darling, I promise. And what have you been doing?"

We chatted for a long time, and I realized Carolyn missed me. When she and Liz were leaving, she told me how much she loved me. That produced an instant warm feeling in my chest. I told her that I loved her also.

The following week they removed me from intensive care, and there was a constant stream of visitors, flowers, and cards. I wondered if I had died, would I have gotten these many flowers? I asked hospital personnel to take some of them after a day or so and place them in the rooms of patients less fortunate.

On Friday I got a visit from Harold Kapinsky and Ron Jacobsen. It was not just a social visit, as they wanted some information about what transpired that evening.

"John, why was Reitbrock at your home that evening?" Harold began.

"He was working with Wertz and Antonoff on securing Dan's research. His organization is a front that provides cover to their true operation."

"But why did he come to you—he must have known that you turned over all the information to the GBI?" Harold queried.

"He knew of the copy and was working on the hunch that I retained the copy. He wanted it, then he was going to kill me."

"And how did the whole shooting come down?" Ron chimed in.

"I knew my loaded shotgun was under the couch from where I had it after the break-in. I tricked Reitbrock into cutting the ropes binding my feet and me to the chair. The rope binding my hands was soaked with blood, and that allowed me to slip my hands out. I shoved him hard, and he fell behind my desk. I got the shotgun, and when he got up, fired, hitting him in the arm. When he got up a second time, I fired again. I then passed out."

"You're a lucky man, John. Your landlord heard the shots and called the police. They were there in five minutes and found you. They tell me that had finding you been delayed much more, you would have died," Harold related.

It was two days later, and Liz got to my room about five thirty in the afternoon as usual. She would bring me a dessert, as my extraordinary hospital meal came around five o'clock. She knew the peaches, pears, or fruit cocktail in syrup would not be the proper end to my fantastic gourmet dinner. This evening she brought a piece of apple-cranberry pie she made the evening before. I devoured it with barely a breath between each forkful.

Liz would usually stay until six thirty or so, and we would catch up on the day. Today I had to finally tell her something that ate at me since regaining consciousness.

"Liz, I have to tell you something, which will be very hard, but I just cannot keep it bottled up any longer. It is just for your ears."

"Sure, John, get it off you shoulder."

"Your voice and gentle touch were the triggers that tripped me into consciousness, and had you not been there, I may have still been unconscious." Then I hesitated.

"That's wonderful, John, but I sense there is more."

"Yes. Just before waking, I had a very bad dream. I know dreams are silly, but this one was very real and very disturbing." Again, I hesitated.

"I want to hear it, John."

"Okay. I was a spectator to an event—a very tragic event." Again, I paused.

"I can tell this is very hard for you, John, but please tell me."

"Well, here goes—I hope you don't think I'm crazy. I was a spectator to the end of our race—the human race—homo sapiens. That's crazy, right?"

"No, John, it is obviously causing you some concern."

"Well, it seems that the governments around the world went on a massive Take Care of Our Citizens—Cradle to Grave campaign in order to satisfy the demand of the citizenry. It also insured their continuing governance.

"The problem is that government produces nothing. They allocate the excess resources that are produced by their citizens. As a result, government is dependent on the productive citizens to produce excess so they are able to reallocate them to those who do not produce enough to sustain their lives.

"As the number of government dependents grows, the number of producers declines. At some point, the government has so few producers it becomes very difficult to meet the promises to those who depend upon them. Ultimately, the government begins to default on its promises.

"Its dependents begin to force the government to supply, which it cannot, and collapses. Suddenly the dependents find themselves without the basics: food, shelter, clothing, and health care. Anarchy results, and there are marauding gangs who take for themselves the basics from anyone who has them. They pillage and kill.

"The domino effect follows with all deficit governments—basically all governments—succumbing. The world governments have all collapsed. All services are lost: no electricity, no water, and no gasoline. Fresh foods cannot be kept and rapidly spoil. Food and water in the large cities cease to be available. Gangs are formed to find food and water. The gangs pillage everything available, even going into the jungles to find isolated, self-sufficient tribes, which they destroy.

"After a few years, all resources are consumed. The gangs are incapable of producing new supplies of food. They gradually die off. What remains of the human race are a few thousand hermits who live in the wilderness and are not found by the gangs. They live off the land and live out their lives alone, and unheralded, the last one dies, leaving the world void of homo sapiens."

"I understand why it is so upsetting, but it was just a dream."

"True, Liz, just a dream. Most dreams are irrational and illogical. This dream was very rational and logical. That's why it is so disturbing, but there is more."

"Oh?" Liz responded.

"Our brains have two sides, both affect our behavior. There is the emotional side, which we have plenty of when we are born. The logical side we develop during our life. The Chinese call it the yin and yang. A person who develops both equally and completely reaches a state of wisdom."

"So what does that have to do with the reality of your dream?" questioned Liz.

"Please let me finish this, and I think you will understand. We are born into emotional state called wonder and awe," I continued.

"Throughout our lives, we develop courage and, eventually, some of us reverence. This places our emotional brain at the last step to wisdom. Our logical side gathers knowledge, which leads to right judgment, and with some of us, understanding. It is understanding which allows us to open the door to wisdom, a state achieved by only a very few."

"Golly, that's some really heavy stuff," exclaimed Liz.

"Not really. Let me put it into context. Let's say that you are being chased through the forest by some bad dudes who are intent on possibly killing you. As you are fleeing, you see a huge, wind-fallen tree, under which you duck to hide, hoping the bad guys pass you by. Suddenly you see a snake coiled a few feet away, and you hate snakes. Your emotional brain tells you to get out of there, but your logical side tells you if you do, the guys chasing you will probably capture you.

"Let's say, though, instead of a snake, you encounter a mother bear and her two cubs in their den. The mother bear is glaring and snarling at you and about to attack. If you stay, you will certainly be killed, but if you continue to run, you have a chance of getting away.

"In the real world, we all have things we want. As children, our emotional side demands our wants be satisfied by the older people around us. As we get older and more capable, we are confronted with the choice of getting our wants satisfied by ourselves or demand that others provide us with what we want.

"Then we realize that we can use others as instruments to give us the things we want with very little effort on us without realizing the full impact such actions will have on us over time. When this becomes the norm, our society will break down."

"Okay?" Liz said in a totally confused, quivering voice.

"I have never told you, but in December, I had a dream where I was in church, and a girl with CP was illuminated by a holy light which cured her condition. When I was alone, in the dark and floating in the Pacific, while half asleep, this girl came to me. She extended her hand, and I reached out and took it. At that instant, I realized it was you.

"Well, my dream ended with this girl standing on the beach with the lush green forest and mountains behind her.

Also behind her were a few hundred other people. The dream ended in a flash of light, and I woke, looking at your beautiful face."

"I don't know what to say, John, but I am flattered that you dreamt of me while out there."

"That's when I knew if I survived or not, we would always be together. If not in the flesh, in spirit, and I fell completely asleep."

"I really do love you, John," Liz said while she placed the index finger of her right hand over my lips.

It was just before Thanksgiving, and I relaxed in my den. I decided to dig something out of the memorabilia drawer in the file cabinet. While rustling though the drawer, I came upon *Clear and Present Danger*. My memory faded quickly, and I sat back in my La-Z-Boy and refreshed the memories of those events. Be very careful of which people you allow to tell you how you should live your life. Everyone you meet has an opinion, but few really know just what's best for you.

My thoughts went to Dan being awarded the Presidential Medal of Freedom in late May. I traveled to Washington with Liz at the request of the President. Liz was the only one receiving the medal that day, or so I thought. The President awarded the posthumous medal to Dan, which Liz accepted. After the usual pleasantries, he asked me to step forward.

"John Castano, I, as President, do award you the Medal of Freedom for your heroic actions in bringing down a threat to the United States of America and to the preservation of freedom for all its citizens."

After the story appeared in the local news about the ceremony and my part in the entire event, I received a call from Greg Steinman.

"John, Jim, Mat and I had a meeting, and we would like you to come back to the firm. You're a key man in our future."

"Oh, it wouldn't have anything to do with the news these days, would it?"

"John, you feel we are that shallow?"

"You tell me, Greg. Two weeks ago, I wasn't worthy of consideration, and now I'm just so important to the firm?"

"I guess that's your answer?"

"Right on, Greg. Give my best to Jim and Mat."

In June, Paul and Susan were married in Des Moines. Gloria was the maid of honor, and I the best man. Liz attended the wedding as my guest. At the rehearsal dinner, she had the opportunity to talk with Gloria. I introduced them, and Gloria was very gracious in talking with Liz, but I expected she would be. It was a hard time for Gloria, as she had just ended her relationship with her physician friend.

Liz was also very gracious, as she did not question the relationship between Gloria and me. The two seemed to hit it off very well, but both are made from the same kind of stuff. We ended the weekend on a very positive tone.

On the way home, Liz explored the relationship between Gloria and me. I assured her that she was the only spark in my life.

Then I said, "Gloria is a wonderful person, and we had a great time in Mexico. She has a strong respect for me, and I for her. There was the opportunity to make our friendship much more personal, but the only person I could think of in those circumstances was you. I could not deceive Gloria."

Liz slowly brushed the back of her hand over the side of my face.

In July, Albert Wertz and Hillary went to trial. Wertz was convicted on two counts of murder one. He was sentenced to two consecutive life terms. UFAC will not have the services of this general, and he will never again see the light of freedom.

Hillary was convicted of assisting in a murder after the fact. She pleaded for leniency. During the sentencing, testimony from the Boilens swayed the judge, and she received a sentence of five to fifteen years.

An investigation found that UFAC was indeed an anti-American organization and had been spying on other researchers at various university campuses. Several of their leaders were arrested, but the organization managed to survive, focusing solely on animal rights. UFAC got into raiding farms for the purpose of liberating the prisoners and remains active.

Alexi survived but suffered a skull fracture and broken nose. He was convicted of espionage and treason and sentenced to federal prison for the rest of his natural life. Jerome and Foley were also convicted of espionage and treason, and both got life sentences. The GBI and Defense Department used the information gained from Antonoff, Jerome, and Foley to identify and close down several other cells set up to obtain classified research for sale. Antonoff's superior was the organizer of the entire spy-for-money operation and was convicted and sentenced to life in prison.

A few days after his conviction, I asked to see Alexi, and he granted my request. I just wanted to try to understand why he sacrificed his freedom and could have lost his life just to realize a few thousand dollars. The meeting took place in the Hennepin County jail the day before his transfer to the federal prison.

I came away from that meeting with no clear understanding what motivated Alexi. I asked him if he really would have killed me and why he set Phil on fire.

"I don't know John. I really liked you and did what I could to protect you from my less scrupulous associates.

But had I let you go, I certainly would have been arrested. When you ran from me that night, I didn't shoot to kill you. I just wanted to stop you. I don't know what I would have done had you not disabled me."

"You know about Reitbrock. Did you put out the hit on me?"

"No, John. I think he was freelancing." He continued, "I did kill Petroff, only in the hospital. After you guys left the junkyard, I knew the cops would be there soon, and I wouldn't be able to explain the killing. I set him on fire and got the hell out of there hoping that would be the end of it. Then I found out he was in the hospital. I killed him in the hospital before he could talk. I slipped a sizable dose of a potassium chloride solution onto his IV."

"Why did Wertz kill Danfurth?"

"Danfurth caught him in his office looking for the file. He ran out before Danfurth could get security. He had never met Wertz but asked some students if they knew who he was, and one IDed him. I think when Danfurth asked me to the cabin that weekend, he was going to tell me about Wertz. That was when Wertz decided to kill him."

Before leaving, I took A *Clear and Present Danger* from my briefcase and handed it to Alexi. I told him to open it. He did so, looked at it for a bit. I said that was his bullet. He closed it and started to handed it back.

"You keep it, and you ruined a pair of gloves and my new top coat."

"John, you are a lucky man." He smiled.

Paul Runyon played no role in the caper. His dispute with Dan was over a large expenditure he wanted the department to make in order to have a gas chromatograph in the department. Dan felt that there was not enough need for the device, and they could use the one in the department of chemistry when they needed one.

Ollas Sorenson, Dan and Liz's neighbor, was not involved in the plot. Ironically, the tree he was so concerned with was rotted out in the center, and a wind burst during a summer thunderstorm toppled the tree into Sorenson's backyard, doing little damage. Liz agreed to pay for the removal.

Lynn and Scott did decide to adopt, and I assisted in the process. Their first child was a newborn girl whose mother and father placed her up for adoption. The second was a three-year-old boy whose father was killed by the boy's mother, and she was serving a forty-year to life term. I really felt good about the whole thing, as the two children will grow up in a loving family, and Lynn and Scott will live a fulfilled life together.

We are occasionally confronted with a situation that requires that we react in a manner not consistent with our true nature. Forced to react, we must always do so with a strong sense of rationality. To act irrationally in such a situation is asking for disaster.

POSTSCRIPT

It was Friday night, and I was on the corner of Nicollet Mall and Seventh in downtown Minneapolis waiting for the beginning of the Holidazzle parade—Macy's Christmas-light parade. It was a cool sparkling night, December 16, 2005. I was reflecting on my earlier conversation with James. It was his birthday.

He and Deatra adopted Hillary and Brett's baby boy. They agreed to name him Brett. He was born in June 1990, just one month after they gave birth to their first girl they named Madelyn Joy. She was named Joy as she brought so much magical life into their family.

Hillary was released early from her sentence and became extended family to the Boilens and their son. She visited them three or four times a year. She completed college with a Master's degree in social work and now works in social services for the health department.

James and Deatra had a third child in 1992, and they named her Chloe Breze. She was named Breze as she was such a wisp of a child who looked as fresh as a mild summer breeze. James became a partner in the law firm, and Deatra worked part-time for the clinic. To all the kids, I was Uncle John.

I took a position with the attorney general's office in 1990 and have worked there ever since. Eventually several months after my leave of absence was over, my old firm offered my position back. I politely refused. If someone tries to shoot you in the back, you don't turn your back to them a second time.

I felt a tug on my coat sleeve.

"Daddy, Daddy, the light parade is coming."

"Yes, Jameson, I see them."

"Lift me up, Daddy."

I lifted Jameson to my shoulders. which gave him the best view in the house. Mrs. Castano returned just in time and grabbed onto my free arm as tight as possible.

I turned my head and said, "Who called?"

"Carolyn. She wanted to let us know her flight was scheduled to arrive tomorrow at ten eleven in the morning and wondered if we would pick her up."

"You betcha!" I answered in the affirmative. "Why do airlines always have such exact arrival times? 'Ten eleven.' There is nothing exact about airline arrival and departures. They should list it as 'This flight usually gets to the gate around ten thirty,'" I proposed to Liz.

She ignored the comment, as do most wives.

Carolyn was a sophomore at Northwestern and plans to major in physics. She wants to get her doctorate in aerospace. She was following in Daddy Dan's footsteps, as she calls him; she calls me Daddy John.

Liz and I married in 1993 and had a son, Graham, two years later. He was standing next to Liz. Jameson was born December 22, 1999. He's our new-century child. We now live in a modest house on the banks of the St. Croix River just outside Hudson, Wisconsin, which is becoming a rapidly growing suburb of the Twin Cities.

Shortly after we married, Carolyn convinced us to get a dog. We went to a pet shop in the mall downtown, and in the window, there were several puppies; one stood out. It was a miniature schnauzer who spotted us immediately and came to the window begging us to pick her up. We did just that, and we mutually adopted each other. Carolyn named her Sassy.

I reflected on the total unconditional love Sassy provided us. Her biggest desire was always to be with us, and when that wasn't possible, she would greet us upon our return with an overwhelming outpouring of excitement and love. She displayed the purest form of love that exists. I'm convinced that dogs do feel emotions, and love is one.

Sassy would spend hours in the front window, watching people on the river boating in summer, or snowmobiling on the winter ice. Sassy loved that river almost as much as us. She slept between Liz and me every night. We all loved her, and she was a part of our family.

It was spring last year that I said my last goodbye to Sassy. Sassy developed kidney disease, and finally, her kidneys failed. We made arrangements for our veterinarian to come to the house to put her down.

That morning I had to leave before sunrise for an out-of-town business meeting.

Sassy was lying on our bed, where she always slept, too weak to lift her head. By the dim light from the hall, I went to our bed, lifted her head, and looked into her eyes. The sparkle was gone, and she knew. I scratched her chin and kissed her on top of her head then gently laid her head back on the bed. "Goodbye, Sassy." She looked up at me without moving her head, and the look said, "Goodbye. I love you."

We buried her near the river with a small plaque saying, "Until We Meet Again," marking the spot. On a bright, clear day, we can see that tiny plaque from her favorite window. I thought about death being a sunrise or sunset. I knew it would be a sunrise. Suddenly I realized I was really awake.

IN VERUM

A coworker walked by Liz's office, looking through the open door, to see her in tears. He stopped and asked if something was wrong, or if he could do something. Liz just shook her head, but he asked a second time. Without a word, she handed him the newspaper folded in fourths. This article appeared in the Minneapolis paper on January 25, 1989:

Minneapolis Attorney Lost at Sea

John Castano was lost at sea and presumed dead in the Pacific Ocean off the coast of Cabo San Lucas, Mexico. A memorial mass will be said for Mr. Castano at St. Therese Catholic church, 1514 Second Avenue on Saturday, January 28 at 2 PM.

Mr. Castano was a family lawyer and worked for Pauli, Pauli & Steinman. He was vacationing and on a fishing excursion in Mexico with a friend, Paul Greco. He was lost overboard during a sudden, violent storm. It was reported he was wearing a life jacket.

The Mexican coast guard, along with several local fishing boats, conducted a three-day search with no sign of the missing Castano. Mexican authorities have suspended the search and are listing him as deceased.

Just a thought: Is it possible for one to live out their entire life at the instant of their death?

ACKNOWLEDGMENTS

Since this endeavor was one in which, through a fictional story, I revealed my basic beliefs and philosophy through the main character, I relied on my personal experiences to develop the book. I was very familiar with the Twin Cities area as both of my daughters attended the University of Minnesota. Christina, my older daughter, graduated from U of M, and my younger, Gina, attended there for her freshman and sophomore years before transferring to the University of Wisconsin–Madison. In addition, my employment entailed many business meetings in the Twin Cities.

I have to give many thanks to those who helped me in the editing process: Margret "Peg" Grimm, Judy Tyler, and my wife, Carol, who, in addition to editing, has developed the cover for this book.

I also must mention my helpful research companion—Google. I used their resources to validate times, places, weather on specific days, and so on. Without that resource, much of the material in this endeavor would have been as fictious as the story itself.

ABOUT THE AUTHOR

J. A. Commodore, who enjoys writing, fishing, and reading, is a husband, a father of two daughters, and a grandfather of two grandsons and two granddaughters. In his youth, he enlisted in the Navy and later received his BS and MBA degrees. Prior to retiring, he worked four decades as a sales representative. His career and his daughters, who attended the University of Minnesota, took him often to the Twin Cities.

Commodore and his wife, Carol, have traveled for both pleasure and business to multiple countries across the world, where they have met many fascinating people and have seen phenomenal sites. J. A. Commodore and his wife reside in Wisconsin.

www.ingramcontent.com/pod-product-compliance
Lightning Source LLC
Chambersburg PA
CBHW030620310726
48979CB00003B/806
* 9 7 8 1 9 5 7 2 0 3 6 6 9 *